If *Honeymoon* were an old movie it would be *His Girl Friday*. If it were a movie today it would be *My Best Friend's Wedding*. A great old-fashioned romantic comedy gets crossed with a hip, fresh comic romance in this wonderful debut by the talented and highly successful British writer Amy Jenkins.

HONEYMOON

HONEYMOON

A NOVEL

AMY JENKINS

BACK BAY BOOKS

LITTLE, BROWN AND COMPANY

BOSTON   NEW YORK   LONDON

Originally published in hardcover by Little, Brown and Company, September 2000

First Back Bay paperback edition, September 2001

The characters and events in this book are fictitious. Any similarity to real persons, living or dead, is coincidental and not intended by the author.

Grateful acknowledgment is made for permission to reprint from the following copyrighted works: "Can't Take My Eyes Off You" (Bob Crew/Bob Gaudio) © 1967, EMI Longitude Music Seasons Four Music Corporation, USA. Reprinted by permission of EMI Music Publishing Ltd., 127 Charing Cross Road, London WC2H 0EA, and Seasons Four Music Corporation; "My Favorite Things" (Richard Rodgers/Oscar Hammerstein II) © 1959 by Richard Rodgers and Oscar Hammerstein II. Copyright renewed. Reprinted by permission of EMI Music Publishing Ltd., 127 Charing Cross Road, London WC2H 0EA, and Williamson Music. International copyright secured. All rights reserved; "New York, New York!" (Fred Ebb/John Kander) © 1977 EMI Catalogue Partnership/EMI Unart Catalog Inc., USA. Worldwide print rights controlled by Warner Bros. Inc., USA/IMP LTD. Reprinted by permission of International Music Publications Ltd.; "I Will Survive" (Dino Fekaris/Freddy Perren) © 1978. Reprinted by kind permission of Universal Music Publishing Ltd.

For information on Time Warner Trade Publishing's online publishing program, visit www.ipublish.com.

Library of Congress Cataloging-in-Publication Data
Jenkins, Amy.
Honeymoon : a novel / Amy Jenkins — 1st American ed.
p. cm.
ISBN 0-316-65570-8 (hc)/0-316-65588-0 (pb)
1. Honeymoons — Fiction.   2. Young women — Fiction.   3. First loves — Fiction.
4. New York (N.Y.) — Fiction.   I. Title.
PR6060.E5173 H66 2001
823'.92 — dc21   00-035670

10 9 8 7 6 5 4 3 2 1
DESIGNED BY JAM DESIGN
Q-FF
Printed in the United States of America

HONEYMOON

1

W E'RE in this white limo purring through crowded Saturday-night streets. Like in Hollywood. Although it's not Hollywood. This great big fuck-off ridiculous stretch limo is in London's West End — although it's hardly the West and nowhere near the end. This limo is so stretched you can't understand why it doesn't sink in the middle and drag its belly on the ground. This limo is so long you think it can't turn those tight Soho corners without sweeping café society into the gutter.

But imagine this. Imagine it does have to stop at one of those corners. To avoid killing someone. And when it stops, there's this young man — looks like he might be from out of town, all fresh-faced. And he is drawn to one of the limo's open windows, leans down to the window, becomes involved in conversation with the limo occupants, leans into the window, further and further, until finally he is sucked through the window into the limo, head first. The last you see of him being his tattered red sneakers as they disappear from sight.

Because the thing is — you see — this limo does not contain one lonely pop-star riding along in state. This limo contains more girls than you could shake a stick at. Wall to wall feminine flesh, crammed in we are. Girl sardines. I'm in a great white tin of girl sardines. Or that's what it feels like.

And this witless piece of fresh-faced masculinity is wedged into the seat opposite me, squeezed between thighs. And all the girls in the limo — they want me to get off with him. That's what you do at your hen party.

Hen party.

Oh my God. Or, Oh! My! God!, as my sister Ven would say — she's twenty-one. Left to my own devices, I would never have had a hen party. "Honey," Della had said, "sweetheart, left to your own devices you would never be getting married. And now look."

And now look. Well, quite.

Honey, by the way, is my name. Della is given to terms of endearment but not that given. Not two-in-one-sentence given.

So Della went ahead and arranged a surprise hen party. And, actually, I'm quite enjoying it. I mean, I never like the *idea* of just being girls together — like I never like the idea of a salad for lunch — but when it comes to it, it can be quite pleasant. At least they didn't hire a male stripper or truss me up and put me on a plane to Amsterdam. Del rented the stretch limo and invited everyone and we've been driving round London drinking champagne. Or, rather, they have. Champagne gives me a headache.

After a bottle or five, they'd got all girl-powerish, which is how they came to be hanging out of the windows trying to pick up blokes. I wasn't that interested. West End pickings on a Saturday night are notoriously slim. Besides, I'm not really interested in anybody at the moment. Not a foreign body at any rate. They'd been telling me you have to be unfaithful at your hen party, make-out unfaithful at the very least. Della said the French have a word for it — she'd just spent six months in Paris on assignment, she works for Marks & Spencer. She couldn't remember what the French word was exactly, but roughly translated it means "last gasp before dying."

"Charming," I said. "Believe it or not," I said, "I don't want to be unfaithful."

Della looked kind of disappointed at that, but not too disappointed. Because she likes Ed. My intended. Thinks he's a *good thing*. Actually, I think Della's finding it a bit hard to adjust. They all are. It's a tradition, you see, amongst my friends. That I can always be relied upon to fuck things up. By things, I mean life.

We'd all got into Ecstasy but I was the one who was out three nights a week and weeping into my sneakers if I wasn't on the guest list. We'd all had trouble getting into work on time, but I was the one whose favourite *must-go* club was on a Sunday night and ended up losing my job. We'd all had ridiculously loud parties ridiculously late, but I was the one who'd had Paul Trouble Anderson play a 5K sound system in my basement flat and I was the one who got evicted two months later. We'd all had dodgy boyfriends, but mine was the one who cleared three grand out of my Abbey National account and was last heard of behind bars. And we'd all had credit-card debts, but I was the one who got declared bankrupt — well, virtually. I had to do one of those voluntary-arrangement things.

But all that was pre-Ed and now I'm post-Ed and not only born again but smack on the brink of matrimony. I felt a bit like a weary boxer. I'd been up there in the ring, year after year, doing the rounds and now at last someone had thrown in the towel. Someone in the form of a nice, suitable young man called Ed. And all I wanted to do was to bounce on the ropes for a blissful moment and catch my breath while I dreamed of retirement. I did not want manager Della shouting in my ear that I was good for another round. Presenting me with some leery lanky Scottish lad they'd pulled, trying to get me off with him. No thanks, I'm headed for the dressing rooms, me. Not that he was that bad or anything. I think Jennie had him in the end.

When the girls finally realised they weren't going to get any live action, they became resigned. But they started saying, "Okay, who would you be unfaithful with if you could have anyone? Tonight. Right now. If the man you most fancy in the world were to walk out of that restaurant and get into this car. There must be someone." They made suggestions. You know, the usual suspects, the movie stars. They didn't get very far because I'm over fancying men on celluloid. Although I did waver a bit when they got to Ewan McGregor — I once saw him in a kilt at a party.

Then Della shrieked, "I know! The Love of Your Life!" The Love of My Life is what we call this guy I had a wild night with years ago. The story's so old and hoary now it's sort of gone into Legend Land. But with Della and me it's still one of the old favourites.

Jennie, who we only met about a year ago, when we took up Ashtanga yoga for, like, one day, said, "Who's the Love of Your Life?"

So I said, "Does this mean I get to tell the Love of My Life story?" I like doing that because it gives me this nice glowing feeling when I'm telling it. It's like rewriting my life as a movie, with me as the leading lady, and all of a sudden I get a sense of myself as someone who things actually happen to, like in a movie, and when I'm telling the story I sort of believe that I am that character for a few moments. That my life is a bit like a movie, or could be seen that way.

"Yes," they all said, "tell the story." Like they really wanted to hear. Bless them. So I did.

At the time, this is like seven years ago when I was about twenty-one, I was seeing this guy called Paulo. He was Italian and I was just *seeing* him, if you know what I mean. Seeing every bit of him, mind you, but it didn't even cross my mind to have a relationship with this man. He was young and fuckable and vain and kind of middle-aged before his time, though he'd kill me if he heard me say that — with his cheekbones, his Armani suits and his cocaine habit. Anyway, he just wasn't suitable relationship material. Not that relationships were much on the agenda at that point in my life — but I mean we could barely have a conversation. It wasn't a language problem, he spoke perfect English, we just weren't that interested in anything the other had to say. Those were the days when I filled my evenings and weekends having non-relationships with Mr. Unsuitable and wondering why I never met Mr. Suitable. And that was pretty much the story of my twenties.

You know, I wish someone had told me that it was probably a good idea to apply some time and effort to looking for a nice man with an interesting life and prospects and all that while I was still at an age when there were lots of them around and on the market. But no one tells you. It's a bit like when the new season's shoes come into the shops and you go in and ask for a size five and a half in the second week of September and the assistant looks at you like you're nuts and says they've sold out of all sizes except those fitting giants and midgets and you say, "Why have you already sold out in the second week of September?" And they look at you like you're even more nuts to think that they might wish to supply you with this shoe and they explain gently but firmly, "It's a very popular shoe." Or even, "It's a very comfortable shoe."

You see, if you don't learn these natural laws hard and fast you're looking at a very unfashionably shod life. Or a very uncomfortably shod life. One or the other.

Maybe I should have worked out this suitable-man thing for myself. Others did. I think what put me off was the idea that this Mr. Suitable wasn't going to look like Johnny Depp. I couldn't face the non-Johnny-Depp look. But I do wish someone had told me that the distracted man with a dream and a drug habit — the one who keeps looking over my shoulder for something better — is not a sensible route to that warm, fuzzy, thirty-something place where you gambol with children and dogs.

Anyway, I digress. The night I met the Love of My Life, Paulo picked me up in his sports car — I have to admit, I found the sports-car thing quite dazzling. I was like a rabbit in the headlights. Paulo took me to a chic Italian restaurant, all minimal even then, no outsize peppermills. He liked it because they made the vodka martinis like they do back home. Paulo, of course, kept disappearing off to the loo. I declined to join him, partly because I was really quite interested in the food and partly because drugs just don't agree with me. Afterwards, I'm all raw and messy for days. I cry at the drop of a hat. I cry over *Pet Rescue* on TV. I cry when someone wins the Birthday Bonanza on the radio. Oh God.

So, I saw this delicious risotto being delivered to the next table. I've got a thing about risotto. It's like grown-up baby food or something. I can get compulsive around risotto. Luckily, risottos take a long time to cook and a lot of stirring so I don't often attempt them at home. Before I'd thought about it — this is not the sort of thing I usually do actually, I kind of surprised myself — I leant over to the next table and said, "How's the risotto?"

This guy had just taken this great big forkful; I hadn't even looked at him until he turned to me, and he had these horribly blue eyes in this dark face, and he fastened his eyes on mine and we recognised each other. I don't mean that I knew him, I'd never met him before in my life, but we *knew* each other, if you know what I mean. It was like being punched in the stomach, it was like — I'm trying to avoid mentioning electricity here because it's such a cliché, but I guess people talk about electricity for a reason. That's what it feels like.

And he said, "Game."

How's the risotto? Game. That's how it started. I didn't get "game," so I just kept staring at him. In any case, looking away wasn't an option; he had me wired straight into his soul.

"Game risotto," he said. "It's the game risotto."

"My God. What kind of game?"

"I don't know — whatever you guys have been shooting lately, I guess." At this point it registered that he was American.

Paulo, who, I should have mentioned, was present at the table during all of this and not in the loo, coughed politely. He was always polite, Paulo, he was always one great big stuffed-up ball of Armani-suited politeness — except when he whispered unusual requests into my ear during sex — in Italian. It turned out, thank God, that he didn't want to *do* them, he just wanted to whisper them in my ear. So Paulo coughed and I came back to the land of the living, although I was all red and flushed and hot under the collar. And we both went back to our respective dinners and our respective dates.

Mr. Blue Eyes at the next table was with a blonde. Of course, he would be. She was very at ease, she exuded at ease — I put out my antenna for the vibe. Were they an item? I tried to gauge sexual tension. She was all ease. I ordered the risotto.

So the risotto came and I was munching away although, to be honest, I'd lost my appetite, but it was bringing us together, this risotto — it was a love risotto, my love letter to him. And he suddenly leant over and said, "Good game?"

"Very good," I said.

And we were back with the eyeballs things. And this was really getting embarrassing so I glanced at the blonde. And he knew I was saying, "Who is she?"

And he looked at her too and said, "But I'm just a Yankee tourist." Like — what do I know? And she smiled.

So now I knew that he lived in the States and she was the woman he stayed with or saw in London and maybe they had sex and maybe they didn't but there was no "we," which was the most important thing. You may ask, how did I know this for sure, but I did. We were communicating with jungle drums.

Next thing I knew I was leaning over and saying, "Congratulations." And they all three looked at me. And I went, "Did you know that only eight per cent of American citizens hold passports? Congratulations for being one of them."

So then Paulo was doing his coughing thing again and Blue Eyes excused himself and got up and headed for the gents. And I sat there a moment and then it occurred to me that maybe I was meant to get up and follow him. I mean "meant" in a kind of fatalistic, universal sense — I don't mean I thought he was expecting me to follow him. And I couldn't believe I'd even had this thought because — really, I mean it — following people is not the kind of thing I do. So I sat on the idea and then — all this took about a nanosecond — the thought came to me, Well, I *could* just follow him anyway, there's no law against it. It might change my life. Getting up now and going to the loo might change my life. This might be it. The turning point. And if I don't do it, I will never know.

So I got up and went to the loo too. When I got there I hung around in the corridor for a bit waiting for him to come out. But I only managed about a minute of that before doubt struck and the possible awful consequences of what I was doing came crashing down on me. What if I'd read the situation all wrong? And how awful would it be if he came out and found me standing there and just sort of looked embarrassed and walked past? The truly awful thing would be that he would *know*. At this point, you see, we were in the same boat: both of us suspected but neither of us knew. If he were to find me in the corridor, it would mean I had shown my cards first. And that was about as scary to me as embarking on a Channel swim *in January* (i.e., scary even for those sporty types who do Channel swims every day before tea).

So, I was standing outside the ladies, and just being there was making me want to pee — a kind of Pavlovian reaction to that strange lady on the door in the A-line skirt. The gents door started to open and — quick as a flash — I was in the ladies. And then I thought, Okay, I'm leaving this up to Fate. If it's meant to be, it will happen whatever I do. Which was the biggest cop-out, and I went into the cubicle. There was only one.

I'd only spent about half my penny when the door opened and someone came in. I held fire for a moment. I've learnt to do this because it's something they tell you to practise in the magazines. It's meant to exercise your G-spot. Then there was this nervous male cough. And I was sitting there, crucified with embarrassment and struck dumb too. Then the owner of the male cough left. Just like that.

So I came out, expecting Blue Eyes to be waiting outside but he wasn't, he was back at his table, chatting away. And, of course, doubt had got me again, and I was wondering if it was him with the cough. Maybe it was a waiter or something. So I was back to the table, and Paulo, who was not having the best night, shot up and off to powder his nose. And the two at the next table felt they had to talk to me now that I was alone. But the blonde was at ease with it all so by the time Paulo came back we were nicely hooked into conversation. And the blonde started talking to Paulo and I couldn't believe my luck that she would do that. And he was loving it because it was all stuff about how great his cufflinks were and shit. And then, just as Blue Eyes and I were having so much outrageous eye contact that I thought, This is definitely going to get interesting, he said, "I'm going to have to make a move." He pulled out his cash but Blonde told him she'd get it. So he got up and said his goodbyes and I was suddenly in free-fall, a sky-diver, arms spread-eagled, unforgiving earth rushing fast towards my face. Figuratively speaking, of course. In reality I was still sitting safely upright in a minimal chair in a minimal Italian restaurant in central London. But what I meant was I couldn't speak and he was leaving and I couldn't for the life of me work out what was going on.

And as Blue Eyes passed the back of my chair, he did that little cough again, except this time it was more like the start of a laugh, under his breath but not that under his breath. Like there was a private joke between us that only we knew. And then he just walked straight out. And I was sitting there in shock. And the blonde busied herself with getting the bill. And I looked at Paulo, like, did he hear that? But he was checking himself in the window behind me again — and I turned, and he wasn't checking himself, he was watching Blue Eyes hailing a cab outside.

And suddenly I was up. I managed a "Sorry, Paulo." And then I ran. I hit the street and he'd left the cab door open for me. And — well — that was us. In the cab. Driving off into the night.

2

BACK in the limo the girls were all looking at me. Gagging for it. I let a little silence hang. Then I said, "Sometimes I think about the two of them left in the restaurant." Did Paulo move on Blonde? Maybe they got on really well. Maybe they had as great an evening as we did. I never found out because I never saw Paulo again.

"So that's it," I said. "The Love of My Life." And I shut my mouth like that was the end.

"No way," they yelled.

"You can imagine the rest," I said.

"No, we can't," they yelled. Thing was, I didn't really want to tell the rest. Not at my hen party. Not any more.

"Hey," Della said, in her strictest and most scary tones, "they need closure." She indicated girls with mouths hanging open. I let my eyes fall demurely onto those closely packed thighs on the opposite seat. And I murmured that I couldn't go on, that the rest of the story was private. Della rolled her eyes and said, "Oh please," with much emphasis on the "please." In this day and age, you might have noticed, any kind of sensitivity to feeling is regarded as (a) pretentious and (b) tiresome. But the truth was I really didn't want to go on, especially not in a male presence. The lanky Scot was still with us, after all.

"It was precious," I said. "It was beautiful." And it was. I didn't know how else to describe it. I don't know now. In the cab, he'd turned to me and fixed his gaze upon me and in that moment I knew with absolute certainty that I was the only woman in the world. And, of course, we had known each other for years. Years and years.

"Six?" said Martha.

"Six what?" I said.

But it turned out she was asking me about sex. Martha is from New Zealand. I looked at Del. She has always assumed that we — me and he — had actually done it and I had never put her right.

"Actually," I said, "the truth is, we didn't do it." Scream of betrayal from Della. "We didn't really know each other," I said, "we'd only just met."

"But we like it like that," Della reminded me firmly, "the first time is always the best. Everyone says sex gets better but everyone knows it only gets worse, reaching its peak in the first few months of the relationship, then frequently tailing off to nothing at all. In many cases, within a year," she added, with the authority of a rigorously researched government think-tank survey.

"Well," I said, putting lots of superior scepticism into the word and giving it several more syllables than it has, "with Ed . . ."

"Oh God," she said. She sat back and shut her eyes: she didn't want to hear any more.

"If you must sleep with White Van Man . . ." said Jennie.

"Ha!" I said. Because it's true. Della likes nothing better than White Van Man. She's not at all averse to a bit of paunch, tattooed biceps, builder's bum — all that stuff. I've told her she must have had a dysfunctional childhood to like it so rough but she won't have it. Says her upbringing was all Andrex puppies and Mr.

Kipling's French Fancies for tea. Although how they fitted cuddly puppies into that housing project in Beckenham, God only knows.

But it isn't normal, it really isn't. Especially when you take into account how fucking beautiful she is — there's something about Della's looks that makes you say "fucking" before you say "beautiful." Imagine having a friend who looks like a fucking supermodel. You see? There I go again. But seriously.

Recently they got a computer to come out with the perfect female face — i.e., the face deemed most appealing to men, anthropologically speaking. How computers work these things out God only knows but, anyway, this face was in all the newspapers and it was the spit of Della. I swear. When I bought the *Evening Standard,* I thought it was her. I thought she'd finally succumbed to one of those tight-faced women who used to accost us — her, I mean — whenever we walked down the King's Road, claiming they were bookers at a model agency.

In the limo, Della had her eyes closed, waiting for us to shut up. I closed my eyes too. And I had one of those moments when I could feel his presence. He was always with me, like a silent witness to my life. Everything came through him or round him or off him. But sometimes his presence was more tangible than at other times. Sometimes the sense of him ran through my body — the Love of My Life.

"This kills me," he said, "but we're not going to fuck tonight."

For some reason this remark filled me with the sure knowledge of love. "Okay," I said.

"Okay?" he said. Then he whispered, "Don't you want me?"

And I wanted him so much I actually thought I might be sick. We stared at each other, crouching amongst the litter of old coffee cups and brimming ashtrays in the flat Del and I used to share, trying to warm ourselves at the fire I'd lit in the grate. Eventually I gathered myself enough to say, "Right now — you — you can do anything you want to do. Anything at all, including not doing things."

He smiled. "I have to catch a flight tomorrow," he said. "I'd miss it but I have a meeting with Universal and it's a break for me. I don't want to just fuck and leave."

"What are we going to do?" I said. Meaning, with the rest of our life.

"Let's play a game," he said. Meaning, to pass the night.

My thoughts jumped to the battered old Monopoly set in the cupboard because it was the only game we had. I got an immediate sense memory of landing on Park Lane when someone has about five hotels on it — feeling trapped, furious, persecuted, suspecting, in some insidious way, that this is all I deserve in life and all the while having to pretend I don't mind.

"What sort of game?" I said nervously.

"Hold my hand," he said, settling down on the sofa. And he held out his hand. I took it.

I didn't really understand how holding someone's hand could be like that. Like that feeling you get after you've had a long, hard day — that feeling you get after one of those days when there are no seats on the bus and your eyes are too big for your bags in the supermarket so you end up trudging home like some kind of pack-horse and then it rains sideways right into the bit of your coat that's open at the collar, and you feel like you're in some kind of endurance contest with a bit of weight-lifting thrown in and then you get home and put on some music and light some candles and finally, finally, lower yourself one blissful inch at a time into a steaming hot bath and your whole body just goes mmmm. Well, that's what it was like holding his hand. The mmmm bit, not the long-hard-day bit — except I guess you could say the long hard day was my love life to date.

Come to think of it, I don't think I'd held hands with a man for a long time. I mean, as the first move. Of course I'd held hands with a man, but usually only after we'd slept together about a hundred times and adopted just about every position in the *Kama Sutra* and got to that stage where you just about dare to think you might possibly be moving towards a relationship because he's finally stayed for breakfast — and you go to the cinema and at last, at last, the terrifying tenderness of holding hands.

But this was no ordinary holding hands. We held hands for an hour. An hour. During the first bit I couldn't speak. I had to remind myself to breathe. And, talking of electricity, it was like I'd stuck my fingers directly into the national grid.

"What about the game?" I said.

"This is it," he said.

"Good game," I said.

"Tell me about you," he said.

So I did. I told him about my parents being seventies hippie types but uncool ones, left over from the sixties ones. They were school-teachers and they wore Birkenstocks (before they became fashionable, need I say), which were referred to as "Jesus Boots" by my schoolmates. They knew about my parents' footwear because my sister and I were pupils at the school my parents taught at.

I told him how I liked my parents okay at home but somehow at school they were a constant embarrassment to me and I was invited to betray them on many occasions which, of course, I went ahead and did. I told him how my parents called me Honeymoon because that was when I was conceived. And they called my sister Venice because that's where . . . well, you can guess. We shortened the names to Honey and Ven which we could just about live with.

Then I told him how they made us go on these walking holidays all the time in a camper van, sometimes in the Lake District but sometimes in the Australian outback. Which, although you can't deny the amazingness of the scenery, we'd kind of grown to hate due to the overwhelmingly ploddy nature of the enterprise and the distinct lack of television. So we were quite glad the year we got chickenpox and the parents decided to go to Mexico without us. Mum's friend Theresa, who we loved and who lived next door, said she'd take us because her kids had chickenpox too, and Theresa could always cope with anything and make it fun. Like if we were really good — and even if we were bad actually — she'd do handstands against the wall to make us laugh, especially, I seem to remember, after we'd scared ourselves witless watching *Doctor Who* on the telly.

Then I told him how Theresa had come to find us at the local playground one day to take us home and how I remembered that walk because it was the most beautiful spring day, almost like high summer, and the trees blossomed pink and the daffodils nodded yellow and the air was soft and warm and hopeful and she held our hands and gave us Maltesers that made little explosions of sweetness in our mouths and there seemed to be so much love around. When we got home she wrapped us in blankets, even though it was warm, and she held us very tightly and told us that Mum and Dad had been on a plane that had crashed in the jungle and they were never coming back. That, in fact, they were dead.

I was twelve at the time and Ven was six.

When I told him about that, Alex — that was his name — didn't say anything. He just held my gaze — and my hand. Then, gently and firmly, he turned me round on the sofa so that my back was to him and he leant back and pulled me so that he was close behind me, enfolding me, holding me. Tight. Exactly right.

"Are you holding your breath?" he said, after a moment, with some alarm.

"Oh, yeah," I said, "thanks for reminding me." And took in some air.

He said, "I'm not going anywhere" — reading my mind.

So I let the air flow in and out and I let the moments be and be gone and they didn't go too fast or too slow and, like he said, he wasn't going anywhere. We stayed like that for, I don't know, another hour. Just having that togetherness. Just holding and being — and breathing. "Is this still the game?" I said.

"Yes," he said.

"Good game," I said. "Tell me about you."

He told me he was brought up white trash in Birmingham, Alabama, but he'd taught himself to drop the Southern accent and speak generic American and now no one could tell where he was from. He told me his dad was a holy man, a preacher of the gospel who left Alex's mother shortly after he was born and screwed every woman he could lay hands on, including several of Alex's girlfriends on the occasions he came to visit, before dying young of alcohol poisoning. By fifteen his mother had put him out on the street with ten dollars in his back pocket. He worked his way through college and there he devised a system of renting cheap telephone lines and charging them out at a profit. By twenty he had his own telecommunications company. By twenty-two he'd floated the company. By twenty-three he'd been ousted by internal politics and market imperatives and was back on the street — this time with ten million dollars in his back pocket.

So he went to Hollywood and wrote a script. As you do. The script got read with polite interest although never made. So he set up on his own and now produced commercials while hoping to produce features, living the "in your dreams" existence of a Hollywood wannabe.

"I didn't know we were doing our CVs," I said.

"That's my story," he said.

"What about your mum?" I said. "I mean, how did you feel about it all? It sounds so lonely."

"I don't know," he said.

"But it must be so weird to get rich like that," I said.

There was a little silence at that point. "Now the game gets really good," he said. And he tipped us over so that we fell onto the rug in front of the fire and our bodies rolled instinctively together top to toe, greeting each other with a deep satisfaction. We didn't kiss but we were nose to nose and I stroked his cheek. I just love it that men have these hard cheeks, this piece of muscle that goes from the cheekbone to the chin. Women don't have it. I've never met a woman whose cheek I've been in the least inclined to stroke. Alex had good hard ones.

I always used to claim that I never thought of men as sex objects. And, honestly, I don't think I did — but now I can feel it creeping up on me. I guess when I was young those pale emaciated eternal boy types I used to fancy didn't lend themselves very readily to objectification. They were like limp slices of white bread and as my tastes grew more sophisticated I found myself preferring a sturdy loaf of wholemeal. I was probably growing into my sexuality. As I became more woman, men were allowed to become more men. If you see what I mean. And, these days, I find I'm not even averse to the idea of a six-pack. Maybe it's old age. Or maybe I've been brainwashed — all those leery nineties commercials featuring well-preserved professional women drooling over working men's sweaty torsos.

We were nose to nose for at least an hour. I didn't look at my watch but at a wild guess, and judging by the absence of traffic noises, I would've said it was about four in the morning.

"Kiss me," he said. And the words were like a first sip of brandy burning through my body and into my belly. But I didn't. Nor did I realise I'd pulled back until I felt the little draught of air between us. I'd only withdrawn an inch but an inch was a mile in those circumstances.

"Why me?" I said. He looked quizzical so I added, "I mean, do you do this sort of thing often?"

"Pick up strange girls?" he said, without missing a beat. "No. I don't do this often." And, of course, I believed him.

"What's happening?" I said.

"I don't know," he said. We mused for a moment.

"You know when you went to the loo in the restaurant?" I said.

"The 'loo'?" he said, taking the piss out of the word.

"The 'bathroom,'" I said, taking the piss out of the word.

"Yeah," he said.

I looked at him and suddenly didn't dare to go on.

"You followed me," he said.

"How do you know?" I said.

"Because you were meant to," he said.

"But why didn't you say something?" I said. "What if I hadn't followed you out of the restaurant. What would you have done then?"

"I knew you'd come," he said.

"But what if I hadn't?"

Little silence. "Don't you know how to trust?" he said.

Another silence. The CD we'd been playing had finished without us noticing and the street outside was silent. For some reason I couldn't move, couldn't blink, nothing.

"I've heard of love at first sight," he said. "I have heard of it."

More silence. And then he laughed.

"What?" I said.

"You're holding your breath again," he said. I laughed too then, releasing it, and he said, "You're thinking too much." I looked at him and he touched my right temple with his index finger. "It's all going on in here, isn't it?" he said, and then he pulled me back towards him, closed the gap.

He said to kiss him again and I gently brushed the tip of my nose against his.

"Eskimo kissing," I said. I tell you, those Eskimos may be chilly types but they know a thing or two about kissing. And then our lips came together and we kissed properly. Because we did at least do that. And I could feel the hot spring uncapped inside me, bubbling up to become a warm river flowing through me, carrying me away until I become delirious and in danger of losing my head.

Not such a bad thing. My head, you see, is something I sometimes find I can do without.

"And? So? What? He just went back to L.A.?" yelled Jennie, very hard done by, jolting me out of my reverie.

I'd given them a potted version of the above. Della was busying herself buzzing the limo windows up and down. I guessed she wasn't talking to me because of the not-having-shagged business.

"Well, we had breakfast," I offered.

"The sexiest meal of all!" they cried, perking up a bit.

"Well, sort of," I said. "I drove him round to Blonde's — she turned out to be happily married to someone else — and he got his bags and then I drove him to Heathrow and we had breakfast in this Happy Eater type thing in the airport."

"Oh," they said, disappointed.

"No, it was amazing," I said. So romantic — I didn't know how to explain — it was like we'd put on these special glasses and what is usually depressing and garish and loud appeared funny and witty and nice. Boy, were we happy eaters.

"But he was getting on a plane!" they squealed. "Didn't you cry?"

Well, actually, I was laughing a lot, all the time we were having breakfast. He was pretending he wasn't going to go and telling me all these stupid stories about people being scraped out of airline lounges and carried on to planes and how anyone who goes to the gate at the first call is mad as a snake, and anyone who goes at the second call is an eager beaver and anyone who goes at the third call . . . And then they actually called him by name which, despite his bravado, kind of freaked him out. And we sort of half walked, half ran to the departure bit and I didn't cry because I truly felt in my heart that we would see each other again at any minute. It didn't feel possible that he could go away from me. Not really away. Okay, he'd be over the ocean, but we'd found each other now, so we'd have each other. Always.

Always.

3

WE WERE still, can you believe it, cruising around in that goddamn limo. And it was beginning to get a little close in there, it was beginning to get a little old. The air was a heady cocktail of cigarette smoke, Eternity, armpits and whatever industrial bleach they used to clean the upholstery. They don't tell you it smells like school corridors on a Monday morning. They have to disinfect, I suppose, because of the unspeakable things people do on the seats.

"I never saw him again," I said. "It's getting smelly in here," I said.

"Let's tell the driver to go to the nightclub," hissed Della, "it's time."

"There's an intercom," said Jennie.

So Del pressed the button and yelled, "Stop the car."

"That was uncalled for," I said, thinking I'd pushed her over the edge and she was bailing out.

But she just said she was going to ride with the driver. "Too much yin in here. Not enough yang," she said. Fair enough.

The limo pulled over. "I may be some time," she said, and it was, in fact, the last we saw of her for quite some while. She got in again at the front but we couldn't see her because the driver's partition was heavily tinted.

"But how did you lose touch?" said Trish to me. "I mean — how could you? The Love of Your Life!"

"I don't know," I said. Because I don't, actually, I've never really understood it. "Perhaps there was some misunderstanding," I said vaguely.

"What do you mean?" they said. "What happened?"

"Well," I said, "nothing." There was a little silence. "I mean, really nothing. Nothing happened. I never heard from him again."

And that, I'm afraid to say, was the horrible, horrible truth.

When he'd kissed me goodbye for the final time, he'd asked me if I had e-mail.

"No!" I'd said, outraged at the idea. I thought he might have guessed I wouldn't from the state of my and Della's flat. We'd practically only just got an indoor loo. He said in that case it would be a traditional courtship. Letters.

"Love letters," he said. But he kind of said it with irony so I didn't know whether he meant it or not. I guess even then — seven years ago — it wasn't really done to say something romantic and keep a straight face. And these days, well, being romantic without irony is practically against the law. I see it as part of the post-modern thing. Like post-modern buildings, which are spacious and hygienic, meeting all the safety standards known to man, while harking back to the past with none of the feeling. Post-modern romance is similarly spacious and hygienic, while harking back to the past with none of the feeling.

In fact, I'm always arguing about this with Ed, my intended. I'm afraid to say he believes in being romantic without irony and, being Ed, just goes ahead and does it. Frankly, he spits in the wind of public opinion on the matter, buys roses (red ones!), says, "I love you," — all sorts. I'm getting used to it now but, you can imagine, at the beginning it made me think there was something wrong with him.

"There was a postal strike," I told my audience in the limo, and burst into uncontrollable laughter. Della and I always laugh uncontrollably when I say, "There was a postal strike," it's traditional. It's like "Bus crash on Oxford Street." That's what you say when you're late for work. Any humiliation regarding men — "postal strike." We laugh because, of all the excuses made up by all the women who've been let down by men since the beginning of time and, believe me, there have been some damn fine excuses — some subtle, sophisticated, founded in transactional analysis, Venus and Mars, half-hour-long ones — my postal strike has to be just about the most lame and pathetic of them all. It almost ranks with the proverbial dog who ate the proverbial homework.

This is how it goes. At around the time I met Alex there was a postal strike. It affected my postal area. Not all the post but some. The accumulation of undelivered mail became so overwhelming that a rumour went round that bags of mail were taken to derelict areas of the edges of London and burned. Having said that, no one I knew missed out on any mail whatsoever. Everyone got their electricity bills. Absolutely everyone expecting letters of rejection got them.

My love letter never came.

"But Honey — Honey," said Trish, very patient, "why didn't you ring him?"

"I did," I said. "I rang him and I got an answering-machine and a honeyed all-American voice said 'we're' not able to come to the phone 'but if you wanna leave us a message, we'll call you right back.' Emphasis on the 'us.'"

"That doesn't mean anything," said Trish, "flatmates."

"No, no, no," I said.

I knew it all. You know how you do — you know it all. You just know.

"She was blonde, you see, and she had the slimmest little thighs you ever saw and the distance between her knee and her foot was about forty yards and she had a pert nose and never had to wear make-up or a bra."

"How on earth could you know that?" said Jennie.

"I could hear it in her voice," I snarled. "Anyway," I added, "he never phoned me."

"But maybe he sent you a letter and he thought you never wrote back. Maybe he said 'call me' in his love letter and you never did. Maybe he sent you a ticket to L.A."

I looked at Jennie and wondered if she seriously believed I hadn't thought of that. Maybe he'd stood for ages at the arrivals gate amongst all those chauffeurs like wallflowers, holding up their dance cards, searching the crowd for a face. Maybe he waited and waited until finally the people coming through were down to a pathetic little trickle and all the chauffeurs had found their mates and even then he waited until it was only one or two strip-searched drug couriers coming through —

"Jennie," I said, "shut up. You're making it worse. If he'd sent me a plane ticket he would have called."

"But this is all daft," someone said. "You should have just called him again."

"I just couldn't," I said. I said it like I wanted to end the conversation right there, because I did. I didn't want to explain about the feeling I'd had in the pit of my stomach that told me with absolute certainty I'd never see him again. That familiar feeling, which says, "Oh yeah, I remember how it goes now. They act like they love you but they don't really. They go away and they never come back. And what the hell's the point in phoning them when they're never coming back? Because they never are. And that's the way of the world. Always has been. Always will be. End of story."

"End of story," I said firmly and out loud, and hoped they could tell I meant it.

They couldn't. Jennie said, "Well, I think it's tragic. Tragic. Romeo-and-Juliet tragic."

"Hardly the same?" said Martha, which I don't think she meant as a question but being antipodean everything she says comes out like one.

"Yes, it is, exactly the same. Crossed wires, communication failure," said Jennie.

"Like when Romeo doesn't get the letter to say Juliet's not really dead," said Trish.

"Actually I meant when the Fed-Ex gets delivered and Leonardo is too busy mooching moodily to see the van," said Jennie.

Of course I'd like to put down the loss of the Love of My Life to crossed wires — I would, I really would. But deep in my heart I knew the explanation was something far more profound. Deep, deep down, down in my soul, down where you really know things, I knew it was because I wasn't thin enough and I wasn't pretty enough.

I said this last bit to the girls then immediately regretted it because I got the usual chorus of "Of course you are!" "You are thin, you are pretty," which means absolutely minus nothing to the Enuff monster. Although I would like to make it clear — lest you throw this book across the room in disgust — that, by any normal standards, I am neither fat nor ugly. Of course I'm not. That's not the point. The point is — not Enuff.

"Well, it depends, doesn't it?" I said — or was it the Enuff monster speaking? "It depends what you mean by thin." Which put me in mind of the time I'd answered a lonely-hearts voice mail thing because I was fooling around one Sunday and happened to like the sound of this man's voice. He'd advertised for a "slim twenty-something" and the reply service suggested I describe myself, so I said I was slim. Suddenly I felt on very unsafe ground. I mean, what exactly is "slim"? Do you have to be Kate Moss — or will Jennifer Aniston do? So I qualified with "well, I think I'm slim" and then I immediately saw that would make him think I was one of those girls straining at the seams of my size fourteens and being all "it's only natural to have curves" about it. So I added that I was a size ten. And then felt compelled to admit that although I am a size ten in high-street shops, often in more designery shops — not couture or anything — but you know one up from the high street, I'm a size twelve. And I once needed a size fourteen in a French designer store that shall remain nameless. *But,* I urged the lonely-heart fat fascist on the other end of the line to understand, cut does vary, and to this day it is my position that those particular pants were cut very much on the small side.

"Did he ring back?" said Jennie.

"Course he didn't," said Trish, and snorted unattractively.

"Must have been a fault on the line," I said, sarcastic, because in my opinion the important bit in *Romeo and Juliet* isn't the bit when they get their wires crossed. The bit that strikes me as important is the bit when Juliet wakes up beside Romeo and finds him dead.

"Don't you just know that thing?" I said. "That thing when you wake up beside your lover and find him dead?" They all looked at me. "Metaphorically speaking," I said.

It's usually about six weeks into the relationship. Well, with most people it probably happens about six years into the relationship but with me it's six weeks. It goes like this. It's a Sunday morning, the sun is streaming in. You're all tangled up with him in the white of the sheets, sexy and tousled in your love bubble. He's asleep. You wake up slowly and your languid eye falls upon his sneakers sitting innocently beside the bed.

And that's it. Pop goes the weasel. I find empty shoes very upsetting. They have the eerie quality of a footprint in the sand but sadder — the sad imprint of a life in transit. This doesn't apply to all shoes, I should add; it doesn't apply to my sister's shoes lying around her bedroom floor, for example, or shoes in shops. But it definitely applies to the shoes of a man I'm involved with and, weirder still, my own shoes through his eyes. If I've got a boyfriend coming round, I have a morbid fear of him seeing any shoes of mine without my feet in them. As I am obviously unable to wear all my shoes at once, I am compelled to hide the overflow in the cupboard.

So, anyway, there I am, looking at those plate-of-meat sneakers and suddenly it hits me that this man in my bed, this Adonis, this marvellous specimen of masculinity, this dream-come-true is not any of those things. He has feet. He has sneakers. And when his sneakers are empty they sit there unapologetic, holding the memory of his feet, emanating a truly disturbing vulnerability. And there's something about this that makes me realise with absolute certainty that he's — oh God — he's . . . he's a human being.

"You see," I said, "*Romeo and Juliet* says it all. You feel all this passion, it feels so real, and then the love bubble bursts and it turns to ashes in your hands. It's like you woke up and found him dead. Dead and gone. The whole thing was all a big made-up story and there are the empty sneakers to prove it. And you can't even blame him for this disaster, because who made it all up in the first place? You did!"

"What about Ed? You nut!" yelled Trish, beside herself. "You're marrying him!"

She had a point. "I had the six-week love-bubble bust-up with Ed," I said, defensive now.

"And?" someone said. They waited.

"I just couldn't get rid of him," I said. "Ed was Ed — he just kept coming back. He was like thrush or something."

Jennie said she really thought she'd better give me the number of her therapist, except she only got half the word *therapist* out because at that moment the limo lurched violently and the tyres screeched and then it hit something quite hard. We all ended up in a messy tangle of legs and synthetic fabrics on the floor. I was lucky: my fall was broken by Martha — she's been on the Baby Spice jam-doughnut diet, so she provided a soft landing.

I untangled myself. We all seemed to be alive. I couldn't see anything through the limo's tinted windows so I got out. We were in one of those big residential streets in west London and the trees were ranked up in blossom, white against the night sky. The limo had hit one of the trees and been liberally sprinkled with its white confetti. There was something quite bridal about it all. Bridal — virginal.

Virginal, not. Not when Della got out of the front passenger seat adjusting her clothing. "Shit," she said.

"You can say that again," I said.

"Shit," she said.

"This is no time for jokes," I said.

"We were just fooling around," she said, in an exasperated way, easing her flippy bias-cut skirt round so that the bias did its absolute best for her hips. Then she got out her mobile phone and called 999.

I ran round to the driver's door. He was slumped in his seat, appeared to be dead.

"He's not dead," said Della, appearing on the other side of him, phone to ear. "I checked for a pulse. He's just concussed." Della had been through rigorous first-aid training with M&S.

By this time the girls had all de-limoed and were flapping about like a bunch of starlings ousted from a telegraph wire they'd been pleased to call home. There were shrieks when they saw what had happened to the driver.

"Calm down," said Della. "He hit his head on the steering-wheel. He's going to be all right."

"But why wasn't he wearing a seat-belt?" said Trish.

"He just wasn't," said Della, curt.

"For Christ's sake," I said. It took a while for the girls to get it but when they did there was much "What-are-you-like!"-ing and everyone stared at Della, very impressed.

"But, Del, *you* were wearing your seat-belt," Martha remarked.

"You think I'm a law-breaker?" Della said.

I went and sat on a doorstep while they tended to the driver, unbuttoned his collar, loosened his tie, buttoned his fly. A few minutes after the ambulance turned up, I saw Ed crossing the road towards me. His black hair was sticking up at the front a bit, the way it always does. He tries to gel it down but it always pops up again. He's got a big face, big features, a big smile. And he wears specs that make him look a bit like a schoolboy in a cartoon — not unhandsome, though, a sort of good-looking Just William. I suppose the schoolboy thing struck me because his spectacles were slightly awry and his jacket was flapping untidily. He was running.

"That was quick," I said. While he inspected me for damage he told me the boys had taken him for his stag night to the Passion Palace, one of those new nightclubs — and wasn't it lucky because his phone could get a signal there. The Passion Palace turned out to be the proper name for the club we used to refer to as Girls-Girls-Girls, as in "He looks like the type that goes to Girls-Girls-Girls." We knew about it because the club advertised with a flashing sign — saying Girls-Girls-Girls — that stuck up over the Westway.

"It's a lap-dancing club," he said.

"Cool," I said, before he could draw breath. "Madonna goes to lap-dancing clubs. They're very fashionable in L.A.," I said.

He looked relieved but there was a little silence which, for some reason, I found intensely irritating. "Describe the whole thing to me," I said, "from start to finish."

"Not now," he said. "Are you hurting anywhere? How's your neck? You didn't get whiplash, did you?"

"Did you ogle another woman's breasts?" I said. He didn't need to answer, I could tell by his face. "Don't answer that," I said. "Did she have a great body?" He didn't need to answer that either. "Don't answer that. Did she turn you on? Don't answer that either. What was her name?" I said and, needless to say, didn't let him answer. Long story short, when I finally allowed him to speak, it turned out she was called Cherry and she danced for him eight times. Eight times. Eight times!

Ed came and sat down beside me, put his arm around me. Typical, I thought, can't leave me alone for ten seconds. I put my head on his shoulder anyway. I thought that as it was there I might as well take advantage of it. I started to cry. Luckily Ed wasn't taking my crying too seriously, thought I was in post-traumatic shock or something, but all I can remember thinking was that the car crash was the least of my worries.

After I'd had my cry I felt a lot better. The limo driver had come back to life and started an argument with the ambulance people who were trying to get him to hospital. The girls were phoning for cabs except for Jennie who was riding round piggy back on the lanky Scot. One way of getting home. I told Ed that he'd better go back to his stag night. He said his friends had called it a day and that he wanted to take me home. This annoyed me. "Why?" I shouted.

He reminded me patiently that I'd telephoned him with the news that I'd been involved in a car crash.

"Exactly," I said, seeing the loophole in his argument and pouncing on it. "I told you I'd had a car crash. I didn't tell you to abandon ship and come running. I just wanted you to know I'd had a car crash. That's all," I said. "There was no need to come running." I said "come running" as if it were the most despicable activity on earth. I said "come running" as if I was saying "pick your nose and stick the bogey on the wall," which is apparently the kind of thing the Spice Girls did before they got famous. I had this irresistible urge to be just — just horrible all over him. And, honestly, I couldn't have told you why.

"Fuck this," he said, as well he might, and got up and walked off. A few paces up the road he turned round and came back. He always comes back. "Is this about the lap dancing?" he said.

"Don't be stupid," I spat.

"Fine," he said. And off he went again.

I stood up. "The wedding is off!" I yelled after him.

When it was clear he wasn't coming back this time, I paced up and down by the limo for a while and continued the argument in my head in such a way that it came out most satisfactorily in my favour. Della came over. I told her about the wedding being off. She sat down on the doorstep and sighed. I went on pacing.

After a while she started to hum under her breath. Then she started to sing, just quietly, but to sing nevertheless. *"First I was afraid,"* she sang, *"I was petrified. Kept thinking I could never live without you by my side."*

She looked me in the eye — one of her "don't-think-I-don't-know-you" looks. We go back a long way, me and Del. We go right back to the day, aged thirteen, when we performed Gloria Gaynor's "I Will Survive," the whole thing, eight verses and chorus, to several hundred pupils of the St. Barnabas Abbey Catholic School for Boys. Don't be thinking this was some karaoke-enhanced affair. This was me and her on the pavement, belting it out, uninvited and with no accompaniment. Our audience — the boys — leant out of the school windows *en masse* during their morning break. You might think they'd be enthralled but, as it turned out, they lacked the generosity even to manage an appreciation. We had to skulk away to jeers, our tails between our legs.

Afterwards the incident became quite famous and we were asked why we had done it. The only reply we could muster was that we wanted them to know. We wanted them to know that we would survive.

4

IT IS a truth universally acknowledged that a thirty-something single woman in possession of good fortune must (a) be wanting a man and (b) be having trouble finding one. But, if you ask me, it's not about having trouble finding a man, it's about having trouble compromising. Women are no longer forced to compromise, you see, because they no longer need husbands to bring home the bacon. They can simply buy a liver and bacon ready-meal from Marks & Spencer.

By the way, with all these mentions of M&S, you might well be thinking that I have been co-opted by Della and am involved in some kind of surreptitious product placement — that they have agreed to supply me with high-leg knickers in a three-pack for life. This is not — yet — the case and all I can say in my defence is, you try writing 10,319 words about contemporary woman without mentioning Marks & Spencer. Actually, Marks & Spencer really have quite a lot to answer for since women weren't liberated by Germaine Greer, they were liberated by the chicken korma.

It's surprising, then, that, given my love of curries and economy-wash cycles, I find myself with someone who is not only a man but also a husband — or, at least, a husband-to-be. I am surprised too. Believe you me, no one is more surprised than me.

The thing is that I am the kind of person who basically likes to be doing what everyone else is doing. It might take me a while to knuckle under but I always succumb in the end. So, if everyone's getting fake-fur jackets, it's never long before I get one too. And there's no getting away from it: being single kind of implies that you haven't sold well in the marriage marketplace. I have my pride.

You may also be wondering exactly how I stumbled into this happy-ever-after business. You reap what you sow. It's an abundant universe and all that. So, for what it's worth, here are my pearls of wisdom on How to Get a Husband, handily divided into six easy-to-follow steps to heaven.

Step One: Look in the *Yellow Pages*.

Look under Garden Designers, see Garden Services. (Another friend found hers under Drain and Pipe so you might think of looking there too.) Having chosen one because it is local and has no central switchboard with an 0800 prefix, you dial the number. You are told your call is being transferred, then it rings at the other end for ages until eventually a male voice answers. He is on a mobile phone and you have caught him navigating a windstorm off the coast of Alaska in a hot-air balloon. No — you are mistaken: the background noises change and you quickly realise that in fact he is involved in a high-speed police chase round the M25. You ask him if you are interrupting his getaway. It turns out he's actually in someone's garden in Muswell Hill.

Next, you invite him round to give you an estimate on your employer's garden. You make sure it's one of your really bad-hair

days. When he turns up you take one look at him and decide he's
not your type although why he needs to be your type when he's
here to do the garden — and not you — is something you could
not explain if your life depended on it. You note, however, his big
broad smile, his sticking-up hair and his glasses. The smile registers
as "warm, loving, kind to animals." Specs register as "non-smoker,
likes walks in country and good books." All of which rings up as
not your type. The calculation is quite straightforward. You are
nothing if not rational.

You then try to get a rise out of him by deliberately giving him
the impression that you are a kept woman and that the garden in
question — a Chelsea garden, I might add — is yours to do what
you want with and, what is more, you are doing what you want
with it with somebody else's money. You breezily order a Japanese
water garden, you don't blink an eye at the expense and then
remark, when the particular extravagance of the cedarwood deck-
ing is pointed out, "Well, it's not me who's paying." There is something so wildly un-PC about being a kept woman that you feel
pretty wanton and outrageous playing one, and become convinced
that the whole thing — being kept, that is — will be back in fashion at any moment. You are on the cutting edge.

You listen to him telling you how green and beautiful and how
quintessentially "Chelsea" the garden is with its rambly old roses
and wisteria. You shriek, "It's all got to go!" and wax lyrical about
minimalism and acres of grey pebbles. You watch him making
friends with the garden: he touches the plants and describes their
foibles to you, "This euphorbia would love it over there by the
wall," and boring old shrubs that, a moment before, just looked like
boring old shrubs seem not only to acquire personalities but a Bill
of Rights all their own. You begin to feel like some sort of ethnic
cleanser so you offer him a cup of tea and retreat to the kitchen.

In the kitchen, you watch him through the window and note his
big bone structure and decide he's probably got some kind of
natural-childbirth wife in the country and seven children, although

he can't be much older than you. You wait until he comes in, then you give him his tea. You rather hope he'll spit out his Earl Grey with cries of "What's this muck?" but he says, "Oh, good, Earl Grey," and doesn't ask for sugar.

You both sip your tea for a couple of moments, then he looks at you long and hard and says, "Bollocks."

"What?" you say.

"Bollocks!" he says. "You're not someone's wife."

"I never said I was," you say. But nevertheless you are outraged. You put your hands on your hips and ask him how he can tell.

"You don't look like someone's wife," he says.

You take this the wrong way, you are deflated. You clutch at straws. "Couldn't I be someone's mistress?" you say.

"No," he says, very definite. There's something about the way he's looking at you — through you — that makes you decide to drop the line of questioning.

You tell him that he's right and that you work for a manic millionaire movie mogul called Mac and it's his house and his idea for the water garden. And that he's hardly ever in London and that you run his life for him when he is. He asks you about Mac's movies and attempts to kick off a film-buff conversation — asks you what your favourite film is. You fear it is only a matter of time before he mentions Antonioni. You tell him your favourite film is *The Sound of Music* to shut him up. You'll find he immediately asks you out.

In fact, *The Sound of Music* business turned out to be pretty fundamental to the general scheme of the Happy Ever After — so we'll make that the second step.

Step Two: Tell him your favourite film Is *The Sound of Music*.

In the pub he admits that *The Sound of Music* is his favourite film too, and you end up singing a protracted medley. Of course, you know the words better than he does but he's not bad for a boy. He makes you laugh so much you nearly spray a mouthful of lager over him.

You decide you're hungry and you end up in a local Thai restaurant. Things are going so well you can see that, any moment now, he's going to get the wrong idea. Because, of course, he's not your type. But you watch the funny things he does with his face when he's talking and you notice the way his forearms are so broad and straight when he rolls up his sleeves to eat. And you're kind of enjoying all the attention because he keeps asking you questions about your life, your childhood, everything. You answer for a while but you don't want to get on to the my-parents-died-in-a-plane-crash jag because it's usually a bit of a downer, especially for the other party, so you deflect with questions about him.

It turns out his mum and dad died in quick succession less than two years ago but he exhibits none of your sensitivity to feeling and talks shamelessly about how difficult it was, how close they were because he was an only child and how his parents had had him quite late in life. Then he tells you about how he left his girl-friend of five years when they died because he realised he'd ended up losing himself in the relationship. He tells you how he inherited their terraced house in Queen's Park and is now doing it up bit by bit himself.

By the end of the evening he seems quite happy and he tries to get you to say you'll go boating with him on Saturday. You've never been boating in your life and you're not about to start now. You don't even know what boating is. Boating turns out to be going out in a row-boat on the upper reaches of the river Thames and having a picnic.

He won't take no for an answer, and you like him a lot by now so you decide to give it to him straight. You do so — and this was obviously critical to my success, so listen closely, husband-hunters, to Step Three.

**Step Three: Tell him that if you go "boating" with him
you will end up getting involved and that, much as you
like him, it is clearly Not Going to Work Out between
you so it would be best if the whole thing
was nipped in the bud right now.**

He then pretends not to know what you're talking about. He does
a very good job of pretending: in fact, he looks quite convincingly
nonplussed.

You explain slowly and clearly that you are doing him the honour of not beating about the bush and it is quite obvious to you
that the evening has turned into a date of a sort and that should you
spend a long, lazy Saturday on a boat together, drifting and basking
in the sunshine, you will end up . . . Well, you will end up — not
to put too fine a point on it (you lower your voice) — having sex.
And while you are sure that sex would be very nice, the prognosis
for a future between the two of you is not good. You tell him not
to be offended, it's just a matter of not being suited. He looks
shocked, his mouth falls open, he absolutely doesn't lower his voice
to say — in fact, shout would be a more accurate description of his
voice level: "I don't want to have sex with you!" And so, you see,
we were off to an auspicious start. I refused to believe he didn't
want to have sex. I told him so, but to be honest it was hard not to
be the tiniest bit red in the face. We had a brief argument about
whether we were on a date or not. I said, "If a man asks a woman
out for a drink, what is it if not a date?" and I do think I had a
point. He kept saying stuff about making friends but — I mean —
come on!

I do have friends who are male — I do — but they're either gay
or I've slept with them, or if not with them with their best friend,
or they're sleeping with my best friend . . . or something.

Not that any of this was on my mind as I wandered lonely as a
cloud through the streets of London in the early hours of the

morning after the hen party before. It wasn't even on my mind as I put my key into Mac's door and let myself in. I was just glad to be in Chelsea. Chelsea is very comforting. It puts me in mind of the department store Peter Jones, which is in Chelsea, very morally upright — "never knowingly undersold" — and has been known to display all the various types of scissors it carries in neat rows in the window. Some people say that in case of a nuclear attack you should go straight to Peter Jones because nothing bad could ever happen in Peter Jones. Well, Chelsea is a bit like that. Nothing bad could ever happen in Chelsea.

I was headed for Mac's power-showers — and the jacuzzi and the thirty-six-inch flat screen DVD and the cable movies. Mac was out of town but Mac doesn't mind me staying at his. In fact, he's given me my own room and would really prefer me to live there. Then he could have his wicked way with me twenty-four/seven when he's in town.

I chose a CD in the living room, selected "bathroom" as the destination and turned the volume to max. Then I went upstairs, lit the candles and got naked with some enthusiasm, slinging my hen-party outfit on to the luscious Italian marble floor, and set about the serious business of foaming aromatherapy.

If this seems disrespectful, given that I'd just called off my marriage, you should know that I'm a Scorpio and at times of stress I have to get into water. I can't string two thoughts together until I've got into water. It's like baptism or something, I am reborn. Up to this moment I'd just been feeling completely blank. I did catch myself worrying whether the honeymoon was refundable but that was as far as it went. I was probably suppressing my feelings or something. Or maybe it's just that, like I said, nothing bad can happen in Chelsea.

I called Ven — this was possible at two thirty in the morning because Ven was in L.A. being an au pair. We have a theory, Ven and I, that Ven was actually meant to be a valley girl but was sent to the wrong family. She's got all the right bits for a valley girl —

shallowness, blonde hair, curvy long legs, looks particularly good with sunglasses up on her head. I'm more sort of straight and brown. Long straight hair — brown. Long straight body — brown (if I've been anywhere near the sun). Anyway, Ven and I hadn't wanted to be separated but in the end we decided she'd better cut to the chase, go to L.A. and find her roots.

When she picked up I didn't say hello or anything just "The wedding's off."

"Oh. My. God," she said, right on cue. "Tell me."

I told her about the limo and the girls, about the lanky Scot, about the crash, about the argument with Ed.

"Respect," she said, when she heard about the lap-dancing club. "That's my boy Ed." Ven thinks Ed is some kind of god from Planet Nice. When she first clapped eyes on him we were up in Mac's office window and Ed was down in the street unloading his van and Ven was suddenly jigging about behind me hissing, "Who is he? Who is he?" with a very sharky look on her face.

I said, "Who is who?" thinking she was referring to some sleek-looking drug-dealers I rather liked the look of getting out of a BMW on the other side of the road. Then I realised she meant Ed so I said, "That's Ed. He's doing the garden."

"He's gorgeous," she said, with a long linger on the "gor."

It did make me look at him again. "Well, I suppose he's — he's tall," I said, and left it at that. But it might have had some effect in later weeks when she kept murmuring things like "Say hello to Ed from me," and raising a perfectly plucked eyebrow.

Back to the future: Ven's mid-Atlantic accent is cultivating nicely. "I don't buy that you're not marrying the nicest, most decent man that ever walked the planet and was tall and gorgeous thrown in with it. I don't buy the jealous-of-the-lap-dancer bit," she said.

"What," I said, "would you know about relationships?" Silly question. Everything, of course — although Ven doesn't have a sex life. She says she's doing True Love Waits but I think she finds the

men her age just can't keep up with her. Anyway, she doesn't seem
to mind. She says studies show sex is better in middle age. I've told
her it's marriage not better sex that True Love is meant to Wait for,
but she ignored me.

"You don't give a shit about Big Boobie the lap-dancer —" she
said.

"Cherry," I interrupted. "She has got a name, you know, and
there's absolutely no call for disrespect here."

"Cherry-schmerry. Whatever," she said, "I don't buy it."

"I'm not selling it," I snapped back.

"Okay," she said, "keep your lace panties on. Let's go back," she
said.

"Back?" I said.

"Start at the beginning," she said.

I described the evening in broad brushstrokes. She wasn't getting
any clues so she said, "Talking about what? In the limo, talking about
what?" A silence fell. "Breathe," she said. I hadn't realised I wasn't.

More silence.

"Uh — hello?" she said hopefully, after a moment.

I said, "Talking about that guy I met that time, you know the
one that —"

"Alex," she said, curt, "the Love of Your Life." Then she added,
"Aha."

"Listen," I said, and tried to be older sister, "I'm over Alex. It
was a fantasy. I'm not stupid enough to think it meant anything."

"I don't believe you," she said. "We're all stupid enough to think
these things mean something. Especially things like that."

"Tell me," I said, "you're six years younger than me, how come
you think you know it all?"

"Different generation," she said. "More wisdom in the genes."

"Levi's?" I said.

"No," she said. "Calvins. See what I mean?" She paused to
savour her triumph a moment, then went on. "How do you feel?"

"Fat," I said.

When Ven was thirteen she won the Metropolitan Police Quiz Trophy (don't ask) and the local paper came to take a picture of her at school with her statue thing and they asked her how she felt and she said, "Fat," because that's how she felt. She hadn't expected to win and she'd been caught wearing her second-best school-uniform skirt, the one she felt fat in. She wasn't fat at all, she was just in a bad mood about having her photograph taken — we've both always hated having our photograph taken. We're like one of those tribes that think it's stealing the soul.

We'd also noticed that when we felt bad we also felt fat even if we were the skinniest minnies — which we were, actually. Money can be a bit like that too: you can feel broke or flush and it's got very little to do with how much there is in the bank.

Anyway, the fools printed it. The headline was: "Dulwich School-girl Feels Fat." The journalist must have thought fat was some hip new word for happy, like when "bad" meant good for a bit.

"Fat's not a feeling," Ven said.

"Since when?" I said. Ven's changing — I think it might be all those guru cults they go to out in California.

"How do you feel about losing Ed?" she said.

"You know what I keep thinking about?" I said.

"What?" she said.

"Red Ted," I said.

Red Ted was a teddy with a red ribbon round his neck. I got Red Ted when I was three. By the time I was fifteen the ribbon had long gone but he was wearing a red sweater I'd had as a baby so he was always called Red Ted. It's true that Red Ted was also known for his extreme left-wing views but it was basically the jumper that earned him his nickname.

Red Ted's eyes had fallen off and been sewn on and fallen off again and left off and now he was threadbare. He was also in a plastic bag at the bottom of my wardrobe. I rediscovered him one day when I was cleaning out my bedroom — giving it a makeover in prepara-tion for the potential visit of a new boyfriend. In that moment I considered myself the most grown-uppest grown-up there ever was. I was ready to relinquish my childhood without a second thought and, in a fit of unsentimentality, I threw out Red Ted.

But that night I couldn't sleep and I ended up going out in the middle of the night and rummaging through the dustbins. But Theresa had put out the kitchen rubbish in the interim and it proved more than I could do to sift through rotting vegetables and wet coffee grounds wearing only a nightie in a tart November dawn — so I left Red Ted.

The next morning, I overslept as usual, rushed out of the house late for school and forgot all about Red Ted. On the way to school I heard the familiar rumble and clunk of the rubbish truck, like a distant rattling of the gates of hell. My stomach dropped into my boots in the split second before I made the connection in my brain. The truck clattered past me going fast on its way to the depot and there — hanging out of the back, caught in the jaws of doom, practically decapitated — was Red Ted.

I ran after the dustmen wailing and pleading — they didn't hear me. I couldn't keep up with the truck. I went to school. I was late, and when a teacher told me off, I burst into tears. I sobbed and sobbed. I was inconsolable. They couldn't get a word out of me. They thought someone had died. Who I don't know, since most of the important people in my life were already dead and my sister Ven was happily ensconced in Form 2b in the lower school. When they finally got it out of me about Red Ted they said I could go home for the day and referred me to counselling.

Actually, I didn't go home straight away. I dried my tears and made straight for the aforementioned St. Barnabas Abbey Catholic School for Boys. I skulked around outside, sent messages in at break, talked my boyfriend into coming home with me and energetically seduced him for several hours in my new cuddly toy–free bedroom, finally giving the whole thing up as a lost cause just as Theresa put her key in the door.

As for counselling, I went once. I didn't know what to say. We sat in silence for fifty minutes. I assumed that my counsellor, like me, was either too embarrassed or too bored to speak although I later discovered that the silence is some kind of Freudian technique. I didn't go again.

Mistake? Possibly.

"Red Ted," said Ven, "is your inner child." When I said Ven was shallow I should have made it clear that the shallowness is purely affectation: it's in the manner and style, not in the content. Unfortunately.

I felt like saying, "Be shallower," but I just said, "Inner child. Right," at which point I was saved by the bell.

Guess who. No prizes. Ed. I said goodbye to Ven and let him in, went back up and got back into the bath so's I could think straight. He followed me. "What's going on?" he said.

"Nothing's going on," I said.

Silence.

"It's very stressful getting married," I said.

"We're not getting married," he said. "You called it off. Have you forgotten?"

Silence.

"If you really want to know," I said, "I just couldn't stand the expression on your face when you told me about that lap-dancer."

He was relieved, there was a glimmer of a smile, he was . . . I suddenly realised he was pleased with himself.

"There it is again!" I yelled.

"What?" he said.

"The expression!" I yelled. "Yuk!" I yelled. "Smug!"

"Sweetheart," he said, "I love you."

I took a deep breath. I felt white-hot rage spreading from my belly. "Don't do that," I said, "just don't do that." Then I felt another feeling. I don't know what. I remember thinking, If I start crying now I'll never be able to stop, so I submerged myself in the water instead. When I came up all sleek and wet, Ed was right there, really close, squatting beside the bath. I looked at him and all I could think was, Get away from me. "You know when I first saw you," I said, "the very first moment I saw you I thought, not my type."

Ed didn't move. He didn't even flinch. "Explain to me," he said, "how you get from me going to a lap-dancing club — once — on my stag-night to me not being your type for ever and ever amen. It doesn't marry up — no pun intended — and, anyway, I am your type. I have evidence."

"What are you?" I said. "Rumpole of the fucking Bailey?"

"If I wasn't your type why would you give a flying fuck what I did with fifty fucking lap-dancers?" he said. He was enjoying swearing — he didn't do it often — so I thought there might be more but he only added, "Not to put too fine a fucking point on it."

He smiled and I was overwhelmed by an urge to wipe it off his face.

"Ed," I said, quietly, patiently. Pause for effect. "It's quite simple. I've gone off you. I don't fancy you any more and that's the end of it."

He reeled. He was mortally wounded. It put me in mind of that moment in *Raiders of the Lost Ark* when Harrison Ford is presented with a rabidly eager sword-fighter, flourishing a deathly-looking scimitar. Harrison simply gets out his gun and shoots the guy.

Ed walked to the door, which was the idea. Then he came back. He always comes back.

It suddenly came to me that I'd like to be sitting peacefully in a swanky restaurant with some fucked-up young man getting it on with himself in the mirror while generally getting off my case.

"You're trying to drive me away," he said.

"Oh, please," I said and tried to get out of the bath and wrap a towel round myself in one movement. I felt events had taken a turn that required some kind of clothing.

"Okay," he said. "What exactly is it about marriage that scares you so much?" He was always one for these piercing questions on the battle of the sexes. "Are you scared that you'll let me down?" he said.

"Me?" I said. "Let you down?" I said. "Men are the ones that do the letting down. Men leave," I said. I don't know where that came from. Honestly I don't. But it came out with utter conviction — and, by the way, it is not statistically the case: more women leave marriages than men.

"Well," he said, "I've got to be going myself."

And so he did.

5

From: alexlyell@hotmail.com
To: honeypot@webweweave.co.uk
Subject: Hi
Date: 12 April — 11.40 a.m. PST
Mime-Version: 1.0

Honey,

I first started telling you stuff in my car. I thought, what if you were there beside me? I had this idea. This idea that you might be interested.

Sometimes when I'm doing something or thinking about something in particular, I suddenly see a street corner in my head. For no reason. But I always see that one particular street corner when I do that thing. There must be a neural pathway in my brain that links the activity to the image — seemingly arbitrary, but persistent nevertheless. And the pathway gets more and more worn and the brain electricity just keeps on going that way.

You know in parks when paths between paths get worn across the grass because that's the way people want to go, they call those paths lines of desire. Well, the geography of my mind keeps bringing me back to you.

So Honey — my old friend — how's life? How is LIFE?

As for me, life on this side of the pond is fine, thank you. That's F.I.N.E. — which out here stands for Fucked-up Insecure Neurotic and Emotional, but I guess you can pick your own adjectives. How about egotistical? So yes — I'm doing just fine. I find myself in a 3-D world of large metal objects driving very slow and although I am told that I am the same as everyone else I know that I am, in fact, not. Things go on inside me that I must not mention. But I have a well-tailored suit and a very important purpose and my own large metal object to drive around in pursuing that purpose. Oh, yes, life is fine, thank you very much.

Life — at this particular minute — is a suite in the Chateau Marmont looking out on the hills above Sunset. Life is therefore a hotel room, a phoney antiqued coffee table, and a view up a dusty escarpment that has a kind of impermanent air, like a building site.

I am typing into my lap-top. Tom, my director, is giving it large. He has just now humiliated me in front of one of the models. Because she humiliated him. She has some clothes on — not many, but some. Which seems to be the problem. She's keeping them on. She even makes reference to "perverted strips" in casting suites. Tom goes to me, "Alex, perhaps you would care to return from the Planet Alex and tell Ms. . . . Ms. . . . ." gives up, "Tell this young lady about the product." Tom is one of the very few who has noticed my alien status.

I say, "Uh — it's a commercial for depilatory cream for the — uh — sensitive areas."

The model goes, "My thighs are fucking perfect." Doesn't miss a beat. Not impolite, just to the point, like she's giving us her high-school grades. She's about as close as a human could get to a fresh-bloomed tiger-lily — long-stemmed, waxy, golden.

I notice I am a bit hotter under the skin. Do I want her? Well, not exactly but I'm putting some effort into not wanting her. The lap-top is coming in handy. Avoid eye contact. I don't want to start that thing with my eyes. Tom thinks I'm writing production reports for the client.

Cherelle — my girlfriend — says some people have walls of humor and some people have walls of charm. She says all sorts of people have all different walls — and I have a wall of lap-top. Cherelle's not stupid. My lap-top is my first line of defense.

Do you mind me telling you this stuff? I have this idea that you will understand.

This isn't the first time I've written to you, you know. But before it's always been in my head. This is the first time I've committed to print.

Tom's favorite pick-up line: what's the C-word? Blush, stammer — everyone knows what the C-word is. Yah. Commitment.

Tom tells the model she won't get anywhere with that attitude but I know Tiger-lily's got the job. Now she said no to him, Tom will have to see those thighs. They say the brain is the biggest sex organ of them all.

Then it occurs to me that someone somewhere in this universe gets to go to bed with this woman. Maybe tonight. Maybe someone gets to go to bed with her tonight. I get kind of hung up on that idea until I remember that I've slept with similar creatures. The memories slip, I can't catch hold of them. I guess the occasions were like that too.

Is it okay if I write you about all this? Not that you'll read it most likely. I looked you up on the net. The closest I came was "honeypot" in London. Unlikely to be you but I'll try it anyway. Send it out into the ether. Did you know, a thought is an energetic impulse that never dies? Apparently it travels on and on forever. If I'm honest I've even picked up the phone and dialed your number. There's a strange voice on the line — I guess you've moved.

Take care,
Alex

From: alexlyell@hotmail.com
To: honeypot@webweweave.co.uk
Subject: Hi
Date: 12 April — 8.43 p.m. PST
Mime-Version: 1.0

Honey,

In the car Tom goes, "You know I saw Pete Sampras on TV and he was talking about all the sacrifices you have to make to be truly great — all the fucking sacrifices. It was real sad, man."

"Yeah? And?" I said.

"Reminds me of me," he goes.

Saved by the cellphone — Cherelle.

"I just saw Madonna," she goes, "coming out of Tommy Hilfiger and guess what?"

"What?" I go.

"Her stomach bulges when she bends over!"

"Why was she bending over?" I go.

"To pet a dog. It bulged right out."

"Pot belly!" Tom suddenly yells — I had Cherelle on the speaker. "Alex, don't you just love a pot belly? Isn't it the biggest turn-on? Have our people call Madonna's people and set up a meeting."

Cherelle laughed, but I know she doesn't really find it funny. I know she totally believes that I might go off with Madonna at any moment. That Madonna would leap at the chance to spend time with a groovy guy like me.

"You're gonna see Madonna for the commercial?" she says. She's not stupid, Cherelle, she just loses her place sometimes. Like she's half-way through a book but she's so totally caught up in what might happen and what has happened that she forgets what page she's on.

"No," I say, "I'm not seeing Madonna for a pube-removal commercial."

"Gotta go, babe," says Tom, "got another call coming in." Then he cuts her off and mutters, "Jesus," to himself. "Must be your fucking mother," says Tom. Then he yells, "Pull in! Pull in!"

We'd only got like a couple of hundred yards down Sunset. "Come on," he says, "we'll have a fucking drink in the Sky Bar."

When we're in there Tom says, "Thing is," and stirs his margarita energetically, "you get a guy like you going along quite happily," he hunches his shoulders and does an imitation of me moseying along quite happily, "and then suddenly — bang-boom out of nowhere, man — you're toppled. You're gone. And you know when that happens — when that happens there's only one thing for sure, she's your mother."

"Cherelle and my mother are totally different," I say calmly. When Tom gets like this it's best not to give the thing any energy.

"It's not like Cherelle's got the ass of the century, if you know what I mean," he continues, undeterred. "No disrespect to Cherelle's ass, man — it's a cute ass — but it's like there are a million cute asses out there. Why that ass? That's what I'm saying. Why that ass? She's your fucking mother. Have a drink, will you? Oh, shit, I forgot."

At this point he looks sadly into his margarita. He misses his old drinking buddy. He's lonely drinking on his own. He's not an asshole. I know he seems — well, fuck it. I'm not going to defend him but he's not an asshole, believe me.

I look up and see that Tiger-lily is over by the bar. We meet eyes. The place has filled out — I thought it was on the wane but it seems pretty busy tonight. Tom catches my expression as I look down. I try to think of something neutral — muesli, muesli, muesli — but it's too late, he's read my thoughts. His head whips round and he clocks Tiger-lily.

His largess goes into a whole new gear. She is ushered over, and her friend; he gets them seats and drinks — Diet Cokes. He tells Tiger-lily she got the job.

She says, "Course I fucking did." And then to Tom, "How come you're such an asshole?" Which he loves.

And I like it too, to be honest. I like her for being so cool, so self-contained and frosty cool. And complicated. Looks like it would take a nice long time to get to know her.

Tom gives it some for half an hour. Makes them laugh. I try to work out whether the coincidence of her being here is meaningful in some way. It's like I could handle it in the casting, but now she's fucking here in the bar. And I'm trying to pretend I'm not on a string that Tiger-lily's holding the other end of. But it's no good.

Eventually, while her friend is whispering in Tom's ear, I look at Tiger-lily and smile the smile — the conspirator's smile.

She leans across the table and goes, "I'm taken." She shows me her ring, says she doesn't wear it to castings. Then she smiles again and asks me do I want to do a line with her?

"Why me?" I said — pathetic, I know. But that's what I said.

"Takes one to know one," she said.

"I want you to promise me that you'll look after yourself," I said. That surprised her. Even her.

"What?" she said.

"I know you're beautiful and all that shit," I said, "but you don't have to kill yourself over it."

"Okay," she said, laughing at me now.

"I know it hurts," I said.

"I like you," she said.

"I like you too," I said. Then I left.

The minute I was outside I got on the cellphone and asked Cherelle's dad for his daughter's hand in marriage. He said he'd call when he got through with his dinner meeting.

So I got in the car and headed for the Bourgeois Pig. Which is not a name I have for Cherelle's dad but a café in Venice. I'm here now — amongst the wannabes, fluttering at their keyboards, lapping at their lattes. They have power points by the table here. It's L.A.

Here comes The President.

Take care,
Alex

From: alexlyell@hotmail.com
To: honeypot@webweweave.co.uk
Subject: Hi
Date: 12th April — 10.23 p.m. PST
Mime-Version: 1.0

Honey,
I'm home.

Home is a West Hollywood condo with a pool.

The President is what I call Cherelle's dad. He is actually a president although that's not saying much — L.A. is teeming with presidents. You can't move for presidents.

So he said I could marry her. Of course it's a little quaint asking the dad first but, knowing the family as I do, believe me, I need him on board.

To give him credit, he didn't hesitate. But he did sigh — kind of. Asked me to treat her good. Said I was a decent enough guy, that kind of thing. Moving swiftly on to — "Hey! Alex! Tell me what's hot?" Which is kind of what people say when they run out of conversation around here.

I don't know why a studio president is asking me — me — what's hot. I'm cold as a witch's tit. I guess he's just trying to be nice.

I told him Tom and I want to remake *Chitty Chitty Bang Bang* for today's kids. He said, what did I think *Back to the Future* was? I talked him into some kind of interest anyway — with the car as a space rocket. He recommended a book called *How to Write a Movie in 21 Days*. Yikes.

It's almost past Hollywood's bedtime. Cherelle will be home soon.

I never thought I would end up with Cherelle. But all the time I went along as if I would end up with Cherelle.

I've given up living dangerously — you probably worked that out for yourself. If I sat down next to you, the beautiful stranger, in a restaurant today, I'd look the other way. But the thought remains, there must be more than this, something louder, something brighter, a half-glimpsed possibility — maybe that was her but look again and she's gone. And all the time my feet keep on walking towards Cherelle, always come back to Cherelle. Cherelle's like my default setting.

I gave up living dangerously when I nearly gave up living. I went to a horrible place inside me. I could never have believed it was so horrible — I could never have believed it was inside me. Don't ever go there. Promise me.

But it's okay, I made it to rehab. No big deal. It's not exactly headline news out here: *Hollywood Nobody in Cocaine Habit Fiasco.*

Blame the cocaine. In rehab I found out it wasn't the coke took me to the horrible place, it was the other way around. Now I have to live with myself. By the way, in case you're wondering, I wasn't high when we met in London.

One day, in the treatment center, I was at the reception desk making a phone call and there was this pretty girl there with straight brown hair down to her butt and these huge Barbie eyes that looked like they'd been drawn on by Disney. She was in there with an older man and she was beautifully turned out, lips, nails, fancy watch, etc., except she was slurring her words to hell and every now and then it looked like she forgot to hold her head up and it just slumped down onto her chest and gave her a big shock.

I heard her say to the man, "Don't do this to me, Daddy," but with no conviction whatsoever. If you were directing her in a scene you'd want to say, "Once more, with feeling."

Then the dad said, "This is the best thing I could ever do for you, baby," but also with no conviction whatsoever. The two of them were like they were in some kind of bad soap opera, just going through the motions. And then the dad said, "'Bye," and walked out and she said, "Fuck you, Daddy," to his back and then the nurses led her away. God, they were bad actors.

So that's how I met Cherelle. The next time I saw her she was back haranguing the nurses and saying, "If I don't get my Walkman, I walk." When you check in they confiscate anything that might give you pleasure, all your escape equipment. But Cherelle didn't "walk," she jogged ten times around the perimeter fence every day with no audio stimulation whatsoever.

One day Cherelle came and sat next to me in a lecture. A sex lecture, as it happens. They were explaining about healthy relationships. Real basic stuff that you'd think anyone would know. Well, it was like they were teaching us Greek.

The lecture went something like this:

Stage One: getting to know someone — discuss movies, play tennis, that kind of thing (tennis featured large in stage one, worrying for those of us with no Ivy League education).

Stage Two: exclusive dating — holding hands, kissing.

Stage Three: non-genital sex (your guess is as good as mine).

Stage Four: genital sex (self-explanatory).

I got the impression that months were meant to go by between stages.

The air kind of thickened between me and Cherelle as the lecturer talked. I remember the lecturer said something about how normally we're all inclined to get straight to the genital sex. I thought that if she called it "genital sex" one more time I'd never be inclined to get to it again.

Afterwards, Cherelle goes, "Do you want to have a coffee before Shame-busters?" It really cracked me up the things you heard people saying in rehab. I kind of enjoyed it, once I got used to the idea — especially when we'd be lying by the pool or playing volleyball and this crackly voice would come out of the Tannoy system saying stuff like "Moving into the Light starting now in Room 22."

We did have coffee together, me and Cherelle, decaff, of course. It turned out she was in for Xanax. So we got there under and over the counter respectively. Nicely matched, you could say.

I guess she grew on me. Part of it was I thought that if I was going to do this what's-your-favorite-movie-wanna-have-a-hit thing, I'd better do it with someone who knows I'm talking about tennis. And I liked her. Cherelle had this kind of certainty thing going for her. Like she's certain of her rightful place on this earth. You felt you were in a safe pair of hands with Cherelle. And she knew what was what. Cherelle knows everything from where to get the best real-estate deals to where to get the best eyelid tucks. Not that she's into cosmetic surgery herself — but if you have to have it, she wants you to have the best.

As you know, Tom says Cherelle is my mother. Personally, I don't see the resemblance between Cherelle and Mom. For one thing, Cherelle knows how to dress. For another, she doesn't come from trash. Cherelle is well connected.

Beat.

That's what you write when you want to indicate that the actor should pause for effect in a film script — "beat."

She just got back. She's been out spinning and having juice with a girlfriend. Cherelle says spinning is a kind of inspirational-group exercise-bike-riding class. Apparently you get given all these positive messages about how wonderful you are as you ride. When she first told me about it, I assumed it was the bike that talked but it turns out there's a real live instructor.

So now I guess I go ask the girl to marry me.

Wish me luck,
Alex

6

I DIDN'T even go to bed. I put my crumpled hen-party dress back on — thought it lent a suitable air of tragedy — and drove down to Theresa's. I found her at the stables.

"You're up early," she said.

"Not early," I said, "late. I'm up late."

"Oh dear," said Theresa. "We'll have a cup of tea, will we?" She's from Ireland, Theresa.

I knew Theresa would be up at dawn. Her husband, Roland — heard of but never seen in my day as he was always off travelling around the world compiling the eccentric tourist guides he published himself — had suddenly amazed everyone by selling his company to some media giant for a couple of million. He'd moved the family out to Essex and Theresa supposedly never had to lift a finger again in her life.

Except Theresa being Theresa couldn't sit still for one minute and her youngest, Molly, had developed a passion for ponies and now Theresa, who didn't know a hock from a forelock, was up at the crack every morning mucking out before the school run.

"This is Smoky," she said. "He's lovely except he's a bit naughty about gates. He bolts if he sees a gate."

"Could be awkward in the countryside," I said. "Quite a few gates."

"And this is Stirrup. She's the biggest sweetie — but don't stroke her, she bites if you touch her mane."

"Sweetness itself," I said.

In the kitchen, she put the kettle on then ran an eye over me, a knowing eye. She assessed the damage. With some precision, I could tell. "That's a nice dress," she said.

"Trees," I said, because that's what we called her when we were little, usually in that wheedling voice that heralds the request for an ice-cream or a comic or whatever and she'd retort, "Money doesn't grow on Trees, you know," and then buy it for us anyway.

The wheedling voice was because "That's a nice dress" was not the innocent remark it might appear. Theresa knew the story behind the dress. She knew the whole story — story of my life. And, lest we forget, she was going to call my attention to the dress. You see, she knew all the chapters in the Book of Ed and, just because of the writing on today's page, she wasn't going to let me ignore the rest.

Which brings me to the story of the dress and, in fact, this might be a good moment for Step Four in my foolproof guide to husband-getting.

Step Four: On your second date, appear in a public place wearing a pair of oversized men's pyjamas and bird's-nest hair.

First, though, stay up all night mourning a woman you never met who looked good in baby pink. Wash your face pale, crying for the girl who married the prince and blew the happy right out of ever after.

In the old days, you see, they had Cinderella and, okay, she beat her ugly sisters to the bride's bouquet but only after she had suffered, swept her ashes, survived a wildly dysfunctional family and dragged herself home at midnight several times. Thus illustrating that only when you have found your true self can you earn eternal union with your soul-mate.

But Cinders went out of fashion — something to do with the outfits, I expect — so we got Princess Diana instead. Diana went at it arse over tit. Got the dress and the prince first, only later scattering her ashes all over us. Thus showing those who might have misunderstood Cinderella (or only seen the Disney version) that fairytale weddings and great legs and Prince Charmings don't buy you self-love and proving yet again the most profound spiritual maxim of our time: *There is no such thing as a free lunch.*

So, you go to Kensington Palace where they are laying the flowers. You go because this is a historical thing. A historical hysterical thing. You go so you can tell your children about it. That's your excuse — because, you see, you're not totally out of the closet about your fascination with Diana. I mean, you're not sure if you're allowed to be fascinated by Diana *and* be the kind of person who reads broadsheet newspapers — or intends to read broadsheet newspapers anyway, even if you don't often get round to it because you're so busy reading about Diana in *Hello!*

When you get to Kensington Palace you find that strangers are talking to each other. Extraordinary. It's like Britain during the war. Blighty. You befriend a young woman from Leeds who is making a mandala (her word) for Diana from flowers and candles. She has tears streaming down her face. The depth of her grief leads you to think that maybe her mother died in a car crash too, but when you ask it turns out her mother is alive and well and a living nightmare in Sheffield — your mandala friend had to move to Leeds to get away from her.

It's the night of the long shadows — the blazing TV lights give every standing figure a twenty-foot menacing black one — and the news trucks lined up along the street point their satellite dishes into space like gaping mouths and talk to us of our togetherness on this small planet and this one day when something happened that reminded us we don't run the show. Something happened that made us look up collectively for a moment and think, Here we are gathered together and, hey, so what's it all about, then?

And in this orgy of flowers, candles and tears, you become convinced that Diana was, in fact, a saint, a modern-day saint. The patron saint of fucking-up while looking good. Which is no mean thing to be patron saint of since, in this day and age, there are an awful lot of contenders in the field.

And the weirdest thing is that you keep having this strange, nagging feeling that if only you had been more on the ball somehow — if only you hadn't gone to bed and, even worse, *gone to sleep* — you could have prevented the whole damn thing. It's not that you think you're God or anything, it's just that you keep forgetting you're not. And you keep thinking of the kids — the poor kids.

You don't leave Kensington Palace until five in the morning when it's getting light. You decide to go and crash at Mac's as that gives you an extra hour of sleep in the morning. You sleep for what feels like about twenty minutes until someone introduces a high-pitched power drill into your left eardrum. The doorbell.

Again and again. You must prevent this torture so, eyes gluey, you head blindly in the direction of the door doing the loony-bin shuffle in a pair of your employer's stripy pyjamas. You open the door to your future husband with bird's-nest hair.

He starts off with the sort of polite-smile thing he's been doing since the I-don't-want-to-have-sex-with-you fiasco. But that lasts for about one second and then he just grins a lot. It's totally infectious so you grin too and then you start to giggle and so does he and you both do that helplessly for a while, and then it grows into extreme hilarity and you go out on to the doorstep to get more space to stagger around roaring and then you say, "I can't believe Diana's dead," and you suddenly understand how fine the line is between howling with laughter and howling with grief. This brings you up short.

"Come on," he says, "you need some breakfast."

So you turn to the door to gain access to much-needed grooming equipment at which point you discover you're locked out. And that's how you end up in the local café in the aforementioned state of disarray mumbling things apologetically like "It's not her exactly, you see, it's symbolic — she's our inner princess." (Got that from Ven.) And "It's the kids, I feel so sorry for the kids."

At which point he gets his mobile phone out and puts it on the table in the little gap between his baked beans and your sausages. "I think you should call your mum," he says.

I looked at him. I said, "My mum's dead." He went white. "Don't worry," I said, "ages ago."

"Oh," he said.

"She was in a plane crash," I said, "with my dad."

"Oh," he said again. "A plane crash? How old were you?"

"Twelve," I said.

There was a little silence so we both heard the penny dropping. It dropped about a thousand miles.

Then I got up and went to the loo. I cried a lot in the loo. You're probably thinking it's not possible that I could have gone through the entire night following Diana's death and it not occur to me that I had lost my parents in a similar way, but it is possible because that's what I did. I'm not saying that I didn't know, somewhere on the edge of my consciousness, but I didn't *know* know— in-my-heart know.

And now I wasn't crying because of my mum and dad, nothing as obvious and corny (and sane) as that, I was crying because I just felt like shit. Shit, did I feel like shit. Yuk. I hate that. I hate it. So I kept crying. I thought it was probably good for me. And I kept thinking, That was a good cry and wiping my face and heading for the door, then more tears would come and I'd wipe my face again, and think, That really must be it, but no — and so it went on. I must have been in there for about a year. When I finally got back to the table I thought I was okay but it all started up again. I wasn't sobbing or anything, it was just all very watery. Tears pattering onto my sausages like a light — but persistent — summer rain.

I said to Ed, "Pretend this isn't happening."

Ed leant towards me a bit and whispered conspiratorially, "Having feelings?" He said it like he might say, "Herpes flaring up, is it?" or something equally unmentionable.

"I'm really sorry," I said, "I don't know what's wrong with me."

"Keep your voice down," he hissed, "you never know who might be listening." I looked over my shoulder. "They have surveillance equipment everywhere," he said.

"Who?" I said, completely lost.

He looked at me very sternly. "The feelings police," he said. "Come on," he said and took my hand.

"Where we going?" I said.

"We have to get you something to wear," he said.

"Okay," I said, imagining an old pair of work overalls from his van.

"A dress," he said. "I'll buy you one."

"Whaaaaaat?" I said.

"You know, dresses," he said. "Things that girls wear."

"I don't," I said. Then I added, "Why a dress? Can't you see I'm crying? Are you some kind of pervert?"

"Haven't you ever been bought a dress before?" he said.

"No, I haven't!" I said, in the kind of self-righteous tone you'd use if someone asked you whether you'd stolen from a blind man before.

After we'd been in Harvey Nichols for about ten minutes I asked Ed if he was gay. He just ignored me. As we were going up the escalator, he said, "If you don't wear dresses, what do you wear? Separates?"

"Separates?" I said. "That's a word I haven't heard in a long time. You sound like something out of *Are You Being Served?*" He didn't rise to the bait so I added, "Anyway, I think this whole dress-buying thing is sexist."

"Sexist?" he said. "Now, that's a word I haven't heard in a long time."

I shrugged. I was embarrassed. He had a point. "Well, you know," I mumbled, "assigning traditional gender roles . . ."

"What, like I'm a man and you're a woman?"

"Yeah!" I said, a fresh prick of outrage perking me up a bit.

"Ah," he said, nodding and looking me in the eye. "You're confused," he said. "It's not sexist. It's sexy."

My pyjamas got a lot of admiring looks from the shop assistants and one in the DKNY section actually wanted to know where I got them.

Then there were a lot of indulgent smiles all round when it was realised that a man was buying a girl a dress. I felt like screaming, "He's not my boyfriend and I don't wear dresses!" Just to pull the rug out. But I didn't because I was kind of enjoying the strangeness of being this person who wore dresses. Up until then I had been acting like God had leant out of the sky one day and said, "Honeymoon Holt, it is decreed that you are different from all other women. You don't look good in dresses."

And now suddenly — with no struggle — what had seemed to be a great monolithic truth just evaporated, reminding me of the way the Berlin Wall came down quietly overnight and everybody was, like, whew, that Communism lark was a bit of red herring, wasn't it?

I even found a dress I really liked — silky, silvery, simple — I still wear it, wore it at my hen party. Then I got a hairbrush, some cotton underwear and a pair of flip-flops. Ed had to pay for it all, of course, as I didn't have so much as a bent sixpence to my name.

Afterwards, we got into his van and headed west and Ed said, "Guess what? Boating on the Thames." But it was nice, I'll give him that, it was nice. We drifted about and trailed our hands in the water and I told him a bit about things. Theresa had done her best to keep the memory of my parents alive but there wasn't a grave to visit or anything and, to be honest, the whole business was hardly my or Ven's favourite subject. We were at the age when you have very little time for it. Death, that is.

All we really had left in the end was a bunch of funny old-fashioned photographs — photos that made those two irreplace-able people peering out at us seem funny and old-fashioned in themselves.

But that day, talking on the river, was the day when Ed and I made friends.

You see? I always knew it would lead to trouble, this making-friends business.

"Trees," I said, when we were sitting in Theresa's cheerfully mod-ern chequered kitchen with our cups of tea, "do you and Roland still have sex?"

"Twice a week," she said, without missing a beat.

"Really?" I said.

"Yes," she said, "we've always been quite good on the sex front."

"On every front," I said.

"Oh, no," she said. "He drives me nuts."

"Really?" I said.

"Now he's here all the time," she said. "Well," she said, "at least it wasn't one of those elaborate weddings. You just need to cancel the register office and the table at the restaurant. It'll be the work of a moment. And the dress you can keep and wear anytime. You should count yourself lucky, really."

"And there's the rings and the honeymoon," I said, feeling she was being somewhat previous.

"Well, yes," she said, "but it was hardly the Royal Wedding."

"I thought you liked Ed," I said, in a small voice.

"I do like Ed," she said, "but he's obviously not The One." I thought I detected a note of sarcasm in her voice. "Roland told me this story," she went on. "He got it from one of those new-age business gurus he's into. A man lives in a village and one day a terrible flood comes so he goes up on to the roof of his house but he knows he's going to be all right because he believes in God and he knows God is going to save him. And after a while a boat comes along. There's room for one more person in the boat and everyone in the boat urges him, 'Come on, get in the boat.' But he waves the boat on, says not to worry, God is going to save him. So that boat goes off and the waters rise higher but the man isn't at all worried because he knows God is going to save him. And then another boat comes along and the people in the boat beg him to get in but he tells them the same thing, waves the boat on, then another boat comes but he still won't get in and then the waters rise higher and higher until eventually he drowns."

"Well, that's very uplifting," I said.

"I haven't finished," she said. "So the man goes up to heaven and he meets God and he says to God, 'What the hell happened here? I thought you were going to save me!' And "God says, 'What do you think all those boats were? You eejit!'"

I considered this for a moment. "God said, 'You eejit'?" I said. "God's Irish, then?"

"Everyone knows God's Irish," she said.

"Well," I said, "that was a very enlightening story, thank you." She ignored me. "Has Roland gone religious?" I said.

"No," she said, "he thinks he's Richard Branson is all."

"So, what are you getting at?" I said.

"You, girl," she said, "you're going to get up to heaven and you're going to say, 'Hey, where the hell was my boat?' And God's going to say, 'What about Angus and Steve and Jeff and David —'"

"You call those boats?" I yelled, interrupting her. "They're the most leaky, rickety, stinky excuses for boats I've ever seen in my life!"

"No, they —"

"Angus," I said, interrupting her, "to take a case in point."

"What was wrong with him?" she said.

"He had a folding bicycle," I said.

"Folding bicycle?" she said.

"Yes," I said. "I rest my case."

He'd turned up to our first date on one of those bicycles with weeny little wheels. Not manly. Not manly at all. Then, to make matters worse, he'd folded the bicycle up into a scary sort of box shape and brought it into the restaurant where it sat with us at the table exuding an evil presence.

"You're ridiculous," said Theresa.

"And Steve suddenly shaved his eyebrows off," I said.

I suppose I should've been hip to it — I mean he was quite a cool guy, a DJ or something. But it was like being in bed with a snake.

"And the one with the tooth?" I said.

That was my "older man" although he can't have been more than forty. He was a guitarist with long, steel-wool hair (I was going through a music-biz thing at the time). One night his cat died and he buried it under the moon. Then the next day he came home with a diamond set into his front tooth.

"And the one with the twenty-four-hour erection?" I said.

"Well, he can't have been all bad," she said.

"And the one I'd already been to bed with but we'd both forgotten until —"

"Stop," yelled Theresa suddenly. "I can't stand it. I must have brought you up wrong. Why does it all sound so dreadful?"

"It's the way I tell 'em."

Theresa got up, put some cornflakes in a bowl and placed them in front of me. "Anybody would think you'd never been in love," she said. "I remember a few heartbreaks."

"They don't count," I said. "All two of them."

"Why don't they count?" she said.

"Because they left me," I said.

"They do too count," she said.

"No, they don't," I said. "I mean, on the boats theory — they don't count as boats — they were the ones who urged me to get on board then found there wasn't room for me after all." Then I said, "Anyway, I'm glad I'm not married to either of them — with hindsight. There was one boat, though, that kind of sailed past in the night . . ." I trailed off.

I was surprised that I suddenly felt real pain: it was lodged somewhere between my chestbone and my throat. I tried to go on looking normal but my face went funny in the effort.

Theresa looked at me in amazement. "Who?" she said.

I didn't answer.

"Tell me," she said.

"Oh, you know," I said, "that soul-mate thing." I was embarrassed by the cliché but my subconscious obviously had no such snobby objections: as I said the words I felt the pain getting worse. "You know when you feel like something went wrong," I said, "you wonder if God got his wires crossed because what was meant to happen never happened? And he was The One and now it's never going to happen and you're going to die and you only live once."

"Who is he?" she said.

"It doesn't matter," I said. She looked at me. "Honestly," I said. "He's not around, he's long gone."

"Are you serious about this?" she said, incredulous, angry even. She looked at me a moment. "You are. Aren't you? I can't believe it. Where did you get this 'The One' business? It's completely daft. And, anyway, just because David and — who was it — Simon were technically the ones that ended it, that's not the whole story. I mean, maybe you drove them away."

Silence.

"They're all boats!" she said.

"Don't shout," I said.

"I'm not shouting," she said. And she wasn't, actually, but it was all sounding very loud to me. Then in a smaller voice, she said, "Don't you love Ed?"

I thought about it. "Well," I said, "I feel love for him if I imagine he's had some awful accident or something. If I imagine him lying dying in the road I think about how I'd run to him and hold his hand and tell him I loved him and how I'd will him back to life with my love."

Theresa laughed. "Well, there you go," she said, "that'll do. You love him."

"But — I don't know," I said, "I don't know if there's enough passion. I mean, he's so kind and good and wise and decent and hard-working and — er — clean and sexually functional and non-smoking, and he talks about his feelings and makes me laugh and I don't mind the way he dresses and he can cook and change the sheets on a bed."

"Oh, God, surely there must be something wrong with him," she said, crossly.

I thought for a while. "He supports Aston Villa," I said.

She smiled at me. There was one of those motherly looks in her eye. "You know what?" she said. "Sometimes getting what you want is the hardest thing of all."

7

DROVE back up to London and when I pulled 2B into Mac's garage I saw that Della was waiting for me on the doorstep. I got out of the car.

"Where's NOT 2B?" I yelled.

"What?" said Della.

"The Jag," I said, indicating the empty parking space next to my car — or, rather, the car Mac provided for me to drive. When he bought the cars the Jag's number plate was meant to be 2B and my little runaround NOT 2B. But there was a mix-up and the plates came out the other way round.

"That kills me," said Della, "that to be or not to be shit."

"Well, it's been stolen," I said crossly and let us into the house.

"Hello, nice to see you," said Della. "Nice of you to come round and check up on me like a real best friend should."

"Oh my God," I said. I was looking at the tatty old leather cricketer's bag — cabin-size of course — sitting in the hall. "Mac's back."

I went into the kitchen. She followed me. "He never does this," I said. "He never springs it on me."

"You're still wearing last night's clothes," said Della. "What happened?"

"Ed came round," I said.

"Oh, gooooood," said Della.

"No," I said. "He came. He went."

At that moment, there was a car's central-locking bleep-bleep from outside, the front door slammed and Mac came into the room. Actually, to say he came into the room doesn't really do it justice, it's more like he became the room. He's like a vacuum, Mac, sucking in everything around him. Even though he's strangely small. Small and stocky but hard as a rock with receding grey stubble hair and a big nose. Women just throw themselves at him. He's very compacted, Al Pacino–like. It's always the short ones that conquer the world.

"Hey, you slob," he said to me, "I had to go out to get milk." He heaved four enormous Planet Organic grocery-bags onto the table. "I went health," he said. "Uma just gave me the biggest lecture about the shit I eat." He put three cigarettes in his mouth and lit them all.

I'm joking, he only put one cigarette in his mouth, but with Mac you always feel that one isn't enough. The cigarette looks so small and puny in his thick stubby fingers — a little white stick staying manfully alight in the whirlwind of his presence. Manful until he's finished with it, that is: he usually drains the thing in about three drags.

"Here," he said to me, pulling a box out of one of the shopping-bags, "I got you a grow-your-own-wheat-grass kit — you gotta get into this shit. Then we can juice it and give ourselves shots. Hi," this to Della.

"Hi," said Della, eyes like saucers. She'd never had the Mac experience before.

"Mac," I said, "you didn't tell me you were coming."

"I didn't know I was coming, baby" — his Glasgow burr mingling nicely with the L.A. drawl — and launched into a manic account of the last twenty-four hours, which involved Paris, Winona and Concorde, not necessarily in that order. Della flinched visibly every time he dropped a name. I just switched myself to automatic and made coffee. My life was in ruins, I hadn't been to bed yet and now Mac was in town. I tried to calculate which way was up.

When the coffee was done, I rifled the bags for milk. There was none. "You forgot the milk," I said to Mac, interrupting him mid-flow.

On the way to the corner shop I got on the mobile and called around to break the news — it was Sunday so I spoke to a lot of machines. The idea was to set up a string of meetings for Mac the next day. Mac liked to think he enjoyed time off chilling out around the house but I knew that, within minutes, he'd be climbing the walls making our lives a misery. Then I remembered there was a première in London that evening and a party so I RSVP'd for that. Then I thought, what the fuck, and went all the way to Starbucks and got us really nice coffees.

When I got back Della was alone in the kitchen. "He's in the shower," she said. I took Mac's coffee up to his bedroom. Della and I had ours in the kitchen.

"Does he, you know," said Della, "does he actually fuck film stars?"

"I don't know," I said. Which was true. I didn't.

"I had no idea," said Della.

"What?" I said.

"Well," she said, "that he was — that he's . . ."

"He takes a bit of getting used to," I said, a bit defensive, "but he's got this crazy enthusiasm for everything and I like him actually and, you know, he likes me. After the attempted-rape incident we kind of made friends."

She looked blank. "I told you about it," I said, "didn't I? I must have done."

"No," she said.

"You've forgotten," I said.

"I haven't," she said. "I never forget attempted-rape incidents. They're one of my favourites."

I thought about it for a bit. "Oh," I said, "it must have been during the Cold War." The Cold War was the eighteen months when Della and I weren't speaking.

"It was a couple of weeks after he hired me," I said, "and he'd just bought this house and we were in the bedroom because the decorator had put in the wrong blinds and one minute we were standing beside the bed and the next minute I was on the bed and he was on top of me. The usual," I said.

"Bloody hell," she said. "That's sexual harassment."

"Oh, no," I said, "it wasn't that subtle."

"So, what did you do?" she said.

"I told him to fuck off."

"Cunning," she said. "I never would have thought of that."

"So," I said, "we just got up off the bed and carried on talking about the blinds."

"The man is short," she said. "There's no getting away from it. Vertically challenged. But did you never, did you not — wasn't there ever a moment when you thought — I mean, he's a very powerful man."

"Del," I said, "apart from anything else, if anything had gone on between me and Mac there's no way I'd still be here in this job three years down the line."

"The McJob," she said.

"Yeah," I said, "the McJob." Della only called it that because she was jealous. And who could blame her?

At that point Mac reappeared and I went straight to the coffee machine, knew he'd need refuelling. He'd obviously hit the phones already because he told me to get him tickets for the première and I said I already had. He didn't blink an eyelid. He was busy talking about limos and restaurant tables and whether Cate was in town.

"I've always wanted to go to something like that," said Della. We both looked at her — for slightly different reasons.

"And?" said Mac.

"And," said Della, "I want you to invite me."

"Your wish," said Mac, "is my command," and chain-lit his next cigarette.

I was saying goodbye to Della outside when she suddenly re-noticed I was still wearing my dress from last night.

"What about Ed?" she said.

I said, "I don't know, maybe it's my fault. I've had him on a pedestal, you know, and it's a long way to fall—"

She interrupted me. "Are you talking about the lap-dancing?" she said.

"Yeah," I said. "I suppose he's gone down in my estimation."

"Funny," she said. "He's gone up in mine."

"'Bye," I said.

"You'll see me tonight," she said, as she left.

And I did: Della going up the red carpet. She dressed down in a look-at-me sort of way — black leather, lots of leg — made the luvvies in evening dress look like they were stuffed. She also wore shades so that the photographers couldn't see that they didn't recognise her. They shouted to her, "Excuse me, love, who are you?" Della just took off her shades, yelled, "Nobody!" and cackled with laughter. They took her photo anyway.

I'd had a bit of an outfit crisis since all my clothes were at Ed's flat and my hen-party dress looked like it had seen better days. Which it had. In the end I went and bought a vermilion pink slip for twenty-five quid from the antique clothing store on the King's Road and wore it with a little cashmere cardi I kept at Mac's for when it was cold.

The film was a drag but the party after bore no relation as they so often don't. Everyone seemed to be having a good time. Every-one else, that is. I wandered about feeling left out while at the same time avoiding all the people I vaguely knew for fear of long shouty conversations about trivialities.

I only really see the point of parties if they're about getting high, getting a job or getting laid. Parties like this, I mean. And, these days, I'm not big on the getting-high stuff, plus I've got a job and I like it. I did shark around a bit, purely out of habit, but it wasn't exactly an appropriate moment to get laid.

I saw Della for about five seconds at the beginning. "You do realise," I said, "you'll be in the paper tomorrow under the head-line 'Who's That Girl?' or, worse, 'Who's That Girl with Mac?'" I didn't think she was really listening so I added, "If you'd wanted a million-dollar contract with Estée Lauder you only had to say."

"Bitter?" she said. "Resentful?" she said.

"No, no," I said.

"I've told you already," she said, "if I wanted to struggle in and out of clothes all day, I would." That was about the last I saw of her. She's not a clinger, Del.

Eventually, I got talking with a stout, grey-haired man. He seemed very interested in me, which was rather nice — I missed his name when we were introduced. We ended up sitting out on the balcony, me perched on the thick stone balustrade, where it was quieter. He asked me all about my life and I ended up telling him about Ed. We must have talked for at least a couple of hours. He went off every now and then and got me another glass of sparkling water.

It was a balmy evening for once and the view was very London-by-night. After a while, it kind of dawned on me that he wasn't just a nice old geezer with grey hair, he was another human being with a life all his own. So I asked him what he did. He said he was a film director. I asked him politely if he'd made anything I might have seen. He calmly listed his films — they wouldn't have looked out of place on a lifetime-achievement award. In fact, he'd probably got a couple of those.

"Oh, my God," I said. "Sorry. I didn't know it was you. I didn't know you were you."

I stared at him. There was something tricky in his eyes. It came to me that he was very gently, very beautifully, chatting me up. For one split second I was tempted, then he said, "If you ever get over that boyfriend of yours, give me a call."

"I am over him," I said. He didn't answer, just shook his head — sort of. Actually, he moved it one inch to the right, one inch to the left. Then he walked away.

From that moment, it took me about an hour to get to the point where I was dialling Ed on my mobile. He came to pick me up in the van. It didn't seem right, somehow, but he wanted to so I let him.

On the way home I said to Ed that when I go off like that it's because I hate myself and nothing to do with him. He said he knew that.

It annoyed me that he knew that.

"So you haven't been worried at all?" I said.

"Of course I was worried," he said. "I was worried you'd throw it all away."

When we were going up the stairs just inside the door of Ed's flat, he said, "But I knew it wasn't about me."

I turned around. He was below me. "And doesn't that," I said, "doesn't that piss me off."

And it was that simple, that was all I wanted to say. I grabbed him, he grabbed me. We ended up doing it right there on the stairs. We do that sometimes — the passionate quickie.

I know women aren't meant to like it like that, are meant to demand hours of foreplay. I like that stuff too — but every now and then I want to cut to the chase. Before I met Ed I'd always had this fantasy that some day some man would be so wild about me that when he came to see me he'd hardly get in the door before he was pinning me to the wall and kissing me passionately.

Of course, it was never like that, well, not for me, anyway. En-glishmen do a lot of humming and haaing and saying things like,

"What are you reading at the moment?" Either that or, depending on the type, they occupy themselves so completely with their drugs paraphernalia that you begin to think someone made it all up about men wanting sex and that *Playboy* magazine only exists to write off Hugh Hefner's tax.

But, when we finally got it together, Ed turned out to be a pinner-to-the-waller. Nice surprise. I say "finally got it together" because I'm afraid to say that after the dress-buying and the boating, we didn't just melt into each other's arms and become one.

Which brings me to step five in my invaluable guide to true love.

Step Five: Refuse to sleep with the guy for about six months.

To this day, I don't really know why I couldn't to start with. I think it was because we really did become friends. Having thought becoming friends would ruin everything, I now thought sleeping with him would ruin everything — in fact, I was profoundly certain it would. And, anyway, I didn't want to sleep with him because, as I kept telling everyone, "I don't *fancy* him."

"Define 'fancy,'" Ven said briskly, via a satellite hurtling through space somewhere above Brazil.

"Please," I said, "I really don't want to be amateurishly psychoanalysed over the telephone by someone who is firstly only my sister and secondly only a pod," which is what I called her when she was in the womb and for some time afterwards. "You know perfectly well what 'fancy' means."

"But what does 'fancy' mean to you?" she said.

"It means smitten, it means — you know — that punch in the stomach, that woozy feeling, I don't know," I said, "I can't describe it. You know what it's like, we all do."

"But what happens in that split second moment before you get the feeling? What makes you make the decision to fancy someone?"

"I don't make a decision," I yelled. "It just happens."

"Wrong," she said.

"Look," I said, "what's this leading to? Because if you're going to try and make me have sex with people I don't fancy I'm just not having it. It's perverted. I'm sorry. I'd rather be single all my life."

"Exactly," she said.

"I said," I said, "we're not having this conversation."

"But we are."

"No, we're not."

And so it went on.

I kept having dreams where I'd be going upstairs in a house and the rooms would get smaller and smaller and the stairs narrower and narrower until I could hardly squeeze myself through and finally I was in an attic so small I was crushed in like Alice in Wonderland when she grows big, the roof of the house pressing down on my head.

Sometimes in the night Ed would roll over and caress my face, tuck my hair behind my ears, because after a while we did sleep together — *sleep* — when we didn't want the evening and the being together to end. We called it "staying the night" — like when you're a kid and you have your best friend over from school and you're having such a good time that you get your parents to agree to the magical staying of the night.

During this time Ed and I would hug and kiss on the cheek occasionally but that was it. There was no sexual tension to be cut with a knife, no sickening knot in my stomach so bad I couldn't eat. Then one day he was going to visit his great-aunt Ida. It was a Sunday and I had nothing better to do so I said I'd go too. She was in an old people's home outside Bournemouth — a lively, skinny little thing, well over ninety, with Parkinson's disease, a wide-screen television, which she watched all day, and a will of iron. She was quite fascinated by me and, when she wasn't looking at the television, fixed me with the beadiest eye I'd ever seen. It seemed like every time I looked up she was staring at me.

During a commercial break, she suddenly shouted, "I wouldn't bother getting married. Load of old bollocks."

Ed said, "Honey and I are just friends," raising his voice. He made a sign to me to indicate she was slightly deaf.

"You don't have to shout, dear," she yelled. "I may be clapped-out but I'm not senile and I'm not deaf." She turned to me. "Everyone thinks old people are deaf!" she thundered.

Ed said he was sorry.

"What did you say?" she shouted crossly.

In the next commercial break, she yelled, "I was a lesbian all my life. Did you know that?" Then, "Wouldn't bother getting married. Load of old bollocks."

Ed looked at me apologetically. "We're not getting married, Aunt Ida. But if we do I'll make sure not to invite you to the wedding."

"Inviting me to the wedding?" she yelled back. "Wouldn't bother. I'll be dead."

"I'm sure you won't," said Ed, for want of anything better.

"Bloody well hope I am," came the reply.

Her body was all angles, folded up and weathered like a deck-chair left out in the garden for too many years. When we stood up to go there was this moment when Ed and I were standing across from each other on either side of her. I looked across at Ed and felt a sensation running through my body, a bit like when you press your arm against the wall for ages and then you let go and it floats up into the air of its own accord. I was looking at Ed and it was like he'd morphed into this . . . Master of the Universe. I'd had no idea he was so tall and brave and strong. And me too. I was Amazonian. And then it happened — this wave of desire just rolled over me, through me. I don't know how to describe it, it was like a spiritual experience — not that I've ever had a spiritual experience, but I imagine it might be something like that if I did.

Ed and I went out to the car and I didn't really know what to do with myself. I couldn't speak. I think Ed just knew. He didn't speak either. He drove us down the coast road. We got out and he led me down the cliff until we found a grassy ledge and then we were just all over each other as if the last six months had never happened and that was that. The birth of the passionate quickie.

Happy ending. Although I should add that (a) we also got into sex of the long-drawn-out sort, and (b) in case you're thinking of trying any of the above, when we came up from the cliff we discovered an elderly couple with funny expressions on their faces sitting at easels painting the view.

8

I T HAPPENED that Ed was going round to do Mac's garden first thing the morning after the première party and our reunion, and I thought I might as well go with him even though it would mean I'd be at work a couple of hours earlier than usual. I thought I'd have coffee with him in the garden and watch him prune.

When we got there, Mac wasn't up. I wasn't really expecting him to be up actually — he often stays on East Coast time when he's in London.

I decided I'd give Ven a quick call on the off-chance she was still awake. She was. She was doing a course in *feng shui* and she was staying up studying because the exam was in two days' time.

I told her I was back with Ed and she was like, oh — that's good — yeah — no — that's really good.

"Ven!" I said. "What?"

"Nothing," she said, "it's really awesome news. But I knew you'd get back together."

"Since when do you say 'awesome'?" I said.

"Can we start this phone call again?" she said.

"What's on your mind?" I said.

"Well," she said, "it's only that I've got my first professional engagement as a *feng shui* practitioner and it kind of nearly clashes with your wedding dates but it doesn't exactly. I mean, I just wouldn't be able to come to London for as long as I said."

"Can't you just change the date of your appointment?" I said.

"No, not really," she said. "It's a wedding. I've got to *feng shui* the wedding venue."

"When exactly," I said, very stern, "is this wedding?"

"Well, the wedding itself," she said, "is not really that relevant. It's the days running up that are important."

"Ven," I said, "when exactly is this other wedding?"

"It's the same day," she said, "the same day as yours. But don't worry, I'm going to come to yours, of course I am. I don't have to be there for the actual wedding but I do for the run-up. It's just that this is my first big break — I bumped into my *feng shui* teacher at yoga yesterday and she'd just bumped into this woman at Thai massage who wanted to hire her — my teacher — but she's going to be away so she recommended me at a cut rate. But it's good, eh? And I thought your wedding was off," she added.

Long silence.

"I didn't think you were that into this wedding thing," she said.

"Well, I suddenly am," I said. Another silence. "You were meant to be here for my run-up," I said. "And anyway it's not even about the wedding," I said. "Ed and I are going away immediately afterwards. I'll hardly see you." More silence. "I miss you, you know."

"Oh dear," she said, "real emotion. I feel terrible."

She decided she had to go and have Häagen Dazs. Before she hung up she asked me, did I know Häagen Dazs was a name made up by a company and could I imagine making up a name like Häagen Dazs and thinking it was snappy as hell?

I put down the phone feeling like shite. Again! I thought. Again! Yesterday it was one thing and today it's another and didn't God know that my reward for all that shite over the weekend was two or three (minimum) happy-go-lucky carefree days in which I would float around like a working girl in a shampoo commercial — with bouncy hair. I mean, I know getting married stirs things up and I'm willing to have some feelings about it, but not every fucking day. That's asking too much. And no Häagen Dazs to resort to.

The phone rang. Ven again. "Expect to be abandoned," she said. "I just opened my daily meditation book and that's what it said. Isn't that incredible?"

"Expect to be abandoned? By your own sister?" I said.

"Yeah!" she said. "Why not? Here, let me read you this: 'We are all ultimately and entirely utterly, utterly alone.'"

"Well," I said, "that's cheered me up."

And it had actually. First, because from that point of view things could only get better and, second, because she'd called me back.

After a moment I said, "Anyway, how the fuck do you *feng shui* a wedding?"

When I'd put down the phone to Ven a second time, I called Della. She must've already left for work because she wasn't at home so I called her on the mobile. I wanted a more cheerful I-got-back-with-Ed conversation.

"Hi," she said. She sounded a bit muffled then she sounded a bit worried. "Where are you?" she said.

"It's okay," I said. "With Ed, we got back together."

"Wicked!" she said. "Er, Honey, you're cutting out."

"Are you on the bus?" I said, but the line went dead.

I looked at Ed out in the garden. He was pruning madly, hacking away at things, arms flailing. He likes to prune, it's therapeutic, he says, releases pent-up anger. Even when he's got nothing pent-up he's liable to leave the garden looking like it's had a number-one cut. I wondered anxiously what it would end up like today, given the trials of Ed's weekend — a collection of bonsai trees maybe. Japanese, after all. Although it seems to be true that rosebushes cut back to gnarled little stubs grow all the lusher for it. What doesn't kill you, as Ven would say, makes you stronger.

Looking out, I saw Ed ease up for a moment then wave politely at an upstairs window. Mac. I heard his footsteps and the sound of plumbing. I put coffee on and, tucking the cordless phone under my ear, tried Del again. "So who was it last night?" I said when we connected.

"Listen," she said, "I've got to call work and tell them I'm going to be late."

"Just tell me what happened after I left," I said. "Did you make out with a film star?"

"No, not exactly," she said. "We'll talk later, yeah?" I took this to mean it wasn't a conversation fit for the upper deck of the number twenty-two bus.

"Mac didn't give you a hard time, did he? He didn't get all pervy?" I said, as I took the man himself some coffee upstairs.

"No, not exactly," Della said.

I tapped on Mac's bedroom door. Mac said, "Come in," mock-hopefully, which he always does, but our routine is that I just open the door and slide the tray on to the table inside without going in.

"What do you mean, not exactly?" I said, as I shut his door again, at which point I was struck by a most unpleasant sinking feeling in my stomach. "Della," I said, "you didn't — I mean — no, forget it —" The idea was so horrible I couldn't get the words out. "Della," I said, trying again, "promise me you won't meddle with Mac." She did a sort of hysterical half-giggle. "No, seriously," I said, "it's not funny. He's more than even you can chew."

"Herr Kontroller," she said.

"Della," I said, "seriously, promise me you're not going to mess with Mac. This isn't funny. Promise me."

The phone made a horrible feedback buzz in my ear. The bathroom door was ajar and a noise — something — made me reach out and push it gently open.

The back of Della's head: she was lying in the bath, phone to ear. One delicate foot idly manipulating the hot-water tap. I took two steps towards her, barefoot on the marble.

"Herr Kontroller," she said again, into the phone, "you can't make me."

I stood behind her. My phone had a long silver aerial extension. I drew it like a sword. I whipped it over her head and brought it up sharply under her chin.

"Ve hev veys," I said in my best Gestapo — right into her ear.

Della screamed. It was a very long, gratifying scream. It was a bring-the-house-down scream.

I frogmarched her down to the kitchen in one of Mac's dressing-gowns. Mac popped his head out of the bedroom as we passed but popped it back in again quickly when he saw we were together. Del poured herself coffee. We were both on the edge of hysteria.

"You are a very sick woman," I said.

"I enjoyed that scream," she said. "It was like orgasm."

"This could lose me my job," I said. But she just rolled her eyes up to the ceiling, dismissive. We looked at each other across the breakfast bar.

"Well, now we know why they call him Big Mac," she said.

"Do they call him Big Mac?" I said.

"Apparently," she said. Then she said, "Yup," in a businesslike manner, "that's what they call him," and nodded a few times.

I started to laugh. I laughed so much I ended up hanging on to the breakfast bar for dear life.

"Yesterday — right," said Della, in the gaps when I paused to catch my breath, "when you went to get milk, he said he was going up to shower and then he yelled down would I bring him up the papers — I know, it's hilarious. But I thought I'd go up anyway just to check things out and when I got up there I looked in the bathroom and there was this hand sticking out of the shower holding a cigarette." She looked at me delightedly. Her face was absolutely lit up. I hadn't seen Della so excited by anything since she made out with Vinnie Jones.

"He smokes in the shower!" she yelled. "And he leans out," she said, acting it out for me, "and he takes a drag and he goes back in!"

"Oh my God," I said, "you fell for him. You fell for him because he smokes in the shower."

"You've got to hand it to the guy," she said. "So then I — well — I'll draw a veil over what happened next, shall I?"

"Oh, why?" I said. "You've never bothered with veils before."

"Well," she said, "you know you two have a professional relationship?"

"You didn't, did you — do it?" I said. "Yesterday while I was out."

"Well, *I did* — to him, so to speak, as we didn't have much time and then —"

"Again last night?" I said, incredulous. "What's that, then? A long-term committed relationship?"

Ed came in looking for refreshment and Della said, "Hello, gorgeous," and gave him a kiss.

"And why," I said, "did you pretend to be at work when I phoned?"

"Actually I didn't," she said. "You assumed. I'm on a late," she said, and looked at the clock, "but I'd better go. I've got to get home and change."

Ed gave Della a look, taking in the situation, then said, "Well, good luck to you," and gave her a slightly awed smile. I think he finds her scary.

After Della left my ribs hurt from laughing but I was sobering up and the sinking feeling came back so I called her again on the mobile.

"This can't go on," I said. "I could lose my job."

"No, you couldn't," she said.

"Yes, I could," I said. "He'll be all shamefaced and embarrassed, if not now then later. It's bound to happen and then he won't be able to stand the sight of me because I remind him of you and he'll make some excuse — No, he won't, what am I saying? He won't bother with excuses, he'll just fire me and that'll be that."

"Calm down," she said, "I'll probably never see him again."

There was a little silence. Then I couldn't resist saying, "No, but — honestly — what was it like?"

"He's funny," she said, "he turns me on — just here on the left, please," to her taxi driver. "Got to go, Honey." And she was gone.

When Mac came down half an hour later, I was expecting maybe a tiny bit of sheepishness — his (I assumed) frantic sex life had never been exposed to me before — but I should have known better because there wasn't even a hint of lamb. In fact, we had a manic few days' work and I was getting four hours' sleep a night until eventually I said, "Mac, you know I'm getting married in ten days' time."

And he said, "Sure, baby, no worries — I'm outta here tomorrow," in his mad tartan drawl.

As it turned out, he couldn't wait until tomorrow so I got him on an afternoon flight.

I drove him out to the airport in NOT 2B and he sat in the back doing calls until they dried up. Then he startled me quite badly by yelling, "You're getting married!" As if it had only just registered. "No regrets?" he said.

I said I hoped not. He said, what did I mean? Either there were regrets or there weren't. I said I didn't think anything was ever black and white — not a sensible thing to say to Mac who thinks everything is black and white.

"Don't give me that shit," he yelled.

"We're not going there, Mac," I yelled back, "I don't want to talk about it." Then I asked him if he'd ever nearly got married or anything like that.

"Yeah, I've been smitten a few times," he said, "but so far I always made it through."

"So far?" I said.

"Yeah," he said, "fucking thing's like cancer — you can fight it all you like but it always gets you in the end."

There was a little pause as we contemplated this inspiring metaphor. Then he said, "I liked your friend, what was she called?"

"Della," I said.

"You don't find many like that," he said, and I caught his grin in the rear-view mirror.

"She goes out with a dentist," I said. "They've been together for ten years." Total lie. The only people in the world Mac is scared of are dentists. I glanced in the mirror again but he didn't look that interested.

"So what is it?" I said. "I mean, you could have had your pick, right?"

"Yeah," he said, "the most beautiful women in the world." He looked out of the window wistfully. I don't think I'd ever seen him look like that before. "You know what, though," he said eventually, "I'm too damned scared that tomorrow's gonna bring something better along."

After a while he asked me if I knew what he meant. He'd never done that before either — asked for reassurance. I told him I knew what he meant.

"The trouble with tomorrow," he said to me, in all seriousness when we got to the airport, "is that it never fucking comes."

9

From: alexlyell@hotmail.com
To: honeypot@webweweave.co.uk
Subject: Hi
Date: 14 April — 3.55 p.m. PST
Mime-Version: 1.0

Honey,
I'm getting married. Tom just came in here to my office and I told him the news. He huffed and puffed, threw his arms in the air, walked around the room with his chest sticking out like he couldn't even find words to describe how much I'm an idiot. Then he sat down in a chair deflated and said, "You fucking wuss."

So I told him to go have a nice day now.

He said, "I'm resigned."

I said, "You resign?"

He said, "*I'm resigned,* meaning I'm not even gonna argue with you. How'd you pop the question?"

I told him I asked Cherelle if she wanted to take a trip to Vegas.

Tom said, "Aha?"

I said, "Cherelle said, 'What would I want to go to Vegas for?' and so I said, 'To get married.'"

Tom said, "And what did she say to that?"

"Who to?"

Tom said, "Who to what?"

I said, "Cherelle said, 'Who to?' as in 'Who am I getting married to?'"

Tom laughed, said, "That was cute," and then he said, "So you said, 'Will you marry me?' right, and she said, 'Yes,' and you fell into each other's arms, right?"

I said, "Yeah, kind of." I said, "She cried also."

Tom said, "Well, that'd be the charming way you asked her, you asshole. What's fucking Vegas got to do with it?"

I told him I wanted to go to Vegas, do the deed, get it done. I can't do the cakes and the bouquets and shit. Tom looked at me like, Oh, yeah?

Then he goes, "But you're doing it — right? If I know Cherelle, there's no way that baby's not having her cakes and bouquets."

I smiled. "She's having them," I said. "I want her to be happy." But I told him we'd reached a compromise. We agreed on two weeks to get the show on the road. Two weeks, then it's over. That I can live with.

Tom said, "Cherelle agreed to that?"

I said, "Cherelle likes a challenge." Then I told him Cherelle used to work on a show where they made over people's houses — like, they'd go from fifties suburban functional to exotic Moroccan palaces in forty-eight hours — so yeah, she agreed.

Tom thought about it. Then he said, "She's a smart girl. She knows you're only doing this for her sake."

He's wrong — I'm not doing it for her sake. But that's the only way Tom can make sense of it.

In the car on the way to see the client, Cherelle calls me on the cellphone — wants to know what's on my mind. She's just seen her therapist and apparently I behaved strangely this morning, so now I have to tell her what's on my mind.

"Fabulous fucks in my bachelor past," I say.

"You see," she says, "why are you being like that?"

"I'm trying to make you laugh," I say. "Is that a crime? Anyway I'm not the only one behaving strangely round here. I don't have world exclusive rights to strange behavior. Why do you always jump to conclusions about me?" I say.

She doesn't answer but I can guess why she jumps to conclusions. Because there's nowhere else to go.

"Baby," she says a moment later, "speaking of going places, I need to give you the information that I don't want to go to Europe for our honeymoon." That's how she talks.

"Why not?" I say.

"It rains in Europe," she says.

"What about Michelangelo?" I say.

"What do you mean?" she says.

"I mean, yeah, it rains in Europe sometimes but what about Michelangelo?"

"Sweetie," she says, "Michelangelo is cool as shit but this is my honeymoon we're talking about here."

I go, "You wouldn't want to see Tony Hopkins on stage in London, then?"

"London?" she says, with a little edge in her voice — a definite edge.

I say something about isn't it traditional for the groom to whisk the bride away to a secret destination? She freaks out: "You've already made reservations to London!" Raised voice.

"No," I go, "conclusions!"

"Where?" she yells.

"It's a small island off the west coast — you get there by jumping."

"Honey!" she says.

I've told her — I've told her many many times not to call me that. I tell her again. When she hangs up she says, "You're in my prayers."

Did you know that thinking creates acid in the brain that seeps downwards (wreaking chaos in the shoulders if you're not careful) and eventually getting excreted by the pancreas?

Take care,
Alex

From: alexlyell@hotmail.com
To: honeypot@webweweave.co.uk
Subject: Hi
Date: 14th April — 11.15 p.m. PST
Mime-Version: 1.0

Honey,
It is now way past Hollywood bedtime and the honeymoon question has not been resolved. Cherelle came in from her *tae bo* class and said, "My mother is driving me nuts about the wedding."

It seems her mother, who hasn't heard of growing old gracefully — in fact, I doubt if she's heard of growing old at all — turned up at *tae bo*.

Cherelle goes, "I told Mother no white sugar in any of the dishes at the reception and that includes the wedding cake. It's not like it's a big deal — Fanelli's has a great selection of organic naturally sweetened — and she started that thing of hers that white sugar is no different from concentrated fruit juice, which is just her little bit of denial so she can keep on drinking regular Coke. So I said, 'Hello! Fructose has a completely different effect on the body, it doesn't put you on the blood-sugar roller-coaster and she better trust me on that since I am living proof.' And Mother said, 'It's no different from sugar, *darling,*' like she knows best because she's my mom and my generation is just deluding our asses. So I said, 'So who's happier? You or me? Who's thinner, who's richer, who's getting laid?' "

I said, "You didn't say that last bit."

She said, "You're right, I didn't say that last bit," and sat down in the leather recliner with a sigh.

I said, "What's richer got to do with fructose?"

She said, "I dunno."

I said, "You're only richer because your divorced mother was stupid enough to close on a very harsh pre-nup."

She said, "It's horrible when marriage is treated as nothing more than another piece of business."

I ignored that. I said, "Are they the three moral high-horses, then? Happier, thinner, richer? Is that Heaven's righteous reward for not drinking regular Coke?"

"Yeah," she said, "it is, actually." And got up again. "I also work my butt off at the agency and I'm hot."

Cherelle is an actors' agent at one of the big agencies and her career has resuscitated dramatically since rehab. She is, as she says, hot. She has a good eye for sorting the wheat from the chaff (notwithstanding the fact she doesn't eat the stuff).

She looked at me. "You gotta work your shit out, baby," she said. "What are you writing?" glancing at my open lap-top.

"How about Madagascar?" I said. "How about Marrakesh? How about Rio de Janeiro?"

"You've given up on Europe?" she said, wary.

"For you," I said. And I meant it.

"Honey," she said, "hon —" and then she remembered, "I mean, sweetheart. Can't we just go someplace like Hawaii or Barbados or Acapulco?"

I tried to talk her into a bit of culture using the self-improvement argument. Cherelle dedicates ninety per cent of her waking hours to self-improvement. But she wasn't into it, she wants to lie on a beach. I said, "I hate lying on the beach."

She said, "Is it meant to be this difficult?"

I said, "What?"

She said, "Relationships — are they meant to be this difficult?"

I said I didn't know, we should probably do a course, take some more instruction. Refine our skills. She said it wasn't a bad idea and went to bed.

So now I'm sitting here alone, writing you again. I suppose I don't have many other people to tell. I kind of like that I send these e-mails and I know you're not really reading them but they go somewhere so maybe someone's reading them. I'm just happy they don't come back in my face — "Recipient Not Found."

After that first time I wrote you, when I got back from London, and you didn't reply, I started to think maybe I had imagined you. I had this crazy idea that you were going to change my life. Shit. And then I thought I must have definitely imagined you.

I'd sit down and write you but I couldn't finish the letter. Or I'd pick up the phone but I couldn't dial. It was bizarre. It was like when I used to decide to stop smoking and twenty minutes later I'd find this cigarette in my hand.

I found out in treatment there's some little asshole dictator inside me that's running my life and laying down the laws but, me, I don't get to read the statute books — I don't even get to know what the rules are. I mean, I want to change my life. Sure I do — *don't*. Don't want to fucking change at all.

I know it's arrogant to think I'm worse than everybody else. I mean, how come I'm so special that I'm worst? I like to think I'm some kind of alien. It's the hardest thing for me, being ordinary.

Now I'm getting married and that'll make me an earthling if anything will. But that's my mission in life these days. That's what I've learnt. To be an ordinary Joe. That's survival.

But you know how it is. Sometimes I wonder whether I'm on the right mission — I mean, maybe I'm way off course. Maybe Cherelle isn't part of the plan. And then, when I want to really fuck with my head and carry this fucking awful metaphor to the edge, it occurs to me that you might be in this somewhere. Maybe there were two of us sent down, one male, one female. But we lost each other.

Maybe that wasn't part of the plan either.

Take care,
Alex

From: alexlyell@hotmail.com
To: honeypot@webweweave.co.uk
Subject: Hi
Date: 15 April — 9.22 p.m. PST
Mime-Version: 1.0

Honey,
I was once flying over to Salt Lake City and the plane just dropped out of the air, I swear to God. It felt like all the air fell out of me and the little yellow gas masks tumbled down and people screamed and shit — but then the plane leveled out and we kept going.

But the weirdest thing was that nobody mentioned it. Not the crew — no apologetic announcements, no frequent flyer miles offered, nothing. Not even the passengers mentioned it. It was like that was the deal because we'd survived.

I came home tonight and found my mother waiting for me on the stoop. To prove that she's nothing like Cherelle I'll say that she's like a grizzled sunburned skeleton and her tacky gold rings are thick and loose on her fingers and she was wearing a faded purple lounge suit and had the usual Lucky Strike Super hanging out of her mouth. And, as usual, she was drunk.

I took her in and said, "Cherelle'll go crazy if you smoke that thing in the apartment."

She took it out of her mouth and smothered it gently in the lid of her pack, saving the second half. She said Slack Harry had told her about the wedding announcement in *The L.A. Times*. Her eyes were kind of watery. She had a little bag with a Continental baggage check on it.

I said, "Mom, how did you afford to get down here?"

She shrugged, said, "It's a good question, I'm broke."

I said, "What about the money I send you every month?"

She looked around the room. I knew what she was looking for. I said, "You know it's kind of weird to see you without the soundtrack."

She said, "What's the soundtrack?"

"Your own personal theme music," I said, "the clink of ice in a glass." Then I said, "You won't find a drink here."

"You still on the wagon?" she said, like she was surprised. I didn't answer. She knows I bottomed out, went to rehab. They invited her to come and confront me — Family Week, they call it. She graciously declined. "You ain't never had a problem with booze," she said.

"Mom," I said, "you need to go. You need to go now."

"But you've got yourself a bride and I never met her," she said.

"It's true," I said, "Cherelle and I are getting married. And the deal *is*," I said, "that you and I are getting divorced. Remember?"

"The money's not enough," she said.

"No amount of money is enough for a drunk," I said.

At which point the doorbell rang and I picked up the intercom and this little English voice said, "Hello."

And I thought it was you.

It made sense to me — it's like I always knew that one day the bell would ring and it would be you. And it didn't surprise me at all that you should find me on this particular hot Hollywood evening in my banal Hollywood apartment on the point of acquiring a wife. Trapped, you could say, in my small Hollywood life. It didn't surprise me at all — in fact, it made sense. The whole thing flashed before my eyes. You came to save me. I knew you would.

Then the little English voice goes, "I'm Ven, I've come about the *feng shui*." I buzzed her in. I had this idea that I could get rid of my mother — that she would go down in one elevator while the English girl came up in the other. Plus I knew that if a *feng shui* person was here, Cherelle would be hard on their heels.

Mom, of course, had seen this coming and locked herself in the bathroom. Standing outside I heard the fateful clink of a vodka bottle going upside down in a glass.

The English girl called, "Hello." I grabbed some sodas from the frig and met her at the door.

"It's hot as hell," I said. "Let's go down to the pool." On the way I told her Cherelle wasn't home yet.

The English girl said didn't we have air-conditioning? I said we didn't, then kind of snorted at the idea of Cherelle not having air-conditioning — a hilarious idea. So I said, "Er, we do — it's faulty."

When we got to the pool I said, "Look, we'll catch Cherelle as she comes in," and pointed to the gates. Then I got in the pool, it seemed the best place for me.

My plan was that when Cherelle would come she would talk to the girl at the pool and I would go up and extract Mom from the apartment. Ven — the girl — sat on the edge of the pool and dangled her legs in. She said, "You're Al, right?"

Cherelle must have told her that — she calls me Al. Then she said, "Do you want me to talk about the *feng shui*?"

I said, "No, I don't want you to talk about the *feng shui*." And she looked a bit pissed at that so I said, "Talk about London."

And she laughed and said, "You're not going to ask if I know the one person you know who lives in London, are you?" Apparently a lot of Americans say that when they meet her. They say, "You live in London? Do you know John by any chance? He lives in London." Like it's a village. One guy said to her, "What's the population of Britain? Several hundred thousand?" And she was like, uh, fifty-five million actually.

So I said, no, I wasn't going to ask any stupid questions like that. I kind of liked Ven. I liked listening to her voice. We had a nice talk. And Cherelle didn't come and she didn't come. In the end it got too weird keeping on sitting by the pool when it was getting dark so we went up to the apartment and there was Cherelle on the couch with Mom. They looked kind of cozy.

"How did you get here?" I said to Cherelle.

"How I always get here," she said, then looked at Ven and said, "You must be Ven," and looked at her watch.

"We were down by the pool — we didn't see you come in," I said.

"We were talking," said Ven, trying to help. Cherelle shot her a look. This is not a good thing to say to Cherelle. She's particularly suspicious of talking. "You know what talking leads to," she always says.

"Well," said Cherelle, "*we* have also been talking."

And she looked at Mom and Mom kind of lolled her head about in my direction which I took to mean "Fuck you."

I said, "Cherelle, this is my mother, but I gather you've already met."

Ven said, "I'll come back another time, shall I?"

At which point my mother lurched out of the couch and yelled, "Never done an honest day's work in his life!" in my direction.

I looked at Cherelle and said, "I am really sorry about this. I am going to get her a motel room."

Cherelle said, "It's okay," very calm, "Mom is all set up in the guest room."

"Mom?" I said. "Mom is all set up —"

Cherelle interrupted me: "You know something, you have a very irritating habit of repeating what I say. If you are trying to make a point, make it."

This got a cheer from my mother. She was standing precariously between the two of us. "Tell me about it!" she said. She practically sang the words with glee. "I am," I said, "out of here."

Which is how I have ended up back in the Bourgeois Pig writing to you. The English girl was here for a while but she's gone now. She's a sitter for some banker's kids up in the hills. She was behind me when we were coming out of the apartment and it was kind of hard to say goodbye. We had that kind of bonded feeling that people get who hardly know each other, then suddenly they're in a hostage crisis together. We were trauma bonded. I probably shouldn't have told her everything I told her. It's her voice I think. I could talk with her for hours.

Any minute now I'm going to have to go back and face the music.

Think of me.

Take care,
Alex

PS I just ordered another cappuccino.

From: alexlyell@hotmail.com
To: honeypot@webweweave.co.uk
Subject: Hi
Date: 16 April — 1.03 a.m. PST
Mime-Version: 1.0

Honey,

I'm not good at playing by the rules. I used to be proud of that fact but I'm not any more. I no longer think the rules are good enough for everyone else, but not good enough for me. But I also know my limits. I can only take this wedding thing so far. I have nightmares. I wake up sweating — the image is a bride, white and veiled and too tall, sinister like a spook, flying down the aisle towards me. And when her veil flies back her eyes are huge like a bug's and they stare at me with such intensity and such clarity that my fear rises up in my throat as if it will strangle me and I feel certain that I am going to die. I don't know what would happen if she reached me because the dream never gets that far.

I'm scared to make promises I might not be able to keep. But, most of all, I don't like people watching. Shouldn't it be private? I think it should be private.

Don't worry, I've been through it all with a therapist. I know the ropes.

My mother left me when I was five. Did I tell you that when we were doing our little resumés that evening in London? She left me with my dad, ran off with a traveling salesman. By the time she came back, six years later, my father had handed me on to his sister. He was too busy for me. He had a million women.

One night, before my father went, I had a nightmare and got up in the middle of the night. I found my dad having sex with a woman on the couch. I was terrified. I don't know why. My father followed me when I ran out. He was drunk. When he caught me he pinned me to the bed and told me it was because my mother didn't want him anymore.

Those are the ropes. I know the ropes. All the same, I just want to go to Vegas and get it over in half an hour.

But I'm a grown man. I can do things I don't want to do.

When I got back to the apartment last night, all was dark and quiet. I went and sat on the deck to listen to the cicadas. A feeling came over me like I could never move again — between a rock and a hard place. I can't say I was thinking straight: my thoughts were like a ball in a roulette wheel, stuck in the narrow groove, going round and round and never settling.

So it came out of nowhere — thoughts-wise — when I got up and went into the guest room where my mother was. I pulled a cigarette out of her packet on the bedside table. It reminded me of when I used to go into her room as a kid and she was in black-out on the bed and I used to steal her money.

My mother was asleep with her mouth open. She looked about a hundred years old. You wouldn't think it was possible to fuck up your life as much as my mother has. I tried to think of that tortured body starting life as a fresh-baked newborn child. It seemed impossible.

But the strange thing was, it was like she had more presence when she was asleep. And I got stuck there, glued to the spot, in the presence of my mother. Suddenly her eyes flew open, like the way people's eyes open really wide just before they die, and she said, did I know how much it meant to her when she came back from her travels and I was there waiting for her and we were a family again?

A couple of tears squeezed out of the side of her eyes. I thought maybe I would give her a kiss but in the second before I leant forward to do it she was asleep again. Like the whole thing had never happened.

I went out with the cigarette and sat back down on the deck. I didn't really feel like the cigarette anymore but I smoked it anyway. Until that moment I hadn't smoked for two years, three months and thirteen days. I just carried on sitting out there. Eventually, when I thought it was quite possible I would sit there the whole night, Cherelle came out from the bedroom and quietly sat in the other chair.

Which is unusual. It's unusual that she would do it quietly, I mean. She usually hits the ground running. But she didn't speak. Trouble is, I can beat her at the not-speaking game any day of the week. Any day of the century.

They say you've got to want to change.

I spoke first. I said sorry. Then she asked me, very cool, very calm, why did I want to marry her?

The cicadas went into that kind of frenzy they do, like a piece of classical music building to its finale, and I thought about how it all started with me and Cherelle. We got thrown out of rehab — did I mention? — for "fraternization." Nice euphemism. Anyway, I'm not sure there isn't something brotherly, so to speak, between Cherelle and me. We just do our pain differently.

You need to understand something about Cherelle. Cherelle always made the grade in high school. If she wasn't prom queen in fact — her school had outlawed that tradition — she was prom queen in spirit. Cherelle's the girl who took up martial arts and chopped the brick in two with her hand at the first attempt. If Cherelle had a baby it would be the first painless birth — even without Xanax which, it has to be said, helped the brick-chopping along.

So when Cherelle got thrown out of rehab it was her first failure. The first one she was conscious for at any rate.

If you're wondering what happened to the stage-one dating — tennis and holding hands and all that shit they taught us — we wanted to do it, only we got a bit ahead of ourselves. They were crazy anti-sex in rehab. Men and women weren't even allowed to smoke cigarettes together, on account of mixed-sex smoking leading to scenes of passion.

Cherelle and I got to necking one night, in the desert under the stars. But it wasn't until we were out on our ear, in a motel waiting for flights home, that we really got it together. So I blame them. We would never have been in a motel together if they hadn't thrown us out.

When Cherelle asked why I wanted to marry her I said it was to show those bastards who threw us out of Santa Rosa.

I got lucky — she laughed. I said I didn't think she should ask questions like that.

"Can't you say you love me?" she said.

We sat in silence for a while and then I said I was sorry that I couldn't find much compassion for my mother. She told me she thought I was ashamed of my mother but it was okay because she was still going to marry me. She said she'd marry me whatever kind of mother I had because she loved me, and when would I understand that?

We decided it probably wasn't a good idea to introduce the in-laws and that we would put my mother on a plane home the next day. Cherelle wanted to know how we would get her to agree to go. I said, not a problem, I'd do what I always do — bribe her. Cherelle asked if we were all set now and I said we were — all set.

Then she saw the cigarette butt. She freaked. She told me no way was she going to marry my ass if I smoked. Then she went back to bed.

Cherelle has her priorities.

Take care,
Alex

PS Morocco is the mystery honeymoon destination.

10

I WON'T bore you with the details of my wedding plans. But I will say I'd rather cut my head off and fry it in a pan than walk down an aisle in a white dress. I mean, it's not that my objections are political or anything and, secretly, I think I'd look okay in the dress, I just think the whole palaver is way too much pressure on two innocent lovers. This one day of all days that's got to be a fairytale.

Well, in my opinion, life just isn't like that. I've known people to crack under the strain — seriously, completely lose it. I've seen too many terrified brides waiting in the vestibule. And too many grooms who can't meet their loved one's eye. And too many of those awful tense smiles that are just a hiking up of the face muscles and bear no relation to pleasure.

I've seen a bride yell, "Shut up," in the middle of the service because her sister's kids were making too much noise. I've seen a groom go into spasm because his credit card wasn't accepted at the wedding-night hotel. I've seen a best man cracked over the back of the head with a champagne bottle and carted off to the Emergency Room (because he danced too long with the bride).

I've been to nice weddings too, but not very many, and they're always the simple ones. So that's my motto, keep it simple. Ed and I are getting married in our local register office in the presence of a few close friends. Then we're going out to lunch.

Also, I have to say that I'm not that keen on the whole marriage thing. I didn't imbibe that particular fantasy in my mother's milk and Theresa put me off by being very soppy about a mouldering piece of wedding cake she had in a drawer. In fact, she cried when a mouse ate it.

Like I said before, I was brought up to pass my A levels and not much else.

At an impressionable age I read the following sentence in one of my mother's feminist books: "When a woman gets married her sexuality will be sanctioned and her economic needs looked after. She will have achieved the first step of womanhood." And, boy, did it piss me off.

I think that was probably the moment when I lost my innocence. I made a vow never to get married. I wrote the vow on a piece of paper I still have — I kept it in an old cigar box with the four-leaf clover I found when I was eight. The vow said: "I, Honeymoon Holt, do solemnly swear that I will NEVER get married whatever happens — i.e., even if Hutch (he of the infamous partnership with Starsky) asks me. Signed . . ." And then I'd signed and made spaces for myself to sign again every year and renew my vow. I must have doubted my ability to stay on the straight and narrow even then.

Another thing. I don't have any glamorous associations with the state of matrimony. For example, I don't want to be called "Mrs." — it's so unsexy. I don't even want to be "Ms." I like my "Miss" and I'm proud of it.

To be honest, I'm not even that keen on being a "woman" in the sense of "woman" as opposed to "girl." But you can't win with me because I can't stand pompous middle-aged men who refer to grown women as girls either. Still, I find that the word "woman" — and in particular the phrase "married woman" — conjures up

images for me of twinsets and pearls and, not to put too fine a point
on it, large bottoms.

Do I protest too much? Well, maybe, for someone who is about
to tie the knot. I guess I didn't reckon on Ed. By which I do not
mean that I didn't reckon on Ed being so wonderful. I mean that I
didn't reckon on anyone else having a say in the marriage matter.
Ed has always wanted to get married.

In the beginning Ed and I went along quite nicely as girlfriend
and boyfriend. Then one night when we were lying in bed after
lights out he said, "Now we are more intimate . . ."

"Yeah," I said, "now we are shagging."

"I want you to know," he said, "that I'm looking for a long-term
committed relationship with a view to having a family."

We both lay and stared intently at the ceiling. Actually, if I
remember rightly, I was staring intently at a luggage label bearing the
legend LHR, which was dangling, just visible in the gloom, from a
suitcase on top of his wardrobe. Come to think of it, that luggage
label was witness to many seminal moments in our romantic life.

Ed said, "I just wanted to be really direct and honest and let you
know."

"So what are you saying?" I said.

He said, "I'm saying that if that's not on the cards for you then
you should say so now."

"Is it on the cards for you?"

"I just said it was."

"Not necessarily. The end of the sentence could have been, 'I'm
looking for a long-term committed relationship and you're obviously not a good bet.'"

But it was no use. Ed's problem was that he was labouring under
the illusion, bless him, that I was a good bet.

"Can I think about it?" I said.

A couple of days later I rang him from work.

"Hey!" I said. "Does this mean you're going to leave me if it's
not on the cards?"

"I wish you'd say hello," he said. "Everyone else starts conversations with 'Hello, how are you?' stuff like that."

"Oh," I said, "it's a sign of affection. For example, Ven and I never do the pleasantries, we always jump straight in."

"So it means you like me?" he said.

"Yeah," I said.

"Well, that's something," he said. "Crumbs."

"Answer the question," I said. "Would you leave me if I said no?"

"Yes," he said.

"You'd leave me?" I said, incredulous. I felt like saying, "You mean, you could contemplate never shagging me again and still walk upright?" But I thought he might take it the wrong way. (I blame *Just 17* magazine and the tabloids for bringing me up to expect men to be animals when it comes to sex. Sadly, life experiences have forced me to conclude that it isn't the case.)

"Well," he said, "if you're going to America you don't set sail for India, do you?"

"I s'pose not," I said. "But you might see this boat going to India and think, Well, that'll be an adventure, I'll get on the boat and see where it takes me and — who knows? — maybe I'll end up in America the long way round. Or maybe I'll end up somewhere better."

In the end, Della got sick of all the to-ing and fro-ing and took me to a Tarot reader. I don't really believe in that stuff but I'm willing to do anything that involves listening to someone talking about me for an hour. After the session I called Ed again. "Yup," I said, "it's on the cards."

About six months after that Ed suggested we go away for the weekend. He wanted to rent a canal boat. He has a thing for boats, which is slightly unfortunate because they're not really my favourite places. As far as I'm concerned they are claustrophobic and queasy-making and you bang your head a lot — not to mention that once you've got going, there are limited possibilities for getting off.

To be honest, I think my dislike of boats goes even deeper: I once walked past a tanker in dry dock and the vast underbelly part, which is usually in the water, towered above me. It struck fear deep into my soul — I felt a sort of profound shudder inside. I don't know what it was about. Maybe I went down on the *Titanic* in a past life.

Or maybe it was the canal holiday my parents took us on the summer before they died. I had nightmares on that holiday. A sense of foreboding. I kept imagining that we were all going to fall overboard in a lock and have our heads squashed like tomatoes between the boat and the lock walls. I found those locks sinister places.

In the evenings Dad would read to us from *Treasure Island* up on the roof of the boat in the eerie twilight. It was his favourite book, not ours. But it was a holiday honour that he should read to us and we aimed to please. And then, in the night, the scene from the book where the door at the top of the stairs swings open onto a terrifying wave-ravaged precipice would appear in my dreams and I'd plunge over the cliff edge and out of my narrow bunk, falling on top of Ven who had already fallen out of the bunk below. My parents would come in later to find us both in a little heap on the floor — still fast asleep.

Anyway, I told Ed all this and he compromised on a country-house hotel in Kent. Then things went mad at work and when it got to Friday, I took Mac to the airport and he made me get on the plane with him so that we could continue to work during the flight. I'd left a brief message for Ed from the airport saying I'd have to work over the weekend but when Mac went for his in-flight massage, I called to have a proper chat from my seat in Virgin Upper Class.

"Guess where I am?" I said.

"The deck of the *Starship Enterprise*?"

"Not bad," I said. "I'm about a mile high in the sky."

"What?" he said, like, not funny.

"Mac made me get on the plane with him," I said, trying to keep the smile in my voice.

"Fucking hell," he said.

"Sorry," I said.

"I can't go on with this, you know," he said.

"Can't go on with what?" I said.

"This," he said.

"Don't go global," I said. "It's one weekend. We can go away next weekend."

"It's not about that," he said. "It's about your priorities."

I felt myself starting to get angry — or, rather, that's what it felt like. In reality I was probably getting scared. "It's part of my job, Ed," I said evenly. "It happens sometimes. I had to come."

"You didn't have to," he said.

"I did," I said. "Can't you —"

But he cut me off. "Forget it," he said, and put the phone down.

When we got to New York, Mac was trying to close a big new output deal and I ate only crisps and slept about two hours the entire weekend. I was numb, I suppose. When I did think about Ed I felt nothing much more than defiance — I was in a well-that-got-rid-of-him mood although part of me knew that while he was being unreasonable about my work commitments, he did kind of have a point underneath it all about my level of commitment to him. In one of my only spare moments, I called Ven.

"Hey," I said, "we're on the same continent."

"Groovy," she said.

"Ed's chucked me," I said, and explained the situation, forgetting all about him having a point and getting myself worked into a frenzy of self-righteousness in the process.

"Well, I'm not surprised," she said. "The weekend was obviously very important to him. Why do you think that might be?"

"Oh, I don't know," I said. "He's mad for his little excursions. He's like a bloody Boy Scout."

"You're horrible," she said.

"Well, we know that," I said.

"He was probably going to ask you to marry him, you wuss and a half!" she said.

Well, I flew back to London on Sunday night feeling very strange indeed. Mixed feelings, shall we say? Had I snatched defeat from the jaws of victory? Had it been a very lucky escape? Things were confused further by the fact that I was sitting next to an incredibly handsome banker, who kept plying me with drinks. Aha, I thought, my future husband. Now it all makes sense: fate saved me from Ed's proposal so that I might sit next to this man on the plane because he is The One. When I asked him where he worked, he said, "Goldman Sachs," in a tone that implied I would rush him immediately to the loo and give him a blow-job. I was a little muddled by my numbness and his good looks and, despite evidence to the contrary, kept on talking and drinking with him in the hope he wasn't a wanker.

Eventually, in the post-prandial twilight and to the accompaniment of business class snores, he took my hand and put it on the bulge beneath his blanket. I was horrified — you may well think I had no right to be horrified, but I do have this naïve streak sometimes and I hadn't really thought it would come to that.

I removed my hand.

He said, "You're a fucking prick-tease, bitch." But like he thought I was playing, like it turned him on. I felt like I used to feel in the school playground when my mother arrived to pick me up and I would run joyfully towards her at full tilt only to trip inexplicably and fall, the ground rushing up to slap me in the face, crush my nose, rip the skin from my knees and generally remind me that I was not infallible, that life was hard and that bad things happened.

So, don't you get cocky, girl!

It seemed like hours, but it was probably only moments, before I moved to another seat.

Now it was me that was going global. I felt totally alone in the world. I finally received the full impact of the possibility that I might have lost Ed. Ed who would never in a million years say any-thing like that or do anything like that. I was so hung-over and full of self-hatred that I couldn't even cry.

I got a taxi back to my flat through the morning rush-hour feeling extremely the worse for wear. I was living in a not-very-exciting one-bedroom flat in Kilburn at the time, having moved out of Della's at the beginning of the Cold War. It was rented so I hadn't bothered doing much to it. The living-dining-room bit was bear-able but the bedroom was definitely depressing with brown geo-metric wallpaper that seemed to say, "You might think life is meaningful but actually it's squalid and pointless and if you want proof, I'm it."

Living with that particular vibe had made me very untidy on top of everything else — so, all in all, the place was kind of a pit.

Ed, who had been staying with me a lot because he was doing up his own place, kept saying, "Get off your arse and paint it." But every time I thought about it the wallpaper glowered at me and beat me into submission. So I never got round to it.

I put my key in the door but before I had a chance to turn it, the door flew open and there was Ed. Ed and a welcoming smell of brewing coffee.

"I'm sorry," he said.

"Not as sorry as I am," I said.

"You look terrible," he said.

"I must get into water," I said.

"Have a shower," he said.

I nodded, stumbled towards the bedroom and stumbled in. At which point I entered a different world. Physically, it was the smell that hit me first — the most luxurious, special, impossibly delicate smell in the world, the scent of love, you could say — but what registered consciously was what I saw. The room gleamed white and pure and bright, like a nun's cell in a convent in Spain. He'd painted the walls, the furniture, there was a new blind in the win-dow, and then I looked down and the smell and the love vibe all came together: the floor, the bed, every surface was inches deep in pale pink and white rose petals. I gathered them in my hands, I waded through them and sank on to the bed. I closed my eyes.

Ed said he came in a few minutes later planning to ravish me amongst the petals. He found me fast asleep.

After I'd slept for an hour and woken up and we'd talked and explained everything — Ed had called Della to try to get a number for me in New York and she'd given him a talking-to *re,* "You should be so lucky she's got such a cushy job three hundred and sixty days of the year and you'd be stark staring mad not to put up with the other five" — so he'd worked all his feelings out burning and stripping the bad-karma wallpaper and been up at dawn to get the petals from the New Covent Garden flower market, and after we'd eaten and made love about five times in the rosy bower, Ed asked me to marry him and I said yes.

Three days later the petals were smelly and rotting and we had to get rid of them. We shovelled them into bin liners, then Ed made me go round to his parents' old house in Queen's Park and help with some painting he'd got behind on due to spending the weekend decorating mine. (Told you — there's no such thing as a free lunch.)

"I should carry you over the threshold," he said, as he unlocked the front door. The place was his life's work. Or that's what it seemed like. Ever since I'd known him he'd been doing it up — himself. By which I mean really himself. Putting in the central heating and everything. He'd gutted the whole building to start with and what used to be a red-brick two-up two-down built by a charitable trust for the working man was now an open-plan halogen-lit palace that wouldn't look out of place in *Interiors* magazine. You had to hand it to him.

"That would be a bit previous," I said, referring to his threshold remark and quickly stepping inside on my own two feet.

"Why?" he said. "It's the marital home."

"We're not married yet," I said, but something clicked in my head about why he'd put so much loving care into the place over the years.

"Doesn't it spook you a bit," I said, "remembering your childhood living here and it all being so different now?"

"But I want that," he said. "I want a bit of heritage, roots, you know, that kind of thing."

"How quaint," I said. "What is it exactly with this *marrying* thing?"

Ed said, "You can't change your mind, you're wearing the ring." (A sweet little sapphire that had belonged to his mum.)

"I'm not changing my mind," I said, "but when you gave the long-term-committed-relationship ultimatum, you never said anything about marriage."

"I want a family," he said.

"Fair enough," I said, and left it at that.

Ed really liked his parents, you see. He misses them a lot.

11

ON SATURDAY I was at a loose end. Mac was meant to have been in town that day, which is why Della had arranged my hen-night for two weekends before the wedding, but now Mac wasn't coming — because he'd already been — and Ed had gone up to Cumberland to look at a garden that was only open once a year. I went to a late-afternoon movie on my own then walked home in the gathering dusk.

I walked past some mansion flats and in the wide-lit windows saw some teenage girls getting ready to go out, jostling for space in front of the mirror — hair up, hair down, your top, my top, these shoes, those shoes, can I borrow your mascara? Oh, God, nostalgia, dressing up to get pissed on beer on the top deck of a bus. Who shall I pretend I am tonight?

I took a small detour to go past Della's, was amazed to see that her lights were on and her blinds were down. Amazed because it was, after all, Saturday night.

Now, my view of Saturday night is that it's a wash-out and always has been since the last of the wild make-out days of my teenage years. Ever since, I've never had anything to do on a Saturday night. It's the night you're meant to be out on the town and nobody arranges anything for fear that something better might come along and nobody has people around for fear that they'll be doing something else because, after all, it's Saturday night.

Even when I was clubbing, the big nights always seemed to be Thursday or Sunday or something equally inconvenient. As far as I'm concerned, Saturday night is one of those urban myths — yeah, okay, there are a few out-of-towners on the streets but I have a theory that the vast majority of Londoners are sitting quietly behind drawn curtains imagining everybody else out there having a great time because it's Saturday night.

But Della doesn't subscribe to any of the above. I think she thinks Saturday night's as good as any other when it comes to pulling. I rang her bell. No answer. But the lights were definitely on. I rang again. Still no answer. I was dogged. I pulled out my mobile and called her. After about a hundred rings she picked up.

"What?" she said.

"I'm outside your door," I said.

"I'm on the roof," she said.

"What on earth are you doing there?" I said.

Della has a sort of flat bit of roof, which she tries to pretend is a garden by putting a few of those basil plants you get at the supermarket between the chimney pots. But she doesn't go up there much at the best of times and it was actually quite a chilly night.

"I'm considering jumping," she said.

"Don't do that," I said. "Chuck me the key and I'll come up and talk you down."

After a moment, her head appeared just above the front parapet and a moment later a large bunch of keys attached to one of those executive condom holders that were fashionable in the eighties landed at my feet.

When I got up there her face looked a bit red. "That carrot face-pack's stripped you raw," I said.

"Ha ha," she said, but not with her usual edge and jumped on to the little wall dividing her roof from the next. She did look a little precarious up there but at least she had a great view — the sun was going down.

"What's going on?" I said.

"I'm having a night in," she said, like Linda McCartney might have said, "Mine's a steak and chips."

I sniffed. "Why don't you do it on the sofa like everybody else?" I said.

I sat down on some loose roof tiles. I looked around — lots of chimneys, very ye olde London. Another world, actually. I expected Dick Van Dyke to leap out at any moment and do one of those mid-air cartwheels they do in musicals when they don't put their hands on the ground.

"Ven's coming to the wedding, after all," I said, to make conversation. I knew there wasn't any point in asking Della what was wrong. I knew she wouldn't tell me. She doesn't like to admit to any kind of feelings.

I told her that Ven had called to say she had a *feng shui* job and wouldn't be around for the run-up to the wedding.

"Yeah?" said Della. She wasn't fascinated.

"Ven asked me for your number," I went on. "I don't know what that's about — maybe she wants the two of you to plan a surprise for me or something."

Della shrugged.

"Don't let her go overboard," I said.

She shrugged again.

Della said, "You call this talking me down?"

"Mac, on the other hand," I said, "has decided he's not coming — so you're safe there. He's going to some conference in Jamaica."

She didn't shrug, she didn't do anything. She didn't even blink. And so I knew.

"Oh, no," I said. "Oh, no!" I think I wailed it the second time. I put my head in my hands.

"He said he'd call," she muttered.

"Of course he's not going to call," I said.

"Why not?" she said.

I flailed around. My mouth opened and shut soundlessly like a carp's. I didn't know where to start. I said so. "Mac's too busy to call," I said finally. "Mac can't have a relationship. He's too busy having a relationship with — with his own ego. He hasn't got time. He hasn't got room. He hasn't got space. I can't believe I'm having this conversation with you," I said. "I'm teaching my grandmother to suck eggs."

"I never understood that expression," she said.

"He — is — not — an — appropriate — man — from — whom — to — expect — a — phone — call," I said, Dalek-speak.

"This is going to be like one of those movies when the really tough cop goes up to talk down the guy who's teetering on the edge of the skyscraper and in the end the cop just says, 'Go on and fucking kill yourself, you sick little shit,' or something like that and, for some reason, that makes the guy decide not to jump."

"Yeah," I said, "it's going to be exactly like that. Have you considered therapy?"

I'd been to see a nice woman myself for a couple of years a couple of years back. "I'll give you her number," I said. I thought my chances of getting Della there were minimal but then again the suggestion might act as a little ray of hope in the dark landscape of her mind. "She could explain some basic facts of life to you about unavailable men," I said.

"She cured you, then," Della said, and I fear it might have been sarcastically.

I found I was playing with the condom key-ring in my hand, opening and shutting it again and again. The little chamber was empty.

"And some facts about compulsive behaviour," I added.

"Mac makes me laugh," she said.

"Mac told a joke?" I said.

"No," she said. "He just makes me laugh, you know, everything he does."

"So, sort of laughing *at* him?" I said.

"And he's different. As you get older, don't you find," she said, "that everything just gets more and more the same?" Bleak smile.

"I'll make the appointment for you," I said.

And I did. I don't know how it went. I don't even know if Della turned up. I do know that she didn't jump off the roof. She went on saying she would until I reminded her that *Stars in Their Eyes* was on TV — that got her downstairs soon enough.

When I got home Ven called and said she was going to fly into London the Saturday morning of my wedding. She reckoned the flight would get in around ten with a good following wind, so she should make it to the register office easily by eleven-thirty.

I gave a long hard-done-by speech complete with cracks in my voice. I touched on the unpredictability of following winds but I talked mostly about her being my only family member and the most important person to me in the whole world. It didn't do any good.

"I'm your sister, you know, not your mother," she said. "Have you considered going back to therapy?" Ven took herself to therapy at the age of sixteen and hasn't drawn breath since.

"No, I haven't," I said. "I'm not going back to therapy. I'm about to be happily married."

"Pray for wind," she said.

Ven was sure this *feng shui* wedding job was going to be her *entrée* to the L.A. scene.

When we got off the phone I considered jumping off the roof myself but I went to bed instead and when I woke up in the morning Ed was leaning over me with a breakfast tray and a bunch of flowers. "Let's go to the graves," he said.

Ed's parents are buried side by side in a cemetery in Kensal Green and two or three times a year he likes to visit them. The first time he took me was soon after he proposed. I got into a terrible state of anxiety beforehand: I'd never been on a date before that involved visiting my mother- and father-in-law-to-be six feet under. For a start I wasn't sure if I should wear black or not. I tried on about fifty outfits, eventually putting my back out rummaging for a pair of shoes in a chest. The outing had to be cancelled — I couldn't even stand upright until I saw an osteopath first thing the following week.

"This is all very interesting," Ed had said, cryptic, as I lay on the floor in agony.

"I was simply rummaging for shoes," I said. "There's nothing interesting about that."

"Where are your parents buried?" he said.

"They're scattered over Mexico," I said. "They were in a plane crash." He knows that, of course.

"They don't have graves of any sort?" he said.

"No," I said. "It's just because I haven't been swimming this week. I always put my back out when I haven't been swimming for a while."

"Aha," he said. "Is that so?"

When we finally got to the graves two weeks later, we had a really fun time. The cemetery was beautiful with lots of ornate Victorian mausoleums.

Ed did a bit of gardening at the grave, tended the miniature rose he was growing there, and I stood by respectfully and tried not to think of my in-laws rotting. Later we walked around looking at all the other tombstones, enjoying the names — "Oh, look, two sisters, Enid and Ethel, died in their eighties," and seeking out the ones that thrilled us in a ghoulish way, "Oh my God, this little boy died at eleven," that sort of thing.

That's when Ed said, "I think we should go to Mexico for our honeymoon." I knew immediately what he was getting at. "I think it would be nice to honour your parents like that," he said.

"Ed," I said, "I don't think it's a good idea to open that particular can of worms on a honeymoon." I'd never been to Mexico — or anywhere near it for that matter.

"Maybe it's not a can of worms," he said. "Maybe it's a can of . . . beans."

"Baked beans?"

"Refried beans."

"But definitely not jolly jelly-beans," I said.

"You can grow a beanstalk," he said.

"Can we cut the crap?" I said. "I don't think Mexico is a good idea."

"It's my prerogative, isn't it?" he said. "As the groom, I get to whisk you off to an unknown destination."

"Ed," I said, "this is not a joke."

"Trust me," he said.

Autumn was starting, the leaves were very mellow and the cemetery was enormous. It seemed to go on and on and get more and more wild. Ed said he felt horny and tried to drag me into the bushes. I resisted but then I let him kiss me beside an angel monument and he pushed me back so that I was nestling in her marble wing and he kissed me so bravely and tenderly that I said, "Okay, I trust you."

"Look up," he said, and when I did I saw the angel's beautiful cool white eyes regarding me with an infinite serenity. "You see," said Ed. "Your guardian angel."

We kissed again but when I opened my eyes I saw a grave-digger type approaching with a hoe over his shoulder, so I struggled free of Ed's loving clutches and ran away. Ed chased me. I dodged madly between the graves but he caught me in the end. He always did. I hoped the grave-digger didn't think we were too irreverent. After that we found a tea-room and had currant buns.

So nowadays when Ed says, "Let's go to the graves," I think of the currant buns and say, "Yeah, let's."

We had a nice walk as usual and I told him about Ven and he didn't try to talk me out of my disappointment.

He told me about going to Trailfinders to pick up our tickets to Mexico and all the equipment he had bought. He was particularly excited by a syringe device for extracting insect stings. When he suggested I take a backpack, I said, "This is a honeymoon, matey. I'm going in high heels with proper luggage," but we didn't argue about it.

After the tea-room, we decided to rent a video, go home and watch it in bed. On the way home Ed got lost taking a new route to avoid traffic but I didn't complain — I didn't even make him ask the way. (I'd read in a book that asking the way threatens men's virility or something.) At home, we made ourselves something to eat listening to music in companionable silence and when we were in bed, I said, "I'm glad I'm marrying you."

On Wednesday, Della called sounding really cheerful — a new woman, in fact — and said she was going to take me for a pre-wedding juzzsh (pronounced like judge in French).

"You've obviously been to the therapist," I said.

"Oh, yes," she said. "Sorted."

The juzzsh turned out to involve lots of horrendous beauty treatments and female torturers in white coats, saying, "Going any-where nice on holiday this year?"

When we finally go to the steam-room bit at the end — the peaceful bit — women with sleek thighs kept materialising in the mist and saying things to each other like, "You have no idea what I've been through — no idea."

"Married life," whispered Della to me. "So, has Ven called?"

"Yes," I said suspiciously, "she has. She's not coming until the morning of the wedding."

"That's all she said?"

"Yeah, why?" I said. "Have you spoken to her? You're planning a surprise, right? What is it? A confetti bomb?"

"Er, yeah," said Del.

There was a lull in the conversation as we transferred to the sauna.

"Have you thought of telling Ed about the Love of Your Life?" said Della, out of nowhere.

"Why would I want to do that?" I said.

"Because during the ceremony, when they ask if anyone knows of any impediment and all that —"

"Uh-huh," I said. "So, what do I say to Ed? That there was this guy I spent one night with, who, in reality, I don't know at all, and we never saw each other again and I've never really got over it and I've kept him alive in the back of my mind and it's all probably an elaborate defence mechanism to keep me out of real relationships with people who are there for me?"

"Yeah, why not?" she said.

"Or shall I tell him that there's a guy out there who I secretly think might be the one that's meant for me? That I've never felt the like of what I felt for this man for anyone else — including Ed? That when I first met eyes with him it was like I'd been punched in the chest? That if I really thought about what I've lost — really thought about it — I'd cry and cry and never stop crying again?"

"Steady," she said.

"Shall I tell him that when I think about this man's skin and the particular blue of his eyes and the way his shirtsleeves were rolled up half-way to his elbow and the way he arranged his words and — Shall I tell him that I still get a physical pain in my chest when I think of these things seven years on? I'll tell him that, shall I? What do you reckon?"

"Is that what you really feel?" Del said, sitting up suddenly very straight and without any of her usual spin.

I sighed like a train.

"Big sigh," she said.

"Or I could tell him," I said, a bit calmer, "that only two years ago I woke up in the middle of the night and howled for an hour in the certain knowledge that I'd never see this man again."

Little silence. Awkward silence, in fact. Della and I had always joked about Alex but I'd never really talked about it quite like this before.

"Like when you wake up in the night and know for a fact you're going to die," said Della.

"You've felt that?" I said, slightly shocked. Della's not usually one for acknowledging mortality.

"Yeah, I've had that," she said. "Tell Ed the truth."

"I don't know what the truth is," I said.

There was another lull as we transferred to the jacuzzi.

Della said, "If you feel all that about Alex, I think you should go and find him."

"How?" I said. "I don't even know his last name."

"Say there was a way," said Della, "for the sake of argument."

"I couldn't," I said.

"Why not?"

"He might be balding and fat and married with eight kids. Or, worse, he might be looking great and in a meaningful relationship with a supermodel."

"What if he wasn't?"

I thought about it. "The bottom line is," I said, "if he wanted, he could come and find me."

"I still think you should tell Ed something," Della said.

"Why?" I said again, nonplussed by her persistence. "I mean, it's not real, is it? None of it's real. It's just some stupid thing I do in my head. Since when has it been real?"

She didn't have an answer to that.

"Anyway, that's not an impediment," I said, after a while. "If you want legal impediment you should look in my cigar box."

"What's in your cigar box?" she said.

"My vow," I said ominously.

She didn't bother to ask. We sat in silence for a bit, and then I said, "I don't think they say that in register offices, do they, about impediments?"

"You'd better hope not," she said.

On the way home, Della said that now we had to go to this tequila bar she knew to replace some of the lost toxins. After half an hour a classically handsome businesslike-looking chap in a suit turned up — not Della's usual type at all — and put his arm around her in a proprietorial manner. She beamed from ear to ear. He seemed like a nice enough bloke, worked in computers.

When he went to the bar to buy drinks and I remarked on him not being her usual type, Della told me he was an escaped convict, a lifer, but he'd been escaped two years now and had a false identity and a job and everything.

"What was he in for?"

"Murder," she said. "But, you know, it was one of those ones when it wasn't really him who did it, it was his mate. He's a sweetie. Don't worry. He's perfectly safe."

"Uh-huh," I said. "Where'd you meet him?"

"In the waiting room," she said, "at that therapist's you sent me to." After a moment, she added, "You were right about her. She's very good."

12

IMAGINE this. Imagine a cluster of people on the steps of the town hall as seen through a taxi window. Some of them are wearing hats. ("Oh, God, what are they wearing hats for? Tell them to lose the hats. I'm not getting out if they're wearing hats.") Imagine your surprise when these people turn out to be your closest friends. Imagine how strange they look in hats.

Imagine deciding to get married dressed as a mermaid. ("Don't mermaids weep on the rocks for their long-lost sailor lovers?" — Della. "Well, yes, actually.") Imagine being bustled to the sacrificial altar, vaguely aware of a dusty smell, rows of pertly upholstered chairs, red curtains and a tall man with sticking-up hair who apparently you're to spend the rest of your life with. Imagine looking frantically around for your sister and finding she is not there.

Imagine the professional bonhomie of the civil servants attending. Imagine them as midwives, their calm smiles telling you not to worry, they've seen it all before. Somehow the kindness of strangers is more moving than anything. You feel like clinging to the dumpy one in the plum-coloured suit and asking her to save you.

Imagine the formalities beginning and then a kerfuffle breaking out, which turns out to be Ven arriving and huddling up with Della in the back row. You find it hard to concentrate because you can hear loud whispering. And, anyway, you want to go over and be hugged.

Next imagine hearing the Registrar getting to the bit about whether anyone knows of any impediment because — yes — they do have that bit in civil weddings and imagine hearing your sister say loudly and clearly, but admirably calmly, "Well, yes, actually."

We all turn round and stare at Ven who looks flustered and is being nudged by Della. Della then meets my eye across the room and says, very composed, "Could we have a word?"

When we get outside Ven appears behind Della, eyebrows working overtime, and they bundle me into the loo. I wonder briefly why all the seminal moments in my life take place in the loo. I note that Della and Ven both have scarily serious expressions on their faces.

"He's been found," says Della. "Alive and well."

Ven pulls a stiff white wedding invitation out of her bag and holds it up. "You've got approximately eight hours," she says urgently, like her resistance has suddenly gone and it's a relief.

I take the invitation from her and look at it. It takes me about eight hours to work it out. Two strange names, a California address. I read the names again: "daughter Cherelle to Alexander Lyell." "What is this?" I say, feeling really strange now. Frightened, in fact.

"It's the wedding I *feng shuied*," says Ven.

I look at the card again. "Alex," I say.

"It really is him," says Ven. "I met him in L.A."

"He's getting married today?" I say.

They nod eagerly.

"But he's not married yet?" I say.

More eager nods.

"Neither am I," I say.

Frantic head movements as before.

"You've been . . . seeing him?" I say to Ven.

"Well — yeah," she says.

"Talking to him?" I say.

"Well — yeah," she says.

"Ohmygod," I say faintly, trying to take this in.

I must have gone very white because Ven suddenly turns to Della and snaps furiously, "I told you we shouldn't tell her!"

Della snaps straight back, "This man is the Love of Her Life!" She puts a lot of emphasis on those last four words. "Anyway," she adds, "I told you about the Wardour Pact."

The Wardour Pact marked the end of the Cold War between me and Della. The Cold War had started the night I caught Della at Love Ranch dancing with David. David had already made an appearance in the relationship record books — on my side of the page. He came under the designated heading 6(c), One of the Ones That Got Away, sub-category HB for Heartbreaker. What is more, that night at Love Ranch, the ink on his entry was barely dry.

I stopped speaking to Della, even though we were sharing a one-bedroom apartment at the time. I felt so totally betrayed I couldn't bring myself to utter one word. I mean, I said things like "It's for you," when the phone rang but that was about it.

Della never really spoke either. And after a few weeks we had both retreated into very hard shells. I arranged to move out and even then nothing was really said. It was like losing an arm.

Then one day we walked past each other in Wardour Street. And in that fleeting second when our eyes met neither of us could disguise our joy. So we went for a coffee.

I explained to Della that although it had hurt to see her with David it was the betrayal of not having been warned first that hurt most. She said she'd been trying to protect me. I told her what she did had the opposite effect.

In the end she agreed that from then on she wouldn't try to protect me from anything. She'd tell all. And I agreed that I wouldn't just go cold and silent on her again. I'd explain. We shook on it. We called it the Wardour Pact. (Soon followed by the Treaty of Shepherd's Bush, where we rented a flat together again.)

"The Wardour Pact!" says Ven, scathing, and backing Della up against a wash-basin.

"I warned you," says Della to Ven, refusing to be backed. "I told you to be careful what you tell me."

"I had to tell Del," says Ven to me, "what Alex said yesterday. I had to tell someone. I was bursting!"

I can see she's been suffering. I feel a little rush of love. "What exactly," I say, breaking them apart, "did Alex say?"

"He — well, he — he was talking about — well — I'll start at the beginning —"

"Stop," I say suddenly, holding up the invitation to prevent her continuing. "Second thoughts," I say. "Let's just nip this in the bud, shall we?" I tear the invitation in half.

They both stare at me, goggle-eyed.

"It's okay," I say. "It's okay, you silly wusses, what did you think I was going to do? Jilt Ed?"

"The RSVP address on the invite is Alex's address," Della puts in quickly. She's very thorough, Della.

"Is it, really?" I say. I rip the invitation into tiny shreds, step into a cubicle and scatter the pieces into the bowl. I flush.

"Seriously," I say, turning to them, "no more of this Love-of-My-Life business. Okay?"

It seems a good moment to make my exit.

"False alarm," I said to the Registrar, gliding back into place beside Ed, not a hair out of place. Well, that's how I'd like you to imagine it. I probably was a little ruffled and, although it should have been a glide, it was more of a hobble. I blame the mermaid dress.

The dress was bluey-silvery green — kind of scaly — and it changed colour as I moved. It had a fitted bodice and the skirt bit swept out hourglass style then in again quite tightly around my ankles with a little fishtail train.

Does it sound hideous? It wasn't. It was the most beautiful thing I ever saw. But it did make me hobble.

I looked up and found that Ed no longer appeared to me as a stranger. He was familiar and comforting just because he was Ed. What was more, he wasn't angry, he was smiling.

"I'm sorry about that," I said.

"Whatever it takes," he said, and took my hand.

I thought I'd love him for ever for that. My rock in a storm.

"Er, take two," said the Registrar starting off again.

When we got to the vows I realised that the ridiculous interlude in the ladies had been exactly what I'd needed.

Where before there had been befuddlement, there was now razor-sharp clarity. Where before there had been an attempt to maintain a wry knowingness, there was now a willingness to ditch the irony and do it straight. Where before I had thought I was going to cry, but it would have been the kind of crying I do when I watch *The Railway Children* and Jenny Agutter shouts, "Daddy," and runs down the steamy platform in slow motion with her arms outstretched — i.e., sentimental — there were now real tears pricking my eyelids.

I decided that if I was going to do this I was going to do it properly. For Ed. And for me.

So that's what I did.

Afterwards on the steps there were photos. Theresa slipped me a tiny white parcel wrapped in a huge pink bow. Inside was a cameo locket, not the kind of thing I'd ever normally wear but the sheer old-fashionedness of it appealed to me.

"It was your mother's," Theresa said. "Look inside." Inside the locket was a little curl of hair. For a moment I was taken aback. Maybe that sounds awful but for some reason I couldn't bear the thought of the hair being my mother's.

"Is it . . . ?" I said, not disguising my feelings very well. I held the locket away from me, not able to touch the hair.

"It's okay. It's your hair," said Theresa. "It's one of your baby curls. Your mother put it there."

"Oh," I said. That was an entirely different matter. I picked out the curl and examined it.

"I've been saving it for an occasion like this," she said.

I gave her a big hug. She's good at gestures like that, Theresa.

I don't think it was until I was in the loo at the Ivy, staring at myself in the mirror, that I really realised that I had done it. I was married.

I asked myself if I felt any different. Everyone says it's different being married — it just is. I tested the water. I thought about Ed. I couldn't really detect any difference but I thought maybe the side-effects hadn't kicked in yet. I did feel kind of bonded to Ed, though, if only because of having gone through the embarrass-ment of it all together.

Looking at the locket round my neck, I thought, I'm a real woman now.

Don't worry, I didn't take myself seriously.

And, anyway, what would that have made me before? A fake woman? A pretend woman? Well, maybe.

I considered redoing my lipstick and thought I wouldn't bother as I'd just eat it all off again then wondered if this was the begin-ning of letting myself go. I'd been warned against the dangers of married women letting themselves go. In a panic I got out my lip-stick.

I thought about Alex once. Once. And I honestly didn't think about him again. I went up to where the sun was bouncing off the white linen and all my favourite people in the whole world were gathered around one table.

There were Theresa and Roland and Della, my girlfriends Jen-nie and Rachel, who'd come especially from Japan, and my father's mad brother, Richard, and Karim and Philippe, who I used to work with, and Mrs. Ramsey, who used to be my neighbour, and Ed's sister, Matilda, and his grown-up nephew, and his aunt who didn't live in Australia — and Morris. Strictly speaking Morris didn't fit the category "favourite people in the whole world," seeing as he was Della's new escaped-convict boyfriend, but I had that loving feeling and I wasn't going to let his presence spoil things. Anyway, maybe he was innocent — with British justice there was always a good chance. I mean, the Guildford Four were and the Birmingham Six were and so was the guy who yelled, "Let him have it!" to name but a few.

There was another kerfuffle and more whispering when it came to pudding and I assumed there was going to be some sort of surprise. Ed and I held hands and felt like children at a birthday party. I had ordered *tartes au citron* and now wondered idly if they were going to put candles on them or something so I was genuinely surprised when Mac appeared, in dinner jacket, carrying the most enormous canary yellow tiered wedding cake.

It turned out he'd been to Harrods on the way in from the airport, asked for a white cake, discovered you had to order them three months in advance, and persuaded the assistant to sell him one of the display models off the shelf — very much against her will apparently. (But I defy anybody to hold out against Mac for more than about thirty seconds.)

The cake was a bit stale — but it's the thought that counts. It was also enough to feed several armies so we had a slice sent to everybody in the restaurant, and I hope the homeless later dined off it for weeks.

Mac slapped me on the back a few times and said did I really think he was going to miss my wedding, and I said, yes, I really did. Actually I hadn't realised he was that fond of me, but I didn't say that bit.

And then the waiters, who were wreathed in smiles at the sight of him, brought a chair and put it at the table next to Della, which concerned me slightly. But Mac immediately got into a conversation with Morris, so I didn't worry too much.

I squeezed Ed's hand and looked around and had one of those isn't-life-grand moments and thought getting married wasn't so bad after all.

Which brings me to Step Six in my trusty guide to Happy Ever After Living. I should warn you though, Step Six is a particularly challenging one.

Only the truly resolute will manage this step. This step is not for the faint-hearted. Here the faint-hearted will balk. Here the faint-hearted may fall. This step will, as they say, sort the men from the boys.

A word of encouragement: you can do it.

It is possible. I know this because I have done it. Regular daily practice of Ashtanga yoga may help to build the strength and the stamina. Vegetarianism is probably a good idea. Meditation would help, no doubt, and you might try eating soaked linseeds every morning as I hear they make the bowel movements regular.

Needless to say, I had none of the benefits of the above. I did Step Six cold — in fact, I did it on a full stomach following a large, rich lobster lunch at the Ivy.

Step Six is this: Set off on your honeymoon (by all means) but get to the airport late and *miss the plane*.

This is what you do: you let everything go along swimmingly and coffee is served. Then you say jokingly, "Aren't there any more surprises then?" at which point four policemen enter the room, two of them in plainclothes, and arrest Morris, your best friend's convict boyfriend.

You wobble a little here, but you don't lose it. Morris is seen off tearfully and Mac, who appears to have taken a liking to the man, goes with Della to the police station to see if he can help in any way.

But you — you stick like glue to your best-laid plans. Ed is going home to pick up the luggage, which you didn't want to lug around London all day. And you are going with Theresa to her smart hotel to change into your travel clothes in style and comfort. As Ed will be on the other side of town, you are getting separate cabs to the airport.

After showering and changing at the hotel, you get a call from Mac, who tells you he has now been arrested himself. He won't tell you for what but he insists you go down to the police station with his British cheque book, which is in Chelsea, as the police, foolishly in his opinion, don't take credit cards for bail.

You wobble big-time here. But Mac convinces you that you have time to get to Chelsea and back. He waxes lyrical about knowing you're not going to leave him in the lurch — he says you've got loads of time but just in case he'll call his friend the chief executive of British Airways and tell them to hold the flight for you. Uh-huh?

(In Mac's defence, I'll just say he told me later that he was about to close a deal with Morris regarding a bio-pic of his life.)

You wobble. You fall. When you get to the police station, via Chelsea, you find that Mac has been charged with . . . with . . . smoking.

Smoking?

In the No Smoking waiting room.

How unreasonable, you think. But, of course, he pushed them too far.

Mac is holding forth: "Since when has there been no fucking smoking in a fucking nick? These places were designed for smoking! Hasn't anyone see *The Sweeney*? People have had the smokes of their lives in places like this. What in fuck's name has this country come to?"

You give him the cheque book. You ask Della how the police found Morris. Mac answers. He's convinced that the head of the Met was lunching at the Ivy and recognised Morris.

Before you go, leaving Della and Mac together, you give Della a look that's meant to remind her of what you said about her and Mac, and how it's bound to end in you losing your job and how awful she felt last time when he didn't call her and how you told her that Mac can't have a relationship with anyone except his bank manager (with whom he has a very good relationship), but it turns out to be far too much to fit into a look and, anyway, she ignores you.

In any case, you have no time for anything more than a look. You make a wild dash for your cab. You look at your watch, heart pounding, you have visions of the Hammersmith turnpike smooth, inviting and empty — the way it used to be at five a.m. on Sunday morning when you were coming back from a rave. You decide you have plenty of time.

It takes you twenty-five minutes to get down the Strand. Things ease up a bit — you get to Hammersmith turnpike and only then is all lost: it starts to rain. Traffic all over London comes obediently to a complete standstill. It's a natural law, like night following day.

When the cab finally comes off the turnpike you make a last-ditch attempt by getting out of the cab and on to the tube. But you are clutching at straws. The train stops in the tunnel — signal failure at Hainault. By the time you get to the airport the flight to Mexico has not only closed it has taken off. And so, it appears, has Ed.

13

Nᴇᴡ York. You know those tribes who put their young adults through rite-of-passage ordeals in the jungle? Well, when I was sixteen and being horrible to everyone, Theresa packed me off to New York for the summer with one of Roland's nutty travel guides under my arms.

I read the guide on the plane but it didn't tell me that I was going to another planet. When I got to New York, I thought I was in *Blade Runner.* The whole thing was like an acid trip — an altered reality. I was pregnant with possibility and sick with excitement twenty-four hours a day. I lost my head — and eventually my virginity — somewhere on the Lower East Side.

Not that I had "the time of my life" or anything like that. When I got back and I tried to make out to Della I'd had the time of my life, she was very hard on me: "Are you trying to freak me out and make me think I haven't lived or something?"

Actually, I don't think anyone has the time of their lives except in retrospect. For one thing, how can you know until you're dead? And for another, the actual living of the twenty-four hours just isn't like that. It's only when it's all crushed up and impacted by the long lens of perspective that it gets to seem so great. The reality was that I was tripping around New York with the feeling that IT was going on somewhere and that I couldn't get to where IT was.

Theresa had a niece out there, my age — Martha — and I went to stay with her family. They all lived in this cramped apartment and I remember the alien smells the most, the musty atmosphere, the terrifying cockroachy plumbing. Martha's mum was quite strict and kept us on a painfully tight rein. I kept glimpsing tantalising scenes and torturing myself with what I made up about the adventures I was missing. Tall blondes whizzing past in cabs on their way to nightclubs, groovy drama students picnicking in the park . . . whatever.

We did all the usual stuff — went up the Empire State, the Staten Island ferry, the Met, the Museum of Modern Art. Once I found the MoMA I just kept going back, never went anywhere else. The sense of possibility I was discovering inside me was mirrored in those mad big paintings — and they quite literally turned me on.

I fell in love with abstract expressionism and a MoMA tour guide called Barnaby, who stood in front of Rothko, all skinny and complicated in a pair of heavy black-framed specs, and said, "In the beginning was the word."

Christ. I nearly had an orgasm. If this sounds pretentious, bear in mind that this was a girl who had previously renounced all education and culture in favour of filling out quizzes in magazines to see if she was suited to having group sex with the members of Duran Duran.

The tours were free and I kept going to Barnaby's in particular and on about the third one he stood us in front of the Rothko and asked us what it made us think of. There was a little silence and I just couldn't resist saying, "In the beginning was the word."

Barnaby turned and looked at me for the first time — he'd been too wrapped up in his own tortured soul to notice me before. He looked at me with intense gratitude. I got the feeling I'd restored his faith in the human race — not just the human race: life, the universe, everything.

I had been meaning to add, "I got that from you." But after the look he gave me I couldn't bear to disillusion him. From then on, he definitely noticed me every time I attended his tours.

There were certain difficulties about staying with Martha's uncle and aunt. Mrs. Elberman was a real Jewish mama and she was continually moaning about the way we dressed and the way we ate — ice-cream deliveries at two in the morning. And there were certain family chores that were obligatory, one of which was going to tea with a cousin from another branch of the family who had recently come to town. He was apparently twenty-three and had just started out in publishing.

There was a definite matchmaking vibe in the air and Mrs. Elberman made us wear our good-girl clothes. The address we were sent to was in a very insalubrious part of town and we thought the cab driver had taken us to the wrong side of the tracks on purpose to rob us. But "No such luck," as I said when he drove off. By this time I was beginning to give up on having the real New York experience.

Martha was hysterical and jumpy and thought we were going to be mugged any second and was making so much eye contact with all the men passing by to try to establish if they were muggers or not and giving off so many fear pheromones I told her she might as well be carrying a placard saying, "Mug Me!"

In the end I went into a bar and showed someone the scrap of paper with the address on it and they neither mugged nor robbed me but confirmed I was in the right place and that the apartment block I was looking for was right opposite.

So we went in. It must have been a converted factory or something and the communal parts were about as functional as it gets: concrete and steel. All the apartment doors were fortified like they are in London when a house is empty and they want to stop squatters getting in. Eventually we got to a Fort Knox type establishment with the number 14 just legible amongst the graffiti.

We knocked. No answer. We knocked again. By this time Martha was nearly wetting herself and saying Paul couldn't possibly live there. Finally the door was opened by a bride on roller blades. When she threw back her veil with a self-important little huff and said, "Hi, you guys, you're late — the English muffins will be stone cold," we saw it was a he not a she.

Martha gave out a little moan and quavered, "Paul?" for it was he.

I'm not sure the English muffins existed. Paul bladed around the apartment in his bell-shaped bridal gown, knocking down everything that was to be knocked down, and introduced us to his boyfriend Craig, who spent the whole evening at the ironing-board. He told jokes that made even Martha laugh, made us drink Manhattans, gave us cigarettes to smoke and finally dressed us up and took us out to Nell's.

For "something in publishing" read stylist for *Vogue* and one room of Paul's apartment was entirely filled with rails of clothes. I was in heaven and Martha warmed up considerably with the drinks and ended up looking surprisingly fab in top to toe Vivienne Westwood. I wore a tiny little red velvet dress and what Paul called fuck-me heels.

When we got to Nell's the crowd at the door parted for Paul like the Red Sea. I remember being overwhelmed by the glamorously grown-up jaded people and I nearly died to think I might belong. I wanted to discard my youth that instant. I wanted to be jaded.

Of course I didn't realise that it also works the other way around. The glamorous ones might have regarded my peachy youth with a little envy too. That's the trouble with being young; you don't want what you've got until it's gone.

Paul swept us under the velveteen crush barriers and over the hallowed threshold in one simple movement. And as if that wasn't enough to get me high, the first person I bumped into on the dance floor was Barnaby from the MoMA.

I was pretty mashed and my memory might be unreliable but when I run the tape in my head we pretty much go straight into each other's arms. I wish it could always be like that. I wish I could always have that kind of certainty. In affairs of the heart, he who hesitates . . . The thinking went something like this: I'm a goddess, he must want me. Simple.

So we fell into each other's embrace and during a riff in "I'm Every Woman," which was booming out of the speakers at about a thousand decibels, he said, "How come you understand Rothko?"

I told him I had divine powers.

When Paul came over to inspect my catch, he said, "I think he might be one of mine."

Looking back, maybe he had a point. Barnaby could easily have been suffering from some sexual confusion, but that evening he was most definitely *mine*.

"She's a goddess," Barnaby told Paul, very seriously.

I looked at him in much the same way he'd looked at me in the MoMA. "You knew?" I said.

When we got back to Paul's, Barnaby and I had stuttering sex, which was exciting because it was sex and because I thought Barnaby was my winning trophy, but was a physical experience in the way that going to the dentist is a physical experience.

In the morning Barnaby left early to get to work and I found that there was blood on the sheets. When I told Paul he said we should hang them out of the window and be proud but when he saw the look on my face he helped me take them down to the laundry room and was so sweet about it I knew I'd love him for life.

We went back to the Elbermans' in our good-girl clothes and told Martha's mum that Paul had served a mean English muffin. As they drove me to the airport later that day I realised that the grown-ups would never know. They would never know what it was like to truly live.

I treasured having this secret nearly as much as I treasured my hangover as evidence of my rite of passage in NYC.

"I lost my virginity in New York," I said to Ed, as the plane taxied through pelting rain to the gate at JFK.

Ed was green: there'd been storms coming in off the Atlantic so the last bit had been rough — I even heard a stewardess throwing up in the galley, it was that bad.

"I've been looking for it ever since," I said.

"You're funny," he said. "How long have you been thinking that up?"

The remark was not particularly friendly but it was progress. It was the first thing he'd said to me the whole way over.

"But I have," I said, "so to speak. I don't think I've ever been as excited and as alive and as . . . hopeful as the first time I was in New York."

He turned to me, he narrowed his eyes, "Why are we in New York?" he said.

"You know why," I said.

"Come on," he said, "what's all this about?"

At which point I kind of lost it. I particularly dislike Ed's tendency to believe perfectly explicable life events are some kind of elaborate conspiracy against him. "Well, since you ask," I said, "it's all an elaborate conspiracy against you. Mac wasn't really arrested. I wasn't really caught in traffic. In fact," I said, "we're not really married. The Registrar may have looked like a civil servant from Epping but she was actually an undercover agent for MI5."

"Funnier and funnier," Ed said.

"And," I said, "all that part at the airport when Mac behaved like the fundamentally decent and generous bloke he is, that was all a sham."

When I'd got to Heathrow I couldn't find Ed. His mobile wasn't on and he wasn't back at our flat either. I called Della but she didn't have much to suggest except paging him at the airport — which I tried to no avail.

Mac called me back a few minutes later and said he'd got us two seats on the late Virgin flight to New York — that was the closest he could get us to Mexico at this point. And that he'd booked us into a fancy hotel in the city. He must have been feeling guilty because he said, "You can stay in the hotel as long as you want — on me," although I do happen to know that his company has a deal with that particular hotel.

I drifted around the airport vaguely looking for Ed and thinking that whatever happened I was going to get on the flight to New York. The thought of going back to our dreary flat — or to Mac's — made me feel suicidal. Eventually I wandered into the bookshop and found Ed sitting on a kind of armchair he'd made out of a luggage cart and our suitcases, reading a copy of *Men Are from Mars, Women Are from Venus*.

When he saw me he said, "This book says that you are a rubber band. You pull away and you bounce back. It also says that you are a man."

"I see," I said, "I'm sorry."

"Men are meant to be rubber bands," he said.

"Listen, Ed," I said, "Mac's —"

"Men also," he said interrupting me, "put out the rubbish a lot. You don't do that." He looked at me accusingly. "And they go to their caves."

"Right," I said. "Listen, Ed, we've got a plane to catch," and I'm ashamed to say that I looked at my watch. I might even have looked at my watch impatiently.

"You are unfuckingbelievable," he said, loudly enough for the shop assistant to look up.

I explained about the flights to New York. "Please," I said, with all the desperation I truly felt, "this situation can either go from bad to worse or it can go from bad to better." Then I kind of whispered awkwardly, "We *are* married." In my peripheral vision I saw that the shop assistant's head shot up from her inventory-taking or whatever she was doing.

Ed considered for a while then he got up, straightened our bags on the cart, kind of bowed at me, as if to say, "Your wish is my command," then slung the Venus and Mars book back on the pile.

"Ed, I'm really, really, really sorry," I said gratefully.

He looked away, wouldn't reply. So I looked at the shop assistant. She looked away too.

On the plane, after I'd finished reminding Ed about Mac's saving graces he just said, "Mac's a big bully."

"No, he isn't," I said, losing it slightly.

Ed just turned away his head in cold fury, which is about as close as you can come to getting space between another soul and yourself in 747 economy.

I could have kicked myself, actually, if I'd had enough leg room — or even one to stand on, which I didn't. This was no time for anything but supremely good behaviour on my part.

At this point an air hostess stopped by our seats and said, "Are you the honeymoon couple?"

Ed said, "Can you tell?"

"Here," she said, and handed us a real bottle of champagne from first class. "It's complimentary."

"Thanks," I said, "that's really nice," and we sat there for a while in silence, me with the frosty champagne between my legs.

After they had announced that "at this time" there was going to be a delay getting on to the gate and that our agony was going to be prolonged, I eventually said to Ed, "Can you hear voices?" He ignored me. I said, "I can hear voices."

His head came round a millimetre and he grunted.

"Can't you hear voices?" I said again.

Ed said, "What are you talking about?"

"I can hear voices," I said, alarmed.

"What voices?" Ed barked.

"Voices," I said, "little voices."

"Saying what?" he barked again.

"They're saying things like, 'Aren't you tall and handsome!' 'Isn't that a great pair of legs?' 'Nice kind eyes!' things like that," I said. "I think they must be talking to you."

"Uh," he said exasperated, "shut the fuck up, will you?"

"It's not my fault," I said, "it's the voices."

He didn't dignify me with an answer. We sat in silence for a moment and then I said excitedly, "Oh, I know what it is! It's the bottle of champagne!" and I held it up.

Ed looked at me like he was thinking about having me sectioned. But at least he was looking at me, so I gave him the punch-line — "It's complimentary!"

It's hard to play the tragic hero in the face of idiocy.

Ed hadn't exactly laughed at my stupid joke but he hadn't exactly kept a straight face either. He shook his head and snorted and the ice cracked a little. I wouldn't say that things were vastly improved between Ed and me as we came through the terminal into the petrolly warmth and chaos of JFK at night, but at least he was now talking to me.

"What's really funny," he said, "is that you think you're so funny."

I don't actually, but I wasn't about to argue.

Sometimes I think the best thing about New York is the noise. The perpetual car horns and sirens and the yellow cabs clanking over the metal plates in the street and the garbage trucks at night that make a crashing noise like the top fell off the Chrysler building.

Our hotel rose luminous and blue-lit above us as we got out of the cab. It was like a Christmas tree that you could go and live inside. To say it looked inviting and welcoming would be an understatement. But daunting and exclusive as well. "Abandon reality," it seemed to say, "all ye who can afford to enter here."

And, courtesy of Mac, we too were swept through the thundering revolving doors and into the light. The doormen in designer suits were obviously male models earning extra bucks. I thought maybe if you were a rich and lonely lady you could hire one for the evening.

When we got upstairs, Ed took one look at our room — at the vast, high, deliciously made-up bed with its abundant pillows and suggestive luxury and, outside the windows, the drop-dead gorgeous urban sex of the New York skyline by night. The combination is guaranteed to give even the most cross jilted lover an erection — and pulled me down on the bed.

He managed to get me half undressed in about thirty seconds — while kissing me. I don't know how he does it. I suppose he's perfected his technique over the years. He was just running his tongue down my breastbone when he stopped and said, "We've got no condoms."

Yes — we use condoms. I like condoms. Condoms are pay-as-you-go contraception. They're like key-operated electricity meters: you never get a bill in the post.

"Why haven't we got condoms?" I said.

Ed said, "I bought three economy bumper packs at Heathrow." Then added, "That's thirty-six in total."

"Wow," I said, bowled over by his enthusiasm and regretting yet again that I'd messed things up.

"The man behind me was buying one little three-pack and looking at my stash so I said to him, 'What can I say? It's going to be a long weekend.'"

"So where are they?" I said.

"Oh," he said, "when I finally admitted to myself that you'd missed the plane, I handed them out one by one to a package tour of teenage girls going to Ibiza. It was therapeutic."

"We'll order some from room service," I said, and reached for the phone.

"We can't do that!" he yelled.

"Of course we can," I said.

"What? And some bell-boy will bring them up and I'll have to tip him and — I'm not doing it."

"Don't be so English," I said. For a second I thought that Ed was going to be one of those people who go all sort of fearful middle-class-batten-down-the-hatches when they go somewhere new. I imagined him shrinking in front of me, getting smaller and smaller. I wondered if this was a side-effect of getting married. Then I remembered I was meant to be on best behaviour. I made my head stop. I said, "I'll go down and get some."

"Where from?" he said.

"There was a kiosk in the foyer, they'll have some. Don't worry. No one will know."

They did have condoms in the kiosk. The vast open-plan hotel foyer turned into an armchairs-in-a-warehouse-style bar. And there were goldfish scattered around the place in bowls. I looked longingly at all the people — they seemed so elegant and loungey.

"They'll all be dead by the end of the evening."

I looked up with a start. I felt the remark had been directed at me. But no one was there. An elegant couple stood in front of me and slightly to my right, but I could see only their backs.

"They just kind of float to the bottom of the bowl," the man's voice said. He was talking to his girlfriend. They looked well groomed and together.

The thought flashed through my mind, I wish I was her. I wish I was with him. I think I was just wishing I didn't have to be so exhaustingly inside myself the whole time. I wished my life could feel on the inside like theirs looked from the outside. In short, I had one of those moments when you feel everyone else is having a better time than you.

All this just looking at their backs — you must be *very* tired, girl, I thought. I had a feeling the man was very attractive, though. I was wanting him to turn round — my genetic messaging service was beeping, I guess. Now I'm married, I must remember to turn it off.

I had the lift to myself but someone got the button just before the doors had finished closing, and I thought, With my luck, that'll be the elegant couple come to torment me. But it was only a pair of geriatric lovers who told me on the way up — within ten seconds of meeting me the way Americans do — they'd won their trip off a cereal carton in Seattle.

★ ★ ★

I stood in our bathroom, looking at my reflection in the mirror —
again. For a hotel bathroom, this was a pretty nice one. A rhapsody
in white. The towels were luxurious and the water pressure in the
shower so strong it had nearly washed me down the plug-hole.

I stared at myself in the mirror. I'm not particularly vain — or
particularly enamoured of the way I look — it's just that every now
and then I need to, well, check that I'm still there.

Looking at myself all in white — white towel, white towel tur-
ban round my wet hair — it occurred to me again that it was *still*
my wedding night. By flying out to New York I had added six
hours to my wedding night.

I wondered idly if married sex was going to be any different
from unmarried sex. I wondered if we were just going to have sex
because we felt we ought to, it being our wedding night. I wondered whether we'd feel odd doing it now we were married. I
wondered whether the sex tonight had to set the tone for the
whole marriage. We must have sex, I supposed. Surely it would be
a bad omen not to.

So, with all this buzzing idiotically around in my head, I came
out of the bathroom in my white towels with a million expecta-
tions and some trepidation.

The lights were out. Ed was fast asleep on the bed.

I just stood there. I always felt very self-conscious in the presence
of the sleeping. The view outside caught my eye and the glamour
of the city took my breath away again, somehow put my worries in
perspective. It's going to be okay, I thought, and I went to the window and pulled open the glass doors and stepped on to the balcony
to breathe it in.

I went to the edge and leaned right out and I thought about
what a fantastic planet we were on and how small and insignificant
our lives really were. Sometimes when I look out at a view like
that, I kind of believe in God or, anyway, I have this semi-religious
moment when I get perspective on how powerless I am and how

big IT all is and how much possibility there is and how ninety-nine per cent of the time I am blinded to the bigger picture by my own teeny-weeny pointless details.

"Makes you feel like a goldfish in a bowl."

I turned. The man I had seen downstairs was standing on the next-door balcony. He wasn't looking at me, he was looking out at the view. Something inside me lurched. I looked for the woman he was with but it seemed he wasn't talking to her. He was talking to me.

A second before he turned his head I knew for sure. It was Alex.

I was hemmed in by four walls, I was very safe. I still felt like I might fall over the edge. Fall over the edge of the world. I'd stepped into another dimension — or, rather, I had a sense of the world being two-dimensional. I mean, what if the things that seemed so far away were, in fact, just on the other side? What if we lived in a flat world rather than a round world so that just on the other side of despair was joy, just on the other side of deprivation was abundance and just on the other side of loneliness was love? What if the things we want so badly were right there in front of us the whole time? What if we just had to reach our hand through the invisible barrier? It seemed perfectly logical to me. It seemed just right.

"Goldfish," I said, "don't mind being in a bowl because their brains are so small. Every time they go round they say, 'Oh, look at that interesting weed!' and then three seconds later, 'Oh, look at that interesting weed!' They live a spiritual life."

"New York is kind of an interesting weed," he said.

You see what I mean? He got it straight away. He knew what I was talking about. I turned round properly to look at him and we looked at each other for a long time. I thought about how I'd been kidding myself all those years about him, how I'd told myself it was just a stupid fantasy and I was making him out to be all sorts of things he wasn't. And here he was right in front of me and all the delusion fell away and I realised that I had been absolutely right about him. He was the most beautiful man I had ever known. And it wasn't about how he looked, it was about being in his presence and being me in his presence and about the magic in the air when he was there. Like when you are a child and your father picks up a wooden spoon and tells you he can do magic with it and in that moment you absolutely believe him — you *know* that the wooden spoon is magical and the universe is a mysterious and beautiful place and that anything is possible and that life is a mysterious and beautiful thing. And you are glad to be alive.

"You probably don't remember me," he said.

"Probably not," I agreed. "Have we met?"

"I believe so," he said.

"Where did we meet?" I said.

"In London," he said, "in a restaurant. Italian, I think it was."

"Italian?"

"I had risotto."

"Risotto?" I said.

"You had it too," he said.

"So I did," I said. "And then what happened?"

"We — er — we shared a cab."

"We did?" I said. "And then what happened?"

"We played a game," he said.

"A game?" I said.

"Yeah," he said, "a game."

"And then what happened?" I said.

"Nothing happened."

"And after that?" I said. "After nothing happened?"

Alex smiled at me.

"You wrote me hundreds of letters," I said.

"I wrote you one letter," he said. "You didn't reply. You thought it best. I respected that."

"One letter," I said, clasping it to my chest — metaphorically speaking.

I knew I should go back into the hotel room right now and not come out again. But in truth it wasn't really an option. I had to know — I had to know what had happened. The trouble was, if it was good news it was bad news so to speak.

"What did the letter say?"

He thought about this for a while; eventually he came up with, "You don't want to know."

"Well, here we are," I said, holding my arms out like it was a happy ending. "I got married today."

"You did?" he said, and thought about this for a moment. Then he said, "Me too."

"That's nice," I said, politely.

Politely! Oh, God. Now I was falling down a hole somewhere inside me at about a hundred miles an hour. It took my breath away. I felt I ought to grab hold of something but if I did then he'd see I was falling.

He was asking me something but I couldn't hear. I was too busy falling.

"Sorry?" I said politely, when I'd landed safely in hell.

"I said," he said, "'what are you thinking?'"

"I hate you," I said. It was the only thing that came close.

He laughed. "Come here," he said, and stepped up to the balustrade. I knew from his body language that he didn't want us to be heard.

I said, "Look, I'm just going to do a reality check here. I'm going to go back into my room and then I'm going to come out again and I'm going to see . . . I'm going to see . . ."

I went back inside. Ed was snoring on the bed. It didn't help. I took a deep breath. None of it helped. I went out again.

"You're still here," I said.

"Come here," he said. I went.

He spoke quietly, into my ear: "This isn't — this isn't how it was meant to be."

Now I was so close, I could sense a tremble somewhere right inside him. It made me want to put my arms around him and tell him it was all going to be all right.

"I thought about you," he said.

"I thought about you too," I said. I felt like swooning — women swooned so much in the old days because of all the sexual repression — well, I know how they felt. I felt like swooning.

This is better than sex, I thought, which is saying something because I usually think only sex is better than sex. Then it occurred to me: what was I talking about? This *was* sex — sex on my wedding night. And the thought gave me such a jolt that I stepped backwards.

He might well have been following a similar thought process because he stepped back too — in fact, we sort of lurched apart like a magnetic field that turns to repel.

"We'll move," I said.

"No, we will," he said. "I mean, we're leaving in the morning anyway."

"Oh, okay," I said. "So this is it," I said, making sort of cutting movements with my hands. "I don't think we should — you know —"

"You don't want to be friends?" he said. But with a smile so I knew he was joking.

I couldn't laugh, though. All I could do was back away.

14

WHY are you behaving strangely?" Ed said.

"I'm not," I said, positioning myself behind a pillar on the hotel landing and pushing the elevator button about fifteen times. "I just think it's late and we're tired and room service is fun."

Tearing myself away from the balcony must have made that deafening ripping noise you get when you open a particularly clingy velcro fastener, because Ed's eyes had shot open and he'd said, "I'm starving. Let's go out for dinner."

"It's midnight," I'd said.

"So what," he said. "We're in the city that never sleeps."

Out on the landing, I said, "You didn't want to come to New York — remember?"

"But now I *am* here," he said. "Are you hiding behind that pillar?"

"No," I said.

"Is something wrong?" he said.

"No," I said. I had this scenario in my head. Alex and his wife were going to appear and I would be *caught* with Ed. Right then I thought it would be the worst thing in the world to be caught with

Ed. Which says nothing about Ed: there's nothing wrong with Ed and everything wrong with me.

I had it all in my head. We would be in the elevator, the doors would just be closing. It's called Sod's Law and it's the only truly infallible law of nature.

"What's on your mind?" said Ed, looking at my face as the elevator arrived.

"Don't you hate it," I said, "when you're in an elevator and just as the doors are closing some fucker gets in front of the sensors and everyone has to wait while the doors open again? Don't you just hate that?"

We stepped in and I watched as the doors closed. I was so tense I practically screamed when a well-manicured hand shot through the open bit right at the last moment. If I didn't scream out loud I definitely screamed in my head. It was like when the hand comes through the wall at the end of *Blade Runner.* It was like when she sits up in the bath at the end of *Fatal Attraction.* It was like — actually I'm exaggerating. I mean, my life was not at risk, technically speaking. The doors simply slid open again and a handsome young man and his new young wife stepped politely in beside us.

As I said, it's called Sod's Law and it's the only truly infallible law of nature.

I stopped breathing and my eyes glazed over — there's a part of me that thinks that if I do this I become invisible and what's happening isn't happening. Through the glaze, however, I couldn't help but inhale a horrifying if distorted impression of good grooming and wifely pleasantness. I think first impressions are very deceptive. When you first meet someone you see all the good things about them.

"Hi," crooned the well-groomed one, making the word last several syllables.

"Hello," said Ed, gruffly.

"Oh, my God, you're British?" said she.

"Yes," said Ed.

"First time in Manhattan?" said she.

"Yes," said Ed.

"That's so cool!"

"On our honeymoon," said Ed.

"No kidding! So are we."

At this point I think my eyes probably crossed and my knees started to buckle. I couldn't look at Alex but he was clearly doing nothing to rescue the situation. Although when we spilled gratefully out into the lobby and Ed said, "Do you know a good place to eat round here?" and she said, "We're going for —" Alex suddenly came to life.

"Pizza," he said.

She looked at him in amazement. "You know I don't eat pizza, hon — sweetheart," she said.

I noticed that she'd kind of tripped up over the word "honey" — it didn't pass me by. On the other hand it didn't register as anything very much. I think if you'd asked me my own name at that point I probably wouldn't have known what it was.

"*They*'re going to eat pizza," said Alex. "They're in New York — they should eat pizza," he added, unconvinced.

"We're going for sushi," said she. "You guys probably don't have that in London yet."

"Are you joking?" I said. "We have sushi coming out of our ears in London." Everyone looked slightly alarmed at this analogy. "Oozing out," I said.

"Sushi is —" Ed said.

"Not what we want tonight!" I yelled. And with this I grabbed Ed's hand and pulled hard.

Out on the street, Ed said, "Not what we want tonight? I don't remember anything in the marriage vows about unilateral decisions being attributable to 'we.'" He talks like that sometimes, Ed — his father was a lawyer.

"I feel like sushi," Ed said.

And there was something about his tone that reminded me of the difficulties of the day and decided me not to argue.

Which is how we ended up sitting just a couple of stools along from Alex and the well-groomed one at the local sushi bar.

I suppose, technically speaking, that I could have twisted my ankle or claimed to be having a miscarriage or cried wolf in some other way to prevent this appalling turn of events. But first, I'm not very good at pretending, I tend to freeze up like I did in the elevator, and second, there was a part of me that wanted, if not to punish Alex, then at least to pick at the scab. Seven years ago, after all, he had committed the cardinal sin of *not calling*.

And third, although I couldn't possibly admit this to myself at the time because the implications were unthinkable, I just wanted to *be with him*. Under any circumstances. Even these.

I thought I was going to get away lightly until the people sitting between us left and Ed heard the well-groomed one mention *feng shui* to one of the sushi chefs and Ed started saying, "*Feng shui!* Honey's sister does *feng shui* weddings," in his inimitable enthusiastic and unapologetic way. So, of course, the connection was made.

Alex gave me one of his best penetrating stares — like I'd sent in Ven as an undercover agent or something. Ed kept turning to me and saying, "Isn't that amazing?" Cherelle, as she turned out to be called, couldn't get over that we'd ended up sitting round eating Japanese together on our mutual wedding night with Ven providing only two degrees of separation between us. Me and Alex and years, I thought. How many degrees of separation is that?

"I suppose we should be in the hotel shagging," Ed said.

"Shagging!" crowed Cherelle, delighted to come across genuine ethnic usage of the word.

"Sex," said Alex drily. He hadn't said much. I guess he had to say something.

"Instead we are here eating sushi," said Ed.

"Food is the new sex," said Alex.

"I hate to disillusion you," Ed said, "but interior design is the new sex."

"No," I said, "it's the new rock and roll."

"Whatever," Alex said, and we met eyes.

"Sex on the wedding night," Ed said, ploughing on enthusiastically into the conversation, "isn't really an issue any more, is it? Now it's no longer the moment of truth."

"Oh, my God, doing it for the first time after a day like this," said Cherelle. "That must have been high pressure."

"Like scratching off the foil on your lottery ticket," I said, with rising hysteria and after a moment added, "and if you've won it says clitoris."

I stared at my California rolls thinking I must be punch-drunk or something. Then tried to rescue the situation by saying, "So where are you going on your honeymoon?" but nobody heard me.

So, here we are, I thought gaily. The four of us. Eating sushi and musing on the fraught question — though not so fraught as it was — of sex on your wedding night.

"Imagine," Cherelle suddenly said to me, "imagine if you had to go back to the hotel right now, after all the hard work of getting married, and sleep with someone for the first time. I mean, imagine if you had to go back to the hotel right now and do it with Alex!"

I just kept staring at those California rolls. I don't know what Alex did.

Ed said, "I'm not sure we know each other well enough to imagine stuff like that."

Ed woke me up the next morning by sitting up in bed and announcing gloomily, "Well, no Sex on Our Wedding Night." He said it like it had capital letters. "The marriage is doomed," he said.

I wrenched one eye open, then the other — it felt like peeling two hard-boiled eggs. The red digits on the bedside clock roared 5:47 a.m. into the half-darkness.

"It's the middle of the night," I said. "Go back to sleep," and pulled a pillow over my head. For about three seconds I lingered blissfully on the edge of oblivion, my mind skating freestyle like a needle on a record. Then I had a second or two of a kind of far-off knowing and a far-off not knowing of what exactly it was that I knew. Then the needle fell into the groove and the record started to play. Sleep became instantly impossible.

Alex.

I reluctantly removed the pillow from my head.

"Doomed," said Ed again, and leapt out on to the balcony naked to enjoy the dawn view.

I just lay there and did some positive thinking: I can't go on, I don't know what to do, I can't handle this, I give up — stuff like that. And couldn't think of anything that would help matters except possibly Richard Gere coming in and carrying me off. I thought perhaps I wouldn't mind spending the rest of my life being carried to all my appointments by Richard Gere. I thought about how much I hate the way that when you're grown-up you have to carry your own life around everywhere, the whole time. With no respite, goddamn it. I felt like a pack-horse who'd just faced up to the fact it was going to have to carry the Taj Mahal over the Himalayas.

Ed came back in humming "'The Bronx is up and the Battery's down — the people ride in a hole in the ground.'"

I said, "Is that a bit of enjoyment I see before me?"

"Nope," he said, "no enjoyment is to be had at any point."

"Ed," I said, "I really am truly and deeply sorry that I missed the plane."

He just looked at me. I could see he wasn't going to let it go at that. I wanted to scream. Instead I bit the pillow and wrestled around the bed with it and did a kind of massive growly "Arrrrgh!" noise.

"What's that about?" he said.

"I didn't *mean* to miss the plane," I said.

"But you did," he said, "and you can't just expect sorry to make it better. Because you just say sorry and then you do it again."

There was some truth in this. "Are we really doomed?" I said.

"No," he said. "Do the arrrrgh thing again with the pillow. It was quite horny."

"Ed!" I said.

He jumped on the bed and wriggled up beside me. "Do you love me?" he said.

"Yes," I said, in the wary voice I use when someone phones up and says they are from the credit-card company and are they speaking to a Miss Honey Holt?

Ed said, "What's that tone of voice mean?"

"It means," I said, "what are you after?"

"Love," he said.

"I do love you," I said. "It's just that sometimes I wish I didn't. It would make things easier."

"It would?" he said.

"Yes," I said. "It would be less tiring."

"Tiring?" he said.

"And less marrying," I said.

"Ah," he said. "How is it for you? The marrying?"

I considered. I tried to think of a joke. I gave up. "Scary," I said.

"Ah," he said, and sighed. I took the sigh to mean that he was scared too. Then he took my hand and said, "For better or worse." He looked me in the eye and I don't know what he saw there but he said, "What are you thinking?"

"I'm thinking," I said, "we have to get the next flight to Mexico," and I sat up and grabbed the phone.

The hotel travel desk was closed. New York isn't as twenty-four-hour as they make it out to be.

Ed and I had that intense jet-lag hunger that feels like someone's boring a hole in your gut and Ed decided we should have breakfast in a diner. I could see he was getting into the New York thing.

We found a lovely diner with Formica tables and laminated menus so big they could have doubled as life-rafts. Ed had waffles and blueberries and maple syrup, and he definitely approved of the way they kept filling his coffee cup without even asking. I kept saying we should call the airline and see about Mexico but he just said, "Relax — like chill, baby," in a phoney New York accent that was quite cute.

I took Ed to Fifth Avenue and Central Park and we did the obvious kind of walking-about things. Ed got high as a kite. I kept telling him it was New York's famous negative ions but by lunchtime he'd just fallen in love with the city, hook, line and sinker.

We'd been up so ridiculously early that by midday we'd already been out for hours. Ed bought *Time Out* and said he wanted to read it on our bed. He was fomenting plans for restaurants and movies and jazz clubs. I reckoned we were probably safe by now to go back to the hotel so I agreed. "And I'll book flights to Mexico," I said firmly.

At the hotel I tried to get Ed to the travel desk but he just waved his *Time Out* at me and went up to our room.

There were a couple of possibilities flight-wise and I got the airline to hold two seats for us and took down two inscrutable reference numbers.

I was walking back to our room — pondering life's eternal mysteries like why exactly F for Foxtrot and V for Victor and who was Victor anyway? Or is it "victor" as in the person who wins? — when I heard the unmistakable sounds of strangulated public arguing ahead.

"I'm phobic about snakes," hissed the female voice. "There are snakes in Marrakesh."

"The snakes are in baskets," said the male voice, which I recognised, delivering the word "baskets" with some venom.

I couldn't see them because they were around the corner.

"I told you I could never go see *Raiders of the Lost Ark* because of the snakes!" — her.

"Shit" — him. "New York was only a stopover. We are leaving New York tonight!"

"You never ordered me around before" — her, with a wail.

"I never tried to get you to leave the country before" — him.

Little silence.

"Before what?" — him.

Muffled sob — her.

"Before getting married, am I right?" — him. Retreating footsteps. "Where are you going?" — him.

Silence. I waited until I sensed all was clear then walked on, turned the corner and bumped right into Alex. He grabbed me and pulled me into one of those little coffee-machine stations. Next to the coffee paraphernalia there was a cosy alcove where the maids kept their mops — he wedged us in there.

"She'll be back," he said.

His proximity gave out such warmth I got that swooning thing again although I tried to beat it down.

Alex stuck his head up and listened like a prairie rat. Nothing.

"I never got the letter," I said. His eyes came back to mine. "There was a postal strike," I said.

"You didn't call me?" he said. It was question.

"I did," I said. "A woman answered. You didn't call me."

"You didn't reply to my letter."

"I didn't get your letter."

Footsteps outside. Then Cherelle yelled, "Alex!" I jumped. She sounded like she was standing in my left eardrum. We froze.

When she'd gone by I asked him for a second time what the letter had said.

"You don't want to know," he said. "Believe me."

The cold wind of all my worst fears blew up between us. "Let me out of here," I said.

He did. We went out into the corridor. We stood there. In pain.

"We won't see each other again," I said.

"Don't worry," he said. "I'm leaving the city today. I'm leaving the country — in fact, I'm leaving the continent." His suitcase was still sitting there in the middle of the corridor.

"Great," I said. "Me too," I said, and walked straight into his open arms.

Only joking. I didn't walk into his arms. There were no arms to walk into. I turned and walked away.

"The letter," he said, to my retreating back, "said that maybe it was love."

I kept on walking. He'd told me I wouldn't want to know.

Back in our room, Ed was asleep again, the magazine open on his chest. I laid myself down very carefully beside him. I was conscious of my brain being heavy, the way you are when you have a really bad headache and you can actually feel your brain inside your head. I laid it down very carefully on the pillow. It was working hard to contain the situation. It was working too hard. It was moving towards terminal velocity and it went something like this: Okay, you have to stop this. You have to stop this NOW. Take immediate action to become a better person. Write a journal every day and work out exactly what's wrong with you. Identify dysfunctional patterns and *arrest* them. Go back to therapist once a week. No, twice a week. Get evening job to pay for it. Study, educate yourself, read more self-help books, go to night school. LEARN A LANGUAGE! It's despicable that you never mastered a language. Walk more. Go to art galleries. Be kind, reasonable and loving to all people at all times. Exercise more. Do yoga. Eat whole foods and CHEW PROPERLY. Take vitamins. Every day. Be tidier. Get up earlier. Go to bed earlier. Meditation is a good idea. Spend less. Don't think about Alex at all ever again. Amen. If the thought of him should come into your head count to three and say, "Life is a bowl of cherries." Which is an expression Theresa would use when the going got tough. I never actually knew what it meant — officially — so one day I did a survey and went round asking people what they thought "Life is a bowl of cherries" meant.

Della thought it meant that you just get your bowl of cherries in life and that's your lot and you eat them one by one and then you die.

And Ven thought it meant that life was a kind of cheerful, transient, meaningless thing.

I, however, always thought the expression was referring to the way you tend to get one really delicious perfect cherry quite early on in the bowl, which just explodes in your mouth. But that one exquisite experience of exactly the right firmness and exactly the right tartness and exactly the right sweetness is rarely repeated — so you keep eating the cherries to try to find one that's as good as that incredible first one you had. And every now and then, in the course of the bowl, you do find one that is just as good, but because it's only a cherry it only lasts a few seconds so then you're off again looking for another one. In the process, of course, you have to eat all these watery, tasteless, mouldering cherries, and before you know it you've eaten the whole bowl. And you have stomach-ache.

So then I thought, "Life is a bowl of cherries" wasn't such an appropriate motto for my three-second not-thinking-about-Alex rule in case that made me think Ed was a mouldering cherry — which he wasn't — and maybe my motto should be something ghastly like "Life is not a dress rehearsal" but when I thought about that I decided that wasn't at all a good idea because that means "Seize the day" and if I was to seize today I would go right out there and . . . whoops — one, two, three . . . Oh my God. Is this do-able?

In a panic I shook Ed to wake him up. "We have to go to Mexico," I said.

He groaned a bit then opened his eyes. "I love this place. Let's stay for a week," he said, shut his eyes and went straight back to sleep.

I lay down again and closed my eyes. I remember thinking that I must now immediately call downstairs and confirm our flights to Mexico and that's all I remember. I fell into a deep, numbing, jet-lag sleep and when I woke up it was dusk outside. I lay there for a while fantasising about a cup of Earl Grey tea. I tried to turn over and pick up the phone to room service, but sophisticated body movements were out of the question. Sleeping had been a disastrous move. I felt like you do in dreams when you need to run away from something but you're trying to run through treacle and it's drag-drag-dragging you down. So I just lay there and thought about what had happened and why the hell it had to happen. I forgot the three-second rule and thought about Alex being gone and what I might have lost and Ed slept on beside me and I just went on feeling crazy and alone.

In the end I decided to call Della, tell her the whole story and do whatever it was she thought I should do. If she still thought I should tell Ed about Alex, I would tell Ed. At least it would be off my chest.

I managed to summon the co-ordination to dial her home number. No answer — machine. I called the mobile. It was switched straight to message service. I said, "Della, I need you," and left it at that.

Someone knocked at the door. In my daze I had a wild hope it was room service and they'd read my mind about the Earl Grey tea so I stumbled over to answer it. It wasn't Earl Grey tea, it was Paul. He was wearing the most beautiful suit I had ever seen in my life. And he had a little Pekinese dog tucked under his arm.

"Darling," he said.

I just stared at him.

"I'm not intruding, am I?" he said, looking round me and into the room. "How are you?" he asked. "Honeymoon going well?"

This innocent enquiry as to my welfare made me (a) realise I was hanging from the precipice by my fingernails and that it was a long,

long way down, (b) realise that I was extraordinarily glad to see him and (c) cry.

"You know what?" I said. "Give me a hug."

At which point Ed woke up and came to see what was going on and I clung to Paul fiercely like a little girl who doesn't want to go to school and practically tried to hide myself in his skirts.

Paul muttered, "Women's troubles," in Ed's direction several times, with a convincing air of importance, as he hustled me into the loo and shut the door. When Ed banged on it in outrage Paul told him to make himself useful and go get hot strong tea.

"Earl Grey," I managed to call out, between snuffles.

When we were sure he'd gone, Paul handed me some loo paper and said, "Pull yourself together, girl, that's your husband out there."

"It's all been a terrible mistake," I said.

"Try to avoid clichés," he said, "they only lower the tone," and dumped the dog unceremoniously in the wash-basin. He got out a cigarette — French, untipped. "The first night I spent with Honoria I cried all night. The weight of responsibility was terrible. Terrible."

I took it that Honoria was the dog.

"Now, tell Paulie, what's wrong? He's beating you, right? He's keeping little boys? His mistress is in the penthouse suite?"

"No," I said, and couldn't help smiling.

"No? Oh," said Paul, rather flat. "Can one smoke in here?" He threw his head back presumably looking for smoke detectors.

"Remember the Love of My Life," I said.

"He's back?"

"Yes."

"Here in the hotel?"

"Was."

"Gone?"

"Gone."

"Oh, my God."

"Married."

"Oh, my God."

"So am I."

"So you are."

He stared at me, cigarette forgotten. "What to do?" he said, after a moment. And then with rising alarm, "What to wear?"

"Paul," I said, blowing my nose, "I love you for understanding the enormity of the situation. But I am not going to do — or wear — anything."

"Naked?" said Paul. "I love it."

"No, really," I said, "we must remember that Ed is my husband and I'm incredibly lucky to have him."

"Yes," said Paul, "we must remember that."

We gave Ed a minute's silence — out of respect. Then Paul said, "Darling, as you know, I have nothing against Ed. Not one thing. I like him. He's sweet. He's kind — wah, wah. Whatever," impatient waving of unlit cigarette, "but let's face it. We married him on the rebound."

"We did? What rebound?"

"The Love of Your Life rebound."

"Don't be ridiculous."

"Am I being?"

I looked at him.

"Love," he said, "is love is love." He shrugged.

"Don't say that," I said. But I could feel myself falling. Falling for it.

"Oh God," I said, after a moment. "I won't ever see Alex again."

"You weren't ever seeing him again for the last seven years," Paul pointed out. "And what happened? You saw him again."

Then he made a little twirly circle in the air with the unlit cigarette — a tiny little action that nevertheless described beautifully the great paradoxical wheel of life, how things inevitably come around, and how we reap what we sow.

At which point there was a double knock on the door and — unless I was very much mistaken — some muffled giggles. Honoria snuffled around a bit in the basin and stuck her head out in the direction of the bathroom door. I saw that she was wearing a burgundy-coloured bow in her absurd pygmy pony-tail.

"A knock on the door!" I pointed out to Paul.

"Oh, yes," he said, "there's something I should have mentioned," he said. "A surprise."

15

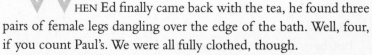

WHEN Ed finally came back with the tea, he found three pairs of female legs dangling over the edge of the bath. Well, four, if you count Paul's. We were all fully clothed, though.

"Bet you're glad to see us," yelled Della and Ven. They were high as kites, both of them, having just flown over on Concorde with Mac.

Ed stood in the doorway and rubbed his already rumpled hair. "Hello," he said.

He loves Del and Ven and he'd never be mean to them. But after he'd said hello, he just turned round and walked away. In Ed language this was about equivalent to him pulling out a Kalashnikov and gunning us all down. A terrified silence fell in the bathroom.

"Go," said Paul, hauling himself out of the bath and parking the dog under his arm firmly, like a clutch bag — except it gave a little yelp. He shooed me out of the bathroom ahead of him and the three of them slunk away, leaving me to face the music with Ed.

Ed was packing.

"Are we going to Mexico?" I said.

"All five of us?" he said.

"They just dropped in," I said.

"I am trying," he said, "I am trying to have a honeymoon here."

"Listen, it's not my fault they turned up," I said.

"Nothing's your fault," he said. *Ergo,* I lose it.

"THEY JUST DROPPED IN!" I yelled. "BECAUSE THEY LOVE ME! NOW THEY'VE GONE!"

"Don't speak to me like that," he said, voice infuriatingly even.

"You know what? I'm fucking sick of tiptoeing around you on fucking eggshells," I yelled.

"Tiptoeing? *Tiptoeing?* When tiptoeing? Interrupting the wedding? Missing the plane?"

"You have no idea."

"*Eggshells?* You're like a bull in a china shop."

"You have no idea" — me again.

Slamming of suitcase, zipping, huffing — him.

"Where are you going?"

"Away from you."

But he stopped at the door. He always does. "Tell me then," he says.

"Tell you what?"

"What do I have no idea about?"

Silence. Eventually, "At the wedding you said 'whatever it takes' — whatever it takes. And now just because Paul and Del and —"

"Have you never heard of the straw that broke the camel's back?"

"I didn't invite them round. It's not my fault Paul and Del —"

"I don't want to hear excuses. I don't want to hear the particulars. There are always particular circumstances. I'm seeing the bigger picture here. I'm seeing the broad brushstrokes. I'm seeing the themes."

"Please can we just go to Mexico?"

"What's that thing you say to me?" he said. "It's the journey. Not the destination" — took his ring off and threw it onto the bed — "something like that." Turned. Went.

I found Della over at Mac's loft apartment. Or, rather, I didn't find her to begin with. At first glance the place appeared to be empty — it's all very open plan and white, but with colourful art on the walls and one of those sectional sofas that can turn corners in an electric blue.

I wandered around for a bit, wondering where she was, until she stuck her head out from under the bed and said that was where she was.

The bed was up on a little podium thing at one end of the room. She was lying under it with just enough head room to swig from a bottle of champagne she had with her.

"Mac's got Tsarina Spooner coming for tea," she offered, as if this were some kind of coherent explanation. Then she burst into fire-hydrant giggles.

"What?" I said — always quick with the zappy one-liners.

"Either you're in or you're out," she said.

"Don't be daft," I said.

"He'll be back any minute," she said. "Either get under here or go."

I thought about it. I had nowhere to go. Beyond that, my mind reminded me of one of those screen savers where the image dissolves and melts and all the little pixels rain down to the bottom. I got under the bed.

"Well, Ed's gone," I said.

"Tsarina Spooner," she said, "has the body of the century."

"I know who Tsarina Spooner is," I said.

There was a little silence. After a moment Del said, "Mac used the L word."

"He did?" I said.

"On the phone," she said.

"Congratulations," I said, although it didn't seem to be quite the right sentiment, like traditionally you're not meant to congratulate the bride on getting married, only the groom. If you congratulate the bride, I suppose the thinking goes, it makes her seem desperate.

"Except Mac thinks the L word is lie," she said.

"You think he might not be faithful to you?" I said, intending sarcasm but Del took it straight.

"Oh, he'll be unfaithful to me," she said. "This is just to prove a point."

"To whom?" I said.

"To him."

There was still no sign of Mac so I said, "Ed's gone," again. Silence. I guess she was thinking about what to say. After a while I said, "Honeymoons suck."

"He'll be back," she said.

"He threw the ring back at me," I said. "So I guess the marriage is off."

"It won't be the first time," she said.

"It will be the first time," I said. "We've never been married before."

"Well, the wedding was off, wasn't it? That's what I meant." She seemed distracted.

"Remember when we used to get all panicky and say, 'There Are No Men'?" I said. "Before Ed."

Della said, "Yeah."

"And we thought maybe it was because we were turning thirty but actually we've been saying it since we were twenty-one?"

Della said, "Yeah."

"But what we really meant was 'There Are No Men That Count.'" Because, okay, there's him, him and him — but none of them count."

"Yeah," said Della, "but we were deranged. We thought you could get guys like in the adverts — you know, cute in a suit. Ha!" she said.

"Well, I don't blame us actually," I said. "When you buy a sofa at Conran you expect it to look just like it did in the magazine."

"What?" said Della — rudely I thought.

"Well, they don't scoff at you when you go in there wanting the sofa, do they?" I said. "They don't tell you to get a life. They don't sneer in your face and say, 'Get real, baby! Sofas like that don't actually exist!' I mean, imagine if they showed you a load of broken-down stodgy sofas with the stuffing coming out — well, you wouldn't even consider those sofas, would you? You'd say, 'Call that a sofa?' Then later you might say 'There Are No Sofas!'" I paused. "Do you see what I'm getting at?"

"I get the gist," she said. "It's a tale of soft furnishings."

"So, walking over there today I was remembering that I always forget that Adam asked me to marry him."

Adam had been my boyfriend at college. With hindsight he could quite easily have been described as cute, and if not literally wearing a suit at the time, at least suitable.

"If I'd married him," I said, "I would definitely have two point four children by now and I would never have said, 'There Are No Men.'"

"Well, there you are," said Della. "There's a sofa."

"Exactly," I said, "but he didn't count."

"Why not?"

"Because he wanted me."

"I see."

"But if I had married him I never would have said, 'There Are No Men' — not once. Because it only takes one."

"Why the fuck didn't you marry him?" said Della, obviously thinking it would have saved her a lot of grief.

"Because I would rather have died," I said. "That's what I was thinking about on the way over — I would rather have died."

Della searched my face for clues. "I can tell you think this is meaningful," she said.

"I'm just realising, you see," I said, "it's not because of them —
it's not because of men — it's because of me."

We fell into another silence. After a while I said, "I saw Him," in
a desultory manner.

"Him who?" she said.

"Him-Him," I said. "The one with the capital H."

"Who?" she said crossly.

"The Love of My Life," I said, in the same desultory manner,
although this time I had the satisfaction of causing Della to bump
her head rather resoundingly on the bed board.

"Whaaaaaat?" she said — she takes after me with the zappy one-
liners.

"For it is he," I said. And, despite my depression, which was
deep, I grinned broadly. There's nothing quite so glorious as telling
someone a truly astonishing piece of news. "Can I tell you again?"
I said. "And you bump your head again?"

"Wherewhatwhenhow?" she said, managing to turn over on her
side to get a better look at my face. At which point we heard the
door go and in came Mac and the babe.

Mac was holding forth loudly about Tsarina Spooner's glittering
future. Tsarina herself, who didn't seem particularly interested in
her glittering future, went straight to the freezer, found Häagen
Dazs, and wandered around the apartment in her Manolos (all I
could see of her) spooning it into her mouth. You can always tell
the really skinny ones by the way they eat Häagen Dazs.

"That's why she's called Spooner," I whispered to Della, who
shushed me like — take this seriously!

So when Tsarina came and sat on the bed, still spooning, Della
and I got a nice close-up — through the lace valance — of her very
sweet little heart tattoo just above her very sweet little left ankle.

"Come here, honey," she said to Mac.

Della looked at me like, here we go. Mac came and joined her
on the bed. There was a silence when we thought they might be
kissing but then there was the clink of spoon on tooth and we

realised she'd given him a mouthful of ice-cream. Then she said, sounding like she'd got the spoon in her mouth, "You want me to blow you, honey?" And there was an even longer silence and I thought, Oh dear Lord, she's undoing his trousers.

But then Mac said, "No, thanks," and Della and I were under there staring at each other eyes big as saucers, the suspense nearly killing us. Because, I mean, he might have been saying, "No, thanks," to another spoon of ice-cream — he might have.

And then Mac said, slowly, haltingly, like someone saying, "Take me to your leader," after having landed his spaceship in a brave new world, "I've got a girlfriend."

Tsarina laughed and said, "So have I. You're gonna have to do better than that, honey. You wanna tell me about your girlfriend? You like fucking her? You want me to tell you about mine?" And Della and I looked at each other like — what drugs was this woman on? She was a pro!

So there was another silence and again we thought the trousers might be coming down but then Mac pulled the rabbit out of the hat, said, "You don't understand. I'm falling in love." He said it like he was about fourteen years old, like he might have vulnerabilities and doubts and needs and all that stuff and it suddenly came to me that he was a human being. I was briefly stunned by the revelation.

But before I'd had time to digest it, I noticed that Della seemed to be having some kind of fit or convulsions or something and I thought I was probably going to have to rush her to ER with the shock of Mac's fidelity.

And now Tsarina was stamping her little Manolo'd foot on to the floor right by Della's head. Tsarina didn't like the L word. Oh, no. "You're boring me," she said petulantly. "You're boring!" which proved too much for Della because her hand shot out from under the bed and grabbed that little tattooed ankle and even with Tsarina spitting and kicking and screaming and running, she just kept holding on to that ankle until she got kind of pulled out from under the bed like a boy riding a dolphin and when she'd stood up she said to Tsarina, "He is boring you? You are boring me! You are the most boring person I have ever met."

And Mac apologised for Della but was getting off on it, I could tell. And no sooner had he seen Del than he'd pulled her onto the bed and put his arms around her — this I could tell by the disappearance of the feet.

"Ha!" said Tsarina.

"Ha!" said Della.

"Happy?" said Tsarina.

"Like a pig in shit," said Della.

"You certainly are," said Tsarina, then totally switched channels. "You wanna smoke some grass?" she said, and plopped down on the bed with them. "I like your dress — who's it by? Cute." Night and day.

Meanwhile I was still lying under the bed trying to script my entrance. I was having trouble. I needn't have worried, there was whispering above and Mac's face appeared in the gap between lacy valance and floor — upside down.

After a few moments of him staring at me I said, "Honeymoons are notoriously difficult things. There is a very high level of expectation and this often results in a certain amount of . . . tension."

And Mac said, "Where's your lover?" and I thought he meant Alex. *I thought he meant Alex!*

Paul and Ven tracked me down at Mac's and put me in a cab back to the hotel. In the cab I told Ven about Ed's desertion. I expected her to do an Oh! My! God! but she just frowned.

"What?" I said.

"Is Alex why Ed's gone off?"

"No," I said, "he doesn't know."

"He knows subconsciously obviously," she said.

I didn't have much of an answer to that.

Paul said, "Now now, girls," rather anxiously. Paul hates anything real.

I said, "Ed's basically had enough because I missed the plane and because you lot turned up and . . . you know — there's a history there with Mac and everything. I'll just stay at the hotel and he'll probably come back at some point. He won't have gone far. He won't just jump on a plane back to London. He's not free-spirited enough. He'll wait for the date on the return ticket."

"He's sensible with money," said Ven.

"God preserve me," I said, "from anyone who is sensible with anything."

"You're mean," said Ven.

"You don't have to live with him," I said.

Paul looked from one to the other of us and said, "Nightmare, nightmare."

"So all those vows we sat through, they meant nothing, did they?" said Ven.

"I'm not the one who walked out," I said. "I wanted to go to Mexico. And the vows didn't mean nothing, but when it comes down to it this is the real world and that was a bit of paper. That's what everyone tries to avoid admitting, isn't it? That's why so many marriages break up at the drop of a hat. Because, I mean, people have good intentions but intentions are one thing. You know, 'The road to wherever is paved with good intentions' — or whatever the expression is."

"Hell," said Paul.

We both looked at him.

"The road to hell," said Paul, "I think you'll find."

"Well, there you go," I said, sitting back in my seat.

"So what's the story with Alex?" said Ven, fairly hostile.

"There's no story with Alex. Nothing happened. He's gone."

"He set her on fire," said Paul.

"Hey!" I said. "Cliché."

"Queens," said Paul, "are allowed to use as many clichés as they want."

Ven looked at me. "On fire is a pretty accurate description," I said grudgingly. "Look — Ed's going is nothing to do with Alex. He knows nothing about Alex. But it's true, it felt incredible to see Alex again." I suddenly wanted her to understand. "I haven't felt like that for — I don't know how long. I can't even describe it. I felt — I felt that kind of oh-okay-now-I-get-it feeling. Now I understand what it's all been about. Now I understand what it's all been for."

Paul said, "Ah, yes, when all those little existential niggles get ironed out —"

"There's nothing like it," I agreed.

"Well, there is," he said. "There's drugs."

Have you ever felt your inner fader slide from plus to minus? Have you ever felt it turn your beautiful Technicolor world to a relentless, dreary black and white? When I truly woke up to the realities of what a mess I was in, I found myself standing outside an empty honeymoon bedroom, looking out at the New York skyline. Alone.

The crisis buzz had gone and I was left with a kind of low-level hum of pain and an inability to drum up even the mildest interest in anything that was going on around me — unable, virtually, to speak. I'd quite liked my life until last night. I'd been doing pretty well until last night. I'd been grateful for — well, you know — life's small mercies, my health, my job, my friends, call waiting, reduced-fat houmous, stuff like that.

And if the truth be told — if the truth really be told — the major source of pain was Alex, not Ed.

If Alex was drugs, I had inadvertently stabbed myself with a needle full of heroin and now I was wandering the flatlands of withdrawal. I had a bad case of that delusional thinking that affects all love-at-first-sight devotees: he must have been on that hotel balcony for a reason. It must mean he's The One. If I'd caught the plane to Mexico I wouldn't have met him again, it must mean he's The One. We ended up in hotel rooms next door to each other, it must mean he's The One. He's the only person who's ever agreed with me that Roger Moore was the best James Bond, it must mean he's The One.

And if he wasn't on that balcony for a reason — well, then, that meant that everything in life was random and nothing meant anything and, uh, actually, don't go there.

And if he *was* there for a reason, well, then, said the voice in my head, I have fucked up. Big time. I've missed the boat. Because now he's gone. I felt the same panic rising inside me as I had when I saw Red Ted being eaten by the rubbish truck and I realised — probably for the first time — that there are some things in life there's no going back on. That you can't turn the clock back and all the king's horses and all the king's men couldn't put Humpty together again.

I didn't know what to do with a thought like that. There didn't seem to be any place to go with it. I thought I probably needed help. I thought maybe if I waited at the hotel long enough Ed would come back. And maybe I'd just tell him about Alex and then I could go to a clinic for mentallers or something and have my brain rewired and then maybe Ed and I could do about fifty years of couples' counselling and then maybe we could get a fresh start.

16

T HE next morning the phone went far too early. I grabbed it.

"Sorry I'm not him," said Della.

I was speechless with sleep and irritation for, oh, several seconds. "That is the most infuriating way to start a phone call," I said.

"Are you all right?" she said.

"I could have done with a lie-in," I said.

"Why? Did something happen last night?" she said.

"No," I said. "No developments. I spent the Night of the Long Knives on my hotel balcony." I'd been out there until about three in the morning which, with my jet-lag, was saying something. Long knives.

I heard her whispering to Mac and then she said to me, "Mac wants a word," and put him on.

Mac said he was going out to the Hamptons for a meeting with — insert name of legendary film director — at his legendary Long Island beach pad and that he thought I'd better go with him.

I took a deep breath. I didn't know where to start: words and phrases like "outrageous" and "how dare you" and "you've

destroyed my marriage already" flashed through my mind. "Mac," I
said, "fuck off!" I felt that summed things up best.

Della came on the line again. "Keep your hair on," she said.

"I'll speak to you later," I said, and hung up.

It wasn't until I'd done my morning meditation that it occurred
to me that Mac and Della had probably been trying to help. My
morning meditation consists of me lying sprawled on my bed staring at the ceiling while the preoccupations of that particular
moment in time go round and round in my head. Not exactly Zen.

"The clothes of your thoughts in the washing-machine of your
mind," Ven once said wistfully, when I told her about my morning
practice. She meditates for real. I said that sounded like a song. And,
anyway, the reality was more like knickers in the spin cycle.

But it became clear to me nevertheless that Mac's idea of cheering me up would be to invite me along for a hard day's work. He'd
probably discussed it with Della and they'd agreed it would be a
good thing. They cared. They loved me! The thought made me
curl into a foetus-like ball and moan loudly. When I'd finished
doing that, I picked up the phone and told Mac I'd meet him in
half an hour.

Good decision. The beach was my best kind of beach. If your
average European beach is honey-coloured Labrador puppy, this
beach was a wild white wolf. Long grass laid horizontal by the wind
and old picket fencing bleached to the bone. Sand, surf, sea and sky
in that order, parallel lines as far as the eye could see. And out there
at the edge of the world a horizon so broad it makes you humble.
You just step on this beach and you can feel your mind expanding.

I walked on the beach while they were having lunch, thinking
thoughts like, if it was "meant to be" with Ed then it would be
with Ed. And how our troubles were but a tiny pimple on the vast
landscape of tortured human relationships. And anyway love was
only God's way of making us reproduce. Stuff like that.

And I thought about Alex a bit — but not really. I seemed to
have limited access in that area, like when something is so close up

in the foreground that you can't really get it into focus or see all of it and you have no way of backing up to get perspective.

I walked for miles and took off my shoes and paddled, then I retraced my footprints in the sand and went back and sent more faxes and took more notes and got more people on the phone. Actually, the legendary film director was almost as inspiring as the beach. He was like a very enthusiastic six-year-old with a very clear head. If he ever fell out of favour in the film business I should think he could get work as a guru. He kind of made you want to serve.

Mac was having a great old time, getting very expansive. He didn't dare light up in the legendary beach-house so he wasn't smoking — something he will only forgo if the smell of box office is very strong indeed. He was mainlining Diet Coke instead and waving the can around excitedly to illustrate his points.

Late afternoon, it came up that they'd both been invited to a big party in the city that night. The LFD said he couldn't face the drive. Mac had me order a chopper. That was the kind of mood he was in.

Which is how I found myself, a couple of hours later, at a definitely rather happening party in the penthouse offices of one of America's biggest magazines. The view was spectacular: the sun had just set over the Hudson and the polluted blood-orange afterglow was bouncing its reflection from one silvery skyscraper to another. Inside the party were more little black dresses and dinky sequinned handbags than you could shake a stick at. I was still in trousers from work, at least they were black. Robotic drinks trolleys were circling the room under their own steam and saying in cute little cyber voices, "Would you like a drink? What doesn't kill you makes you stronger!" or "Get out of my way!" if you stepped in front of one of them.

Being at a party you're not really invited to is a strange experience at the best times. Being at a party you're not really invited to in a strange city when your life is in ruins is downright hard work. I'd just got to wondering whether I should go catch a movie when the gang of three descended. They greeted me like I was the long-lost prodigal.

"Apparently Leonardo is coming," said Paul.

"Oh! My! God!" said Ven.

" 'ad him — rubbish," said Della.

It was nice to see them. But my internal fader, which had dredged up some attractively bleached-out colour tones down on the beach, was fast sliding back to black and white. I told them I was thinking of going back to the hotel to see if there was any sign of Ed. Ven had checked. There wasn't. I said maybe I'd go anyway. They didn't argue with me. They had some respect.

I made my way through the forest of hips, elbows and bags, inventing a pathway where there was none. When eventually I got all the way downstairs to the lobby of the building, I found a vast white marble hall with fountains and trees and bouncers and greeters and, beyond them, a bank of glass doors onto the street. I realised it must have been raining because the lights from the road were smearing red in the glass doors.

I saw a man standing out on the pavement. Lights from the building were catching his hair in the drizzle and when he turned towards me and opened the door it didn't surprise me at all that it was Alex.

He came towards me. He was in a tuxedo — it kills me the way the dress codes are so dressy in New York.

I said, "Good evening," which I thought lent itself nicely to the formality of the occasion.

Cherelle came up fast behind him. "Hi!" she said, like she was over the moon to see me. Seriously. "Are you following us? Are you stalking us? Hey," she said, grabbing my arm and leading me back into the building, "I just saw this really fat guy in the street. He was so FAT! He was blubbing out all over the place."

"I thought you were going on honeymoon," I said. Lame.

"Honeymoons are for enjoying yourselves, right?" she said.

"Right," I said.

"And we're enjoying ourselves right here in the city."

By this time we'd got back to the elevators. "Actually," I said, "I was leaving."

"Oh, you can't go," she said. "You're too funny."

So I was back at the party. But I had only been there for about thirty seconds before sanity dawned: I shouldn't be here. I drank a cocktail or two. I shouldn't do that: it goes to my head. Sanity receded. I danced. I shouldn't do that: it goes to my head.

"At long last love has arrived and I thank God I'm alive." Okay, look — I'm not saying the words of a song were responsible for what happened next. I'm not saying that. But I think if we were going to put the full evidence before the court, if we were going to be searching and fearless in our examination of the circumstances, all the circumstances, then we must allow that they were a factor. They were a factor.

In my defence, I don't see how I'm meant to consume a diet of pop-song sentiment for twenty-odd years and not be affected by it, not one teeny-weeny bit.

"You're too good to be true can't take my eyes off of you." I mean, you hear that stuff all the time but that night I heard it afresh. I suddenly knew what they were all going on about. It occurred to me, with some surprise, that I'd been very shut down for a very long time. I felt this powerful yearning and longing in the songs as if I was hearing them for the first time.

I was dancing on my own — three sips into my third cocktail — and next thing I knew I was being waltzed around by this big stocky drunken man and I was overwhelmed by his strange aftershave and the alcohol on his breath and the thick growth of hair on his neck. I got the sense he went to the gym a lot or was in the Mafia or something. And then he stumbled and my drink fell to the ground. And the next thing I knew Alex was there and I wrenched myself free of the stocky man's clutches and turned to Alex. The man must have seen the look that passed between Alex and me because he drawled something sneering I didn't catch and Alex said something back. And the next thing I knew the stocky man gave Alex a little push that caused Alex to take a step backwards.

I saw Cherelle coming towards us. I saw Alex see her. He backed up and slipped away through the crowd.

Ven materialised beside me. "You're well out of that one," she said. She meant Alex.

"I was never *in* that one," I said.

"Not a happy boy," she said.

"Do you think?" I said, brightening.

"Don't go there either," Ven said, very stern.

I thought I'd follow Cherelle, who was following Alex, but she'd lost him. I left her behind, went across the party and down the corridor. I stopped outside what I thought was the men's room but when I looked up at the door there was a man symbol and a woman symbol standing side by side — hand in hand. I thought maybe it was a sign. I mean, I know it was a sign on a door, I thought maybe it was a sign-sign. Then a woman pushed by me and I realised it was a unisex. I'd heard about them. I went in.

It was so hip in there it could have been the VIP room — you had to be doing drugs to get to a cubicle.

Alex was standing by the wash-basins looking at himself in the mirror. He was in his own world. I stopped. I didn't want to break the glass.

Then, "Uh-huh!" said a man's voice behind me. He had this kind of all-male drawl that left you in no doubt, whatever make of watch he's wearing, that he grew up the hard way. He tapped Alex on the shoulder and said, "You think I was finished with you?" He was, of course, my stocky friend from the dance floor.

Everyone went quiet. Everyone knew immediately that it was a SCENE. An embarrassed atmosphere descended — like you get at the theatre before everyone gets used to the idea of watching grown people pretending.

First off, Alex didn't turn round, which surprised me. Second, I felt real fear — like I knew Alex had gone someplace else with this and for him it wasn't funny any more. Not that it was ever funny but — you know what I mean.

Meanwhile the stocky one had been left a bit high and dry by being ignored. If Alex wasn't going to dance, then he had to invent the steps himself. He glanced at Alex's wedding ring. He said, "You having sexual problems in your marriage you have to interfere with what don't concern you?"

Clearly, in his own private Neanderthal universe, this remark was so far below the belt it couldn't fail to elicit a response. But Alex just finished up at the basin, dried his hands, murmured, "You know what —" and didn't finish the sentence.

Neanderthal man was practically bursting out of his six-pack.

"What?" he said.

We, the audience, were on the edge of our metaphorical seats.

"I don't think I want to be here," Alex said. He turned round and punched Neanderthal man full in the face. There was a gasp from the crowd. Neanderthal man fell onto his butt then sprawled backwards across the floor.

You'd have thought we the audience would have been scared now but it seemed we were just even more embarrassed. The mood was definitely one of embarrassment. It was like sex in public. Violence in the movies is smooth and assured, well choreographed. This was fumbly and shaky. Embarrassing.

Neanderthal man pulled a gun out of his jacket. Okay, so now we were scared. Suddenly everyone had frozen like they couldn't move. I mean, we weren't moving before but now we were in that basic-instinct survival thing — freeze.

Neanderthal man seemed more impressed by his gun than anyone else. He also seemed to be quite frightened by it. He sort of showed it to Alex — didn't exactly point it. But he was still on the floor so Alex just stepped up and efficiently kicked it out of his hand. No one ran, no one moved.

Alex walked over and picked the gun up. When he straightened up he made a gesture with his hand, like, Don't worry, everybody.

He did this with the hand holding the gun and it caused a kind of Mexican wave amongst us onlookers. Perplexed, Alex retreated into a cubicle.

People started to scramble. There were shouts of "Call Security!" and someone said, "Call the police!" and someone else said, "Do *not* call the police!"

Neanderthal man was sitting on the floor. He seemed to have lost all his oomph and sat hunched over and apologetic. "What can you do with a maniac like that?" he said.

I went and stood outside Alex's cubicle. I knocked politely.

"Go away," came the reply.

"It's me," I said.

No answer.

I went back to the dance floor. *"You're like heaven to touch, I want to hold you so much."*

He came out of nowhere. He grabbed my hand and pulled me off the dance floor. He was quite forceful. "We need to talk," he said.

"Oh, sure," I said. Out of the corner of my eye I caught sight of Ven and Della eyeing me nervously from a spiral staircase in the right-hand corner of the room. Cherelle was nowhere to be seen.

"Don't worry," I said wildly, clutching at the wrong end of the stick. "I'm leaving the country! I'm going to Mexico. Alone. I don't care. I have reservations. A beautiful hotel. I may as well go. I mean, this is just a feeling, right? Feelings aren't facts. This is just some weird thing we do to each other, right? All these feelings —" I waved my arms around a bit to illustrate. I was sure he understood. My voice was quite raised. I didn't lower it. No one around us took the blindest bit of notice.

"You don't love me!" I went on recklessly. "I don't love you! I mean, if you loved me you'd have called me. Right? That much is clear. You didn't call me for seven years. Seven years. We don't even know each other. We spent one night! We're deluded. Life isn't like this. Did you follow me here? Maybe you're stalking me! Because, frankly, this is beyond a joke. I mean, what are you playing at? Is this some kind of game?"

"Game?" he said. He looked at me. Blue eyes. Did I say?

In my peripheral vision I saw (a) two security guards running in from the back stairs, hands on gun holsters, the way they do, and (b) Cherelle. "Security behind you," I said, "and Cherelle at two o'clock."

"Run," he said.

So we did. Fast but not so fast that I didn't catch a fleeting glimpse of Cherelle as we brushed past her, a glass of sparkling water in each hand, her mouth hanging open.

Alex caught my hand before we got to the elevators and pulled me into one of those closets where they keep the fire hydrant. It was quite small in there.

"Aren't you going to say, 'We must stop meeting like this'?" I said.

"No," he said, and kissed me. I won't dwell because it would hold up the action. Suffice it to say, the seven-year itch got scratched.

There was a glass panel in the door and during the kiss Della, Ven, Paul and Cherelle galloped past to the elevators like hounds in full cry.

When they'd gone, Alex pulled me out of the closet. "They went down," he said. "We go up."

We were so high in the building the elevators didn't go up any further so we took the emergency stairs.

"Are you okay?" he said, after a couple of flights.

" 'You're like heaven to touch,' " I said, breathless.

"What?" he said.

"It's a song," I said.

At the top we kissed again. It seemed appropriate.

"What happened in there?" I said.

"Have you heard of escape velocity?" he said.

We kissed more — it must have been too much more, because I heard a door banging and four pairs of feet pounding on the stairs below. They'd worked out where we were.

"Come on," he said, and took my hand again.

We ran out onto the roof. The first thing I noticed was that the clouds had lifted and the sky was a glorious deep midnight blue. The second thing I noticed was the helicopter we'd flow in on.

"Perfect," said Alex.

And then, and only then — I swear to you — did I take in the full potential of that helicopter, sitting there in its techno-dragonfly glory.

"We can't," I said.

The pilot waved at me and started the blades.

"Friend of yours?" said Alex.

"Kind of," I said.

Alex wedged the staircase door shut behind us. "What's better?" he said. "We leave them after five years. We leave them after twenty years. Or we leave them now." Then he took my hand and we ran under the blades — like they do in the movies, like I'd always wanted to do.

As we climbed into the helicopter I shouted to Jacob, the pilot, that he'd have to come back for Mac. He shouted that he couldn't take me anywhere without authorisation, he'd have to call in. Honestly, life is sometimes so prosaic.

"Oh, shit," I said.

Alex and I looked at each other and we looked towards the door to the stairs which we knew would be bursting open at any moment. Then Alex dropped his eyes and showed me the butt of the gun poking out of his pocket. He was only half joking.

"Oh, *shit*," I said. "Jacob," I said, "please, please, please."

Something in my voice made him turn around. "Jacob," I said, and put my hand over Alex's — the hand on the gun, "we're on our honeymoon!"

Jacob couldn't hear me, what with the noise of the blades. Anyway, I was probably a bit faint-hearted. I was forced to say it again, wondering if my punishment would be burning in hell for all eternity or just something like a mild case of cystitis for the rest of my life and which would be worse. "We're on our honeymoon!" I yelled again. "Mac told you — remember?"

Jacob's face broke out into a big grin. "Where to?" he said.

Alex shouted, "She's going to Mexico!" Jacob laughed and said he couldn't take us to Mexico but he could take us to JFK. As we lifted off I took the gun out of Alex's pocket and threw it out into a puddle on the roof.

The security guards, Paul, Della and the rest came through the roof door seconds after we'd taken off. We didn't care — the bright-lit skyscrapers were falling away all around us in the clear night air, like a man-made forest of diamond-studded stalagmites — the grandest canyon in the world.

"Fifth Avenue," said Alex. "Are you scared?"

"Scared of what?" I said. "Dying?"

He didn't answer. He was looking out over the Hudson Bay to where the Statue of Liberty held her torch aloft.

"That was me," I said, "for seven years."

He didn't say anything for a while and then he said, "I'm sorry."

"You know what?" I said later. "If I died right now I wouldn't mind."

17

IMAGINE this. Imagine a honeymoon bedroom. Imagine a four-poster garlanded with lace. Imagine rumpled white sheets ruffling gently in the breeze from a ceiling fan. Imagine the dark wooden blades of the fan creaking slightly, comfortingly, as they turn. Imagine the stone-washed Caribbean sunlight outside the verandah doors and imagine the warm sweet Caribbean air. Imagine a soft cotton-wool quietness broken only by the distant plink of marimbas and, almost imperceptible, the languid pulse of waves upon the sand.

Now imagine a young woman lying on the bed, one arm bent at the elbow propping up her head. She is still, very still, and in the heat a fine sweat pricks at the surface of her skin. She watches the ceiling fan wheeling away the minutes and she imagines a young man lying on a bed in a room which is the mirror image of the room she is in.

The young man is incongruous in city clothes — a white dress shirt and black trousers and boots. He is restless, crossing his legs first one way then the other, his hands behind his head. He has the air of someone with serious matters at stake. Very serious. Perhaps he gets up and paces up and down the room like someone might if they had top-secret papers hidden in their suitcase. Not that this particular young man has a suitcase. He has only the clothes he stands up in.

When the young woman has had enough of imagining this — when I've had enough of imagining this, I roll over on my very matrimonial bed to see how the ants are doing. They have doubled in number since I last looked. Back-up has arrived, a second battalion, an army of insects doing military manoeuvres on my hotel room floor. The ants are all engaged in one very important purpose and I wonder how each individual knows what that purpose is. I wonder whether they are born knowing, born with information right there in their DNA as to what to do. I wonder why I couldn't have been born with information right there in my DNA as to what to do. Like Paul was born with information in his DNA as to what to wear.

Then it occurs to me that I probably am — born with information. I'm probably being marched along like an ant by some kind of inevitable genetic destiny and I just don't know it. Things like individual self-determination, chance and choice are probably just some very convincing set-dressing on the part of the great creator.

Which I didn't exactly use as an excuse for what I'd done to Ed but I had to explain things to myself somehow. I had to be able to live with myself and the labyrinthian ant-like workings of my brain went something like this. One: Ed walked out on me first and it's not the first time he's walked out. It's true, I know he doesn't really mean it, but if he wants to behave like that he risks me taking his actions at face value. And now I have. Two: I didn't ask to bump into Alex again. Three: When I first saw Ed I thought — not my type. Sorry to harp on about that. I mean, it was a one-second first impression in what turned out to be years of togetherness. But it is what happened, and it seems meaningful now.

Because now I'm out the other end I can see clearly what I always knew and what I forgot — that I never felt passion for Ed. I never felt he was a dream come true, I never had that over-the-rainbow feeling they sell in the fairytales. And I'd thought that that was a good thing. I thought it was grown-up to give up on princes in shining armour — I scoffed at friends who rode the roller-coaster of joy and despair with their gloriously difficult boyfriends. But now I'd had a taste of the magic again and I knew with certainty that I had been wrong to give up on passion. Passion lights the flame of a relationship, whatever happens to it later. And I kept on coming back to that very first thought I'd had about Ed — not my type.

So now I'm just going to go with the flow, like the ants.

So far so good. The journey down with Alex was like the Great Escape. Am I the only person who thinks airports are sexy places? Probably. I actually applied to be an air hostess when I was twenty-one. I got an interview but my tights laddered before I even left the house and Della convinced me of what I had already suspected: my personal grooming just wasn't going to make the grade. So the two of us sat down and had coffee and endless rounds of toast and fantasised about all the great jobs we were going to get when we actually bothered to go to the interviews.

I think it's the sense of possibility you get at airports — announcements like "Would all remaining passengers for Flight 212 to Bombay please proceed . . ." Makes me think the world is my oyster.

Alex and I had skated across the shiny floors to the airline desks, holding on to each other for dear life in the crowd. All that bustling purpose, all those very ordinary people going about their very ordinary business, all that tedious officialdom seemed only to emphasise our beautiful secret, that we were the chosen ones. And of course, Alex and I had done the airport thing before — re Happy Eating at Heathrow. It was our home from home.

Everything worked out perfectly, which seemed perfectly natural. There was a flight to Cancún in two hours' time. When it came to paying I tried to go Dutch but Alex wouldn't have it, wasn't even amused. I glimpsed a rack of platinum credit cards in his wallet. They gave me a bit of a shock, actually. I had a little rush of admiration and then a jolt of intimidation. I mean, I knew Alex had made all that money but I'd never really thought about the ramifications. I'd never been out with a rich boy before.

We had time to buy toothbrushes and toothpaste — my mind wandered to thoughts of what I was going to do for clothes when we got to Mexico. My mind wandered to the platinum in Alex's wallet. I slapped my mind down in horror. Oh, God, I thought, it's starting already.

I was worried though that there'd be nothing but fluorescent green bikinis for sale in Cancún — even though I felt certain beyond certainty that Alex would love me in a fluorescent green bikini. That he'd love me even if I wore the same pair of jeans for the rest of my life (without washing them).

"Let's find somewhere," said Alex. I wasn't sure what he meant but he took my hand and led me through the departure lounge to the gate and a corner that was vaguely private and "let's find somewhere" turned out to mean "let's find somewhere to kiss."

So, leaning against the plate glass windows, that's what we did. I remember the warmth most, the warmth that came off him, and the cold glass against my back and the noise of the jets rolling back and forth along the runways like waves upon the sand.

It was dawn by the time we got to Cancún Airport where women with babies slung about their bodies like water-bottles tried to sell us hotel rooms for fifty dollars. Alex seemed to know what he was doing so I let him get on with it. He asked me the name of the hotel I'd mentioned. But that was that. I noticed he liked to play his cards close to his chest. He hired a taxi and we headed straight out of Hilton high-rise hell — down the coast to this honeymoon hotel.

After I got sick of staring at the ants I felt like a little girl who'd had her afternoon nap and was ready to go back to the party. I entertained thoughts of putting on my shoe and stamping my foot down in the middle of all the ants — I don't know why I thought about it, I wasn't going to do it. Obviously I wasn't going to do it. Having watched the ants for so long, stamping on them would have been like inflicting my own personal sinking of the ant *Titanic*. Which put me in mind of a time I found Mac out in the garden in Chelsea stamping on ants for pleasure. He said he was pretending they were network executives. I rolled off the bed, winding the sheet around me as I went, and walked out onto the verandah.

I say I walked out onto the verandah, actually I stole out onto the verandah. I had that horrible self-consciousness you get when you're suddenly hyper aware of every cell in your body. I suppose I was scared. When I turned my head I felt I was acting turning my head. Weird.

I did this kind of theatrical glance over to Alex's verandah all nonchalant in case he was there. He wasn't. So I took a careful step towards the rickety wooden rail that divided his verandah from mine. Moving very slowly I craned gently towards his open veran- dah doors until I could just make out the heel of a black boot on the white bed.

Very loud raucous laughter erupted all over me. To say I jumped out of my skin would be an understatement — I scraped myself off the coconut-matting roof. I've always had a well-developed startle reflex. I blame living with Della and all those years of going inno- cently into the loo in the middle of the night to find the double- backed monster heaving away on top of the washing-machine (don't ask). And once it was in the kitchen on the oven.

Anyway, the raucous laughter turned out to be coming from the stocky little hotel proprietor with the handlebar moustache, who had introduced himself as Jesus when we arrived and who was now jumping up and down on the lawn like a hirsute leprechaun. He had a hose-pipe in his hand.

Jesus, you see, thought the fact that Alex and I had separate bed- rooms was the funniest thing he'd ever heard. He said he'd told the whole *hacienda* and apparently everyone had agreed with him that it was the funniest thing they'd ever heard. And, he claimed, the story had spread to the local town whence, no doubt, the strains of hilarity would soon be heard for miles around.

At this point Alex staggered out onto his part of the verandah looking rather rumpled and Jesus took him through the whole joke again with lots of hand gestures and then, his English exhausted, added a long postscript in Spanish which, from what I could make out, appeared to take youth, Adam and Eve and fertility as its theme. When he drew breath Alex said, with some authority, I thought, "We're courting."

I don't think Jesus understood the word exactly but Alex's tone obviously did some good because he looked at Alex with a bit more respect.

"Courting?" he said.

"Yes," said Alex, glancing at his watch, "and for my first move I'm going to invite the young lady to tea. That's what they do in Britain — the country she's from. They have tea."

Jesus seemed enthusiastic about this idea so Alex got down on one knee and invited me to tea. I accepted. Jesus, who was taking it all very seriously by now, said he'd get the kitchen staff to bring it out to us.

I went down my steps and round to Alex's steps and he took my hand and showed me graciously on to his verandah. I was still wearing my sheet.

"Okay," Alex said, "let's see. How do we do this? Stage one — introductions, basic information, what kind of movies do you like, that sort of thing. Stage two — tennis."

"Tennis?" I said.

"Yes, that's what they said in the lecture. Don't you play?"

"No," I said.

"Okay," he said, "already — disaster. You'll have to learn tennis. That could set us back several months."

"Oh dear," I said.

"There must be something else," he said. "What are your hobbies?"

"Hobbies?" I said. "We don't actually have hobbies in England. Hobbies only exist on application forms — you know, like when you're applying to college and they ask you what your hobbies are and you put down Film Studies, which means you rent Tom Cruise videos on Friday night from Blockbuster."

"Let's just start with stage one," he said, giving up, "we'll worry about the rest later."

Jesus brought the tea tray himself. A big white pot, some sponge fingers and a fruit bowl piled high. He was very excited. We thanked him effusively and had trouble getting rid of him.

When he'd gone Alex poured me a cup and said, "Okay, you go first. Ask me a question."

"Like what?" I said.

"Anything," he said, "pick a subject."

"Like what?" I said, unhelpful.

"Uh . . . interests . . . countries you have visited . . . uh . . . pets . . . politics — whatever."

"Shouldn't it just sort of flow?" I said.

"There's a time factor here," he said. "I'll start. What's your favourite country to visit on holiday?"

"Italy."

"Okay," he said. "Your turn."

I sipped my tea and hoicked my sheet up a little. "Er," I said, "have you ever had a pet?"

"Yes," he said, "a snake when I was twelve."

"Oh, okay," I said, nodding.

"You see," he said, "this is good. Okay — my turn. Do you . . . have you . . . oh, okay . . . who is your favourite author?"

"F. Scott Fitzgerald," I said finally, after about half an hour of umming and ahhing and him saying I had to answer quicker or it was going to take all night and me saying, well, define "favourite," and anyway was he expecting me to rate Jane Austen and William Shakespeare in order of merit? But after that we got the hang of it and fired questions at each other relentlessly until we'd drunk all the tea, and by the end I knew all sorts of useful things about him like that he was allergic to strawberries and he drove a German car and he'd never been to Australia.

"Stage two," Alex announced, and looked at his watch. "Come on." Then he grabbed my hand and took me out into the hotel grounds where, for some mad reason, there was a croquet lawn among the palm trees. "Instead of tennis," he said, "do you know how to play this game?"

"As it happens," I said, "I do."

So I tied the sheet firmly around me in a knot and explained the rules to Alex. He had a trial go and swung the mallet like it was a golf club, sending the ball crashing against the stump.

"That easy?" he said, twirling his mallet with disdain. "What's next?"

"I find out whether you're a good loser," I said, and thrashed him, of course. My mad uncle was a croquet fiend — I learnt at the feet of the master.

We went back to the verandah and Alex said he couldn't remember much else of the lecture about courtship but he knew holding hands came into it somewhere.

I said, "I know what happens next. You say you'll call me and then you don't for ten days and I sit by the phone and feel like I'm going crazy."

"Okay," he said, and flung me a banana from the fruit bowl that came with tea.

I sat down on my side of the verandah and put the banana on the table in front of me. "What does the man do during this bit? That's what I've always wanted to know," I said.

"I busy myself," he said, pacing up and down on his side of the verandah, "with a whole range of very important irrelevancies and I really enjoy having you in the back of my mind. I'm like the pilot who goes out on the death-defying mission and keeps himself alive with thoughts of the beautiful woman waiting for him back home. It's like the further I get from you the closer to you I feel."

He went over to the furthest point on the other side of his verandah and sat down on the rail. There was a long silence. I found myself looking at the banana on the table in front of me and hoping it would ring.

"And?" I said, after a while.

He just ignored me — didn't move. Five minutes went by. It felt like an eternity. Eventually he reached over and pulled a banana out of the fruit bowl, held it to his ear and said "Ring ring!"

I grabbed my banana. "Hello?" I said breathlessly.

"Hi," he said, very cool. "You probably don't remember me —"

"Of course I do," I said — too keen. Shit.

"How are you?"

"Fine! I'm fine." Pause. "How are you?"

"Good. I'm good."

"Good."

"So — what's going on?"

"Er, I'm — I'm appreciating this good weather we've been having."

"Yeah?"

"Yeah."

Pause.

"Well, I was just calling to say it was fun playing croquet the other day."

"Oh, yes? Good! It was fun."

"Yeah — and I was just calling to say hello."

"Hello!"

"See how you were . . ."

"That's nice."

"Okay, well, we should do the croquet thing again sometime."

"Yeah. We should."

"Okay, well, see you soon, yeah?"

"See you soon."

"'Bye."

"'Bye."

"Twit," I said, slamming down the banana.

"What?" said Alex.

"That's no fucking good!" I said.

"I asked you out to croquet," he said. "You beat me."

"You did not ask me out to croquet," I said. "You called to 'see how I was.' You called to 'say hello'" — scathing.

"I called!" he said. "That tells you all you need to know! There's no need to castrate a guy by banana."

"Did I?" I said — astonished waving of banana.

"No warmth!" he said. "No give!"

"Sorry," I said. "But to 'say hello' just isn't — just isn't enough."

"Enough for what?"

"The Enuff Monster."

"Okay," he said, after he'd considered my answer for a moment and clearly decided not to go there, "take two." He picked up his banana. "Ring ring," he said.

I answered.

"Hi," he said, "it's Alex."

"Hi, Alex," I said, "how are you?"

"I'm good," he said. "What's going on?"

"What's going on," I said, "is that my brain is completely scrambled. I think I probably don't like you very much because you haven't called me. On the other hand I think I probably love you because you haven't called. Then sometimes I think I invented you and you don't really exist. But mostly I think that I don't exist. And then in the end I just think what the hell."

Long silence.

"You want to have dinner sometime?"

"That'd be great. When?"

"How about tonight?"

"Oh, I'm sorry. The Rules say I would be sabotaging our chances of a successful relationship if I accept a dinner invitation given less than four days in advance."

"The Rules?"

"The Rules of Man-getting."

"Fuck the Rules."

"Okay."

When we hung up our bananas I jumped up and headed for my room.

"Where are you going?" he said.

"What happens next," I said, "is that I go to my room and try on about a million outfits and throw them all on the floor in despair."

Fortunately I didn't even have one outfit, let alone a million, so I went down to the little shop in the hotel lobby. It had those clothes that all tourist shops all over the world seem to have. Universal hippie holiday wear — turquoise-green sea-horse-printed sarongs and suchlike. These clothes have the air of being produced locally by some worthy indigenous woman. But as they're to be found from Spain to Africa to South America they're probably made by some world-dominating franchise.

I ended up with a sarong and simple vest top in a great blue colour. I got a pair of leather sandals as well, with sweet little shells sewn on to them. I added some toiletries and a leopard-print bikini (it was that or fluorescent green) to my purchases and went back to my room and did the shower and hair thing — put some flowers in it. Then I put my new outfit on and decided I downright enjoyed having no luggage and having to "make do." I suppose that's what downsizing is about. It takes a lot of the stress out of life.

The path to the restaurant was picked out by little flames at ground level. It really was the sweetest hotel. The restaurant was on a wooden deck that stretched down towards the sea under a coconut-matting roof. Rickety wooden tables were decorated with bright pink bougainvillaea. Giant prawns sizzled away on an open-air barbecue and the marimbas plinked gently from the beach bar below.

I found Alex sitting at the bar in a new white T-shirt looking out onto the bay. It was funny — just in that split second before I consciously registered him I felt my heart leap towards him. It was as if just the shape of him in outline, the figure he cut, corresponded somehow to a blueprint deep inside me that recognised him as mine.

He ordered me a piña colada, which I tried to refuse on principle but which turned out to be absolutely delicious. Then we went up to the restaurant and ate lobster from the grill. When we weren't staring at each other we watched the sea graduating through the colour spectrum in the failing light to a deep midnight blue. And even though night was falling the air stayed soft and warm around us.

It seemed like we didn't talk very much or maybe it was that we didn't talk about much of significance. I don't think we really wanted to, after the rigours of the day, we wanted to just be. Be in each other's presence. It's funny, but just regarding him was enough for me. Talking, it seemed, might get in the way.

After dinner he said, "Come on," and led me down to the beach. I noticed that he didn't like to tell me where we were going, what we were doing next. If Ed tried to do that I'd wrangle his plans out of him and then I'd have some better idea.

As we walked little sand crabs scuttled in front of our feet and Alex took my hand. "What comes after holding hands on the courtship schedule?" I said.

"Kissing," he said. So we did some of that.

"I know what we've left out," I said, in one of the breaks. "Quizzing each other about recent relationship history."

"Hmmm," he said.

We looked at each other.

"Maybe not," I said.

"Maybe we should just lie on the sand and look at the stars," he said.

"Maybe we should," I said.

So we did that. After a while, Alex mentioned that this was our third date.

"Is that meaningful?" I said.

"Well, the third date," he said, "you know."

"No," I said, "I don't. What happens on the third date?"

"The third date is when you — you know . . ." He rolled over so that he was looking down at me. I wondered what words he was going to pick. He opted for "spend the night together" and a look in the eye.

"Oh, right," I said. "But it's not really our third date."

"Yeah, it is," he said. "First date was tea. Second date was croquet. Third date was dinner."

I laughed.

"Don't you want to?" he said.

"You know what?" I said. "I'm scared to have that thing when you sleep with someone too soon and half-way through you suddenly realise there's something you can't say or something that feels strange and it's because the other person is a stranger, really. And suddenly you feel the gap between the two of you and it's the most lonely feeling . . ." I trailed off. "The most lonely feeling in the world."

There was a long silence while he thought about this. That was one of the things I liked about him. The way he took life so seriously made it seem more meaningful somehow. I got the feeling there were all these things going on in his head which he wasn't telling me.

"I think," he said, after absolutely ages, "we should have the courage of our convictions."

He didn't say, "Because we're soul-mates and it's going to be okay." But that's what I took him to mean.

When we got back to our rooms we stood for a moment at the bottom of the verandah steps and I turned to him and said, kind of muffled into the side of his neck, "Well, for one thing, it is a bit extravagant having two rooms, isn't it?"

"And for another thing," he replied, into the hair behind my ear, "I want to make love to you."

Can I tell you about all the times I imagined you lying by me, lying by my side? I don't mean sex. I mean, to have you lying by my side — that seems like the prize. And the times I imagined us having another of those nights when the world around us ceases to exist because the whole world is right there in your eyes.

And when the bed floats up into the air and out of the window sweeping us into space like a magic carpet, sheets fluttering loose at the edges, we don't even notice. We look up at the stars and the night is far too short for everything we might say to each other. We look down at the insignificant earth and imagine all the millions of people asleep in their beds and wonder how they can sleep when there is so much to be awake for. I never want to sleep again. I never want to break this spell.

But even in all this it comes to me that I mustn't want you too much because it seems to me that if I want you too much you will go away. And even as I am inventing this ineluctable law of nature, I sense the bit of you that I can't see and that I will never know, hidden away by the glare, like the dark side of the moon. Will it be enough, the not-enoughness of it all? And so I cling on to you a little too tight to prevent myself from falling. It's such a long way down.

And when we did make love ("Why use that sickening expression?" I hear Della say), well, whether it was having sex or making love I don't think I could really tell you, I don't think I was even conscious, there was a kind of heightenedness about it that was truly overwhelming and not a little terrifying.

Just thinking about it makes my mind fall off the edge. It's like thinking about space: the earth is in the solar system and the solar system is in the universe, but what is the universe in? Tell me that. The thought makes me dizzy because there's no edge. There are no limits. I need limits. Otherwise I want so much that nothing can be enough.

A pearly warm dawn was seeping through the shutters, and Alex and I were lying together like two pieces of a jigsaw puzzle when I said, "When you come to think of it, I don't really know you. I don't know you from Adam."

"Oh, but you do," he said. And then, after a while, suspiciously, "Who's Adam?"

And giggling is the last thing I remember doing before falling asleep.

"How was the sex?"

"Del," I said, "I'm in a mosquito-ridden phone booth in the middle of the biggest crisis of my life with a stack of phone cards a foot high depicting the various afflictions of various South American saints. Do you think you could drag your mind out of the gutter for just one second?"

"It's an important question," she said. "It's a pertinent question," she said. "Answer it."

"Where are you?" I said.

"I'm in velour joggers," she said.

"I said, *where* are you?" I said.

"I'm in the velour joggers *section,*" she said. "I'll phone you back if you like."

"No," I said. "I'm not giving you my number. I just want you to tell Ed that I'm all right."

"I'm in velour joggers, Marble Arch, London," she said. "Ed's in New York. Tell him yourself."

"Ed's still in New York?" I said.

"Yeah," she said. That's all, just "yeah." But there was something about that "yeah," something that spoke of vast, hitherto-unexplored vistas of Ed. Something that hinted at the fact that Ed's world was still turning and that I hadn't stopped it and even though my biggest fear was having to carry his world, like Atlas, upon my shoulders, I suffered a violent and totally unjustifiable stab of jealousy.

While I was trying to process all this, Della interjected again, "How was the sex?" I'd thought we'd got beyond the stage of giving each other blow-by-blow accounts of our sex lives — I mean, for one thing, with Della's sex life there simply isn't time. And for another, after a certain age — the age when men find out how to do it — you discover that sex is sex is sex. Give or take. When you're young and you have good sex you think you've personally invented the atom bomb, until you find out that Russia and everybody else invented it right along with you.

"Sex is sex," I said.

"That good?" she said.

"Fucking wonderful."

"It better be," she said. "I'd hate to be you when it's payback time."

"Payback time?" I said nervously.

"You never heard of karma?" she asked. "You broke that poor boy's heart."

"Ed?" I said. "Ed walked out on me. Ed threw his ring back."

"He didn't mean it," she said. "Jesus. That's what you get married for, isn't it? So you can do that stuff and not mean it."

"How do you know he didn't mean it?"

"I'm guessing," she said. "He was always like a dog around you. I don't mean dog in a derogatory way."

"How can you not mean dog in a derogatory way?"

"Well, he was dog-like devoted, that's all. You should've counted your blessings."

"Yeah," I said.

"So, what is it about Alex?" she said. "Apart from that Love of Your Life crap."

"Since when has it been crap?"

"Well, you know, you're not meant to actually act on these things. Paula Yates had a picture of Michael Hutchence on her fridge for seven years and look what happened to her."

I let that tasteless remark reverberate in some silence. After a moment Della said, "So, come on, what is it about Alex? What is it?"

"People have spent whole lives trying to put words to it," I said. "And you expect me to be able to explain?"

"Try," she said.

"Well, sometimes I want him so much I feel sick — literally physically nauseous."

"That sounds lovely," she said.

"Ummmm," I said, meaning it and experiencing a rush of euphoric recall that curdled my blood. "I just want him so much. I feel like he's part of me — It's all those things — all those stupid things they say in the songs — *'You're too good to be true'* —"

"Oh, God," she said, "I'm going to have to stop you there. You really mustn't start quoting pop songs."

"Okay," I said. Then, after some deliberation, "Put it like this. With Alex I don't know all the answers."

"Excuse me?" said Della.

"With Ed," I said, "I never didn't know the answer. I always had something to say. It bored me. I bored myself . . . knowing it all. I hated always knowing it all."

There was one beat of silence and then Della laughed. "That's what I like about you too," she said. "Sometimes you say stuff that just isn't what I'm expecting you to say. You can still be my friend."

"Thank you," I said. Then, "You still like me, then?"

"I don't like you," she said. "I love you."

"Del," I screamed, "what's come over you?"

"Nothing!" she said. "Did you think I lent you tights and makeup all those years because I hated you?"

"What's going on with Mac?" I said.

"I've got to go," she said. "Supervisor approaching via cuddly-toy nightwear. Check your e-mail." Click.

18

To: Honey@globalnet.co.uk
From: mmm@wigwam.com
Subject: oh
Date: 3 May — 11.31 a.m. EST
Mime-Version: 1.0

Dear Honey,

I have been having a hellacious time. You are going to have to buy me the most incredible amount of 24 oz sugarfree vanilla ice blended no whips if you even want me to think about being your sister again when you come back. Seriously, you are practically going to have to buy the whole Coffee Bean & Tea Leaf franchise. And you are also going to have to go to therapy because otherwise you are just going to keep on falling over your inner emptiness unless you deal — if you know what I mean.

After you flew off I went back to your hotel room. Well, first there was a hoo-ha with Cherelle, who had completely the wrong end of the stick and thought that Alex was being chased by a mad gunman and that was why he was escaping and in the end Paul had to say, "Darling, Alex *was* the mad gunman."

It turned out that Cherelle had heard about the incident in the bathroom and saw Alex running off and thought he was fearing for his life. I asked her what she thought he was doing with you and she said she'd made all this stuff up about hostages and human shields. It was incredible — she had this whole crazy story in her head. It's amazing how the mind fills in the blanks.

Anyway, I took her on one side and explained the reality and it took her about a hundred years to figure it out — that you and Alex had already met, nothing to do with me. I got the impression it was unfamiliar to her to have a situation where there were elements beyond her control. She seemed to be in shock.

When she finally kind of lined up the relevant brain cells she said, "You mean I've just been jilted?" like now she got to be in the *National Enquirer*. But she didn't seem to really relate, if you know what I mean. I told her these things happen, you know, and she said not to her. Fair enough. Then she said, "You mean he's gone off with the girl with the flat hair?" She kept calling you that. Don't worry — I told her flat hair was fashionable in London. I don't think I've ever seen anyone so flabbergasted. About you and Alex, I mean, not about London fashion. You turned that girl's universe upside down. Later I heard her kind of musing to herself that Kate Moss had flat hair. I think that helped.

Anyway — long story short — she said she was going back to the hotel to call Daddy. I went back there too, to your room. I hope you don't mind — but I hate five-star luxury to go to waste.

So anyway, I'm in this like deep and delicious sleep dreaming about a gorgeous man slipping into bed with me and cuddling right up with me, nibbling my ear and so forth. Until finally it dawns on me — in the depths of sleep — that the nibbling is real. And the tongue is wet! Then this hand closes over my breast and I wake up with a shout to find myself in Ed's arms. Oh. My. God.

Don't worry, we quickly extracted ourselves. He'd thought I was you, of course. I asked him didn't he notice my hair was blonde? But you know what men are like. Oblivious. Well, in some areas. He said he hadn't noticed anything until he — he didn't finish the sentence but he presumably meant that even he couldn't fail to notice that my boobs are so much bigger than yours!

Luckily I was wearing my snowman pyjamas so things weren't as bad as they might have been.

So then we decided we had to order up hot chocolate for the shock and we stayed in bed but with a pillow down the middle between us and, of course, it wasn't long before we got onto the subject of where you were. I gathered all my courage and said stuff like I was sure you would have phoned him but you didn't know where he was and that underneath it all you really love him because I believe that to be true even if you don't love him in exactly the way he wishes you did, but you do still love him and your love is a pure love and — blabbing on.

But it wasn't working because Ed's face got really frowny and in the end he looked so terrified as to what I might be leading up to he asked me to put him out of his misery and I gulped down a big breath of air and blurted out, "Well, the truth is . . . the truth is . . ." I told him I wasn't going to dress it up for him, and he yelled, "What is it?" in anguish. So I took another big breath and I just gave it to him straight. I just said it right out.

"She's gone to L.A. on business with Mac."

Hellacious! I lost it completely — I think it was because he kept sort of wistfully picking up your toenail clippers and stuff like that and saying how much he missed you. But, still, that's no excuse. Honestly, it was like I lost voluntary control of my mouth. The fantasy that I had the power to ruin Ed's life with a piece of information about you and Alex temporarily overpowered me. Ohmygod — I was so conflicted.

Anyway, the hot choc came and after sound and vision were restored Ed pointed out that you have every right to go to L.A. when he had thrown the ring back at you and everything. And that you were probably doing it because you didn't have much else to do and you needed something to distract you. Then, of course, he decided that he had to call you and I had to say that I didn't know where you were staying but I knew it wasn't at Mac's because he had house guests and thank goodness we knew you didn't have your cellphone because it was sitting right there on the hotel desk. Then he went off on this long monologue about how he'd had problems with your relationship with Mac — not anything sexual but about the way you seemed to prioritise Mac. And I said if he was sure it wasn't anything sexual then it probably was something sexual. And there was a horrible moment when he thought I was trying to tell him something about you and Mac but I said I was talking about the subconscious and maybe there was some unacknowledged jealousy there and also a belief in Ed that he is unworthy and that when you prioritise Mac it's because of him, Ed.

But, Sis, what I don't get is the way that you did it. I feel bad that you did that to Ed. I love Ed and would marry him myself if he weren't like a brother to me. What I want to know is why you didn't:

(1) sit down with Ed and Cherelle and come clean — maybe arrange like a six-month "time-out" to reassess?
(2) get your arses to couples' counselling?
(3) take a year out to live on your own and grieve the loss?
(4) institute no-blame divorce from a place of non-compulsivity and self-acceptance?
(5) begin a gentle and gradual courtship with Alex based on true intimacy and shared reality?
(6) pass up a shagfest on a sunny Caribbean beach with the man of your dreams???

AS IF!
But seriously, Sister, I love you whatever.

Ven xxxxxxxxxx

PS I hope you get this although I seriously doubt you are interrupting programming to check your e-mails. It was Paul's idea to e. He wanted to write you himself but I wouldn't let him because he's on the side of Young Love.

PPS Clinical trials have proved that being in love is a kind of madness. It depletes your serotonin levels and manifests similar symptoms to that of Obsessive Compulsive Disorder. You may experience high levels of anxiety and behave outside of your value system thus producing feelings of guilt, fear and shame.

Enjoy!

Jesus had directed me to an Internet café in town. The place had white plastic chairs and sold Coca-Cola in thick glass bottles. I'd had two rounds already. I don't know why, but it seems to taste better when it comes like that.

I bicycled back to the *hacienda* on one of the hotel bikes. This sounds more fun than it actually was. The dusty roads were full of potholes and the bike was so big my feet didn't reach the ground. It had a cross-bar too — I thought I might suffer involuntary female circumcision at any moment.

When I got back I found Alex reading a serious-looking guidebook on our verandah. He wasn't wearing much, just a shirt and his boxer shorts. I had trouble not staring. People go on about women's legs but men's are actually much nicer.

"Where've you been?" he said.

"Sightseeing," I said.

He narrowed his eyes with amused disbelief. Oh God, I thought, of course I can't lie to him. Of course he'd know.

"Shopping," I said, trying a different tack, and produced a bag. I'd found a boutique in town that sold linen bits and bought a couple of sweet little shirts with short sleeves and a wrap-round pencil skirt in black and some wide trousers. They had some tie-dye tank tops too.

"A whole wardrobe," I said.

He smiled. "Show me," he said.

"Are you interested?" I said, amazed.

"Not really," he said. "Unless you're in them."

I sat down in the shade of the cane chair opposite him and we smiled at each other stupidly. We tended to do that.

"So now what?" he said.

"Now we've slept with each other, you mean?" I said, and idly ate a few grapes out of the fruit bowl.

"Yes," he said.

"We get bored of it," I said. Which made him laugh.

"But seriously," he said.

I thought about it. "Well," I said, after a while, "I suppose we could have our first argument."

He grinned at me, daring me. So I yelled, "You bastard!" and flung a peach at him with such force that it exploded on the wall behind his head.

He jumped up in genuine outrage. "What'd I do?" he bellowed.

"Seven years!" I said.

"I wrote you a letter," he said.

"It's not good enough," I shouted. And I found that I really meant it. "Why didn't you call?" I threw a couple of kumquats with that one.

"You didn't reply to my letter!" he said, dodging small orange fruit.

"You should've tried harder!" I screamed back, and sent a kiwi his way.

"I was confused" — getting defensive.

"Seven years! You bastard!"

"Sorry, sorry, sorry," he roared unapologetically, and came at me like a bull. I saw real anger in his eyes too.

I backed up. He got to the ammunition and picked up a couple of apples. I ran for it as they pounded down at my heels. I turned round on the grass. "You wasted seven years!" I yelled, at the top of my lungs. A wave of grief came over me.

"So did you!" he thundered.

"You don't love me!" I howled. "You can't. Or you would have called." I'd gone beyond Method acting. I was consumed with what seemed quite suddenly to be blindingly obvious truth.

At this point Jesus ran into the middle of things, wringing his hands, his hair practically standing on end. "No, no, no," he wailed. "You must be happy." He began collecting up the apples as if that would somehow restore the situation.

"It's okay," Alex said to Jesus, feigning calm. Then to me, "I'm sorry. I have said I was sorry."

"But you're not," I spat back at him. "It's obvious." I turned to Jesus. "He doesn't love me," I said.

"Men and women," Jesus said, and knocked two apples together.

"Jesus," Alex said, "you've obviously got an ear for languages. Translate for me. 'I'm sorry' — *lo siento* — means 'I don't love you'? Is that right?"

"No, no, no," said Jesus to me. "Not right. He say he very sorry."

"Thank you," said Alex. "And tell her it's a free country and I'll take seven years if I damn well choose."

Jesus turned to me and said, "He say you beautiful woman, he scared he love you so much."

The words went right through me. Startled, my head came up and I caught Alex's laser gaze. He didn't look away.

"Tell him," I said, "that I won't stand for being treated like shit."

"She say," Jesus said to Alex, "she say you big important man in her life."

"And tell her," Alex said, "not to give me such a hard fucking time."

"He say," said Jesus, "he think of nothing but you, he want to make love to you all day all night."

"Well, tell him," I said, "that he's pushing his luck."

"She say," Jesus said to Alex, "she want your arms around her, she want your body, she want only you."

This was obviously too much for Alex because he came down

the verandah steps and actually picked me up in his arms. He carried me back to the room while Jesus clapped and cheered behind.

"You're a good man," I said to Jesus, over Alex's shoulder.

Jesus was practically crying with the emotion of it all. He nearly followed us into the bedroom but in the end remembered himself and was contented with carefully closing the verandah doors to ensure our privacy.

Alex dropped me on the bed and I pulled him down with me and rolled over on top of him. "You know what comes after an argument?" I said, and started to undo the buttons of his shirt.

"Us?" he said.

"Good game?" I said.

"Good game."

To: Honey@globalnet.co.uk
From: mmm@wigwam.com
Subject: ohmy
Date: 4 May — 5.40 p.m. EST
Mime-Version: 1.0

Dear Honey,

Things just got worse. I am over at Mac's. Did I tell you he's asked me to *feng shui* his apartment? His toilet is bang in the middle of his love life. It's terrible. I keep telling him to keep the seat down but he can't seem to do it. He says it brings up his mother complex.

Yesterday I woke up to find Ed gone. Yes — we spent the night together but don't worry we had that pillow down the bed like the Great Wall of China. I spent the day round here working on Mac's apartment then I went back to the hotel room. I was desperate for a pee so I barged into the bathroom and caught Ed in the bath. He's obviously quite Free

Willy about these things, didn't seem to mind at all. Seeing him in the bath reminded me of Dad in the bath and how his bits used to float on the surface like carrots in a stew. I'm surprised it didn't put us off for life.

Anyway, Ed eventually came out and went on the balcony in his towel and I was about to rush into the loo when I saw that Cherelle was out there — on the neighbouring balcony. Well, obviously, I wasn't going to miss a moment of that particular show.

As you know, I am studying human behaviour for when I'm old enough to become a therapist. Funny, isn't it, to think I'm too young to be a therapist — even though I know more about life than most fifty-year-olds?

I scooted over to the window and stood behind the blind where they couldn't see me.

When Cherelle saw Ed she put her hand on her hip and said, "You!"

I thought the game was up. I thought Ed was going to guess the whole truth right there and then by the way Cherelle kind of stabbed the air with her index finger when she said, "You!"

But Ed goes, "Hi. How's the honeymoon going?" all charm and calm. Ed has so much trust. He reminds me of a dog that's been fed at six p.m. every single day of his life.

Cherelle goes, "Absolutely fucking fabulous," in this great English accent. (Hidden depths!)

Ed goes, "Good," slightly less confident. He must have noticed the threatening way she'd got her hand on her hip like Ma Cherelle at the Okay Corral.

Ed goes, "Unfortunately Honey got called away on business — which is obviously a bit unfortunate — you know, on your honeymoon, but unfortunately it was unavoidable."

My heart went out to him. Far too many unfortunatelys. You know what? I think he's scared of Cherelle. She just stared at him for ages and I could practically see the situation registering in her head, clunk-clunk-clunk, like the numbers flipping round on an old-fashioned cash register. Eventually she rang up: "Are you serious?"

Ed looked perplexed. Cherelle's mouth was open. Here we go, I thought. Now the beans get spilled.

"Called away on business?" she said.

"Yes," said Ed.

Cherelle snorted out a great big snort of laughter and did a sort of knowing shaking of the head as if she, and only she, was in on the innest joke in the world.

"Perhaps you'd like to tell me," said Ed, "what you're fucking laughing at." I always forget that about Ed. He's like the mouse that roared.

It brought Cherelle up short. By this time I was so desperate for the loo I was doubled over like a frog in a ballet. But there's no way I was going anywhere because Cherelle was changing right in front of my eyes. She was like some kind of special effect — her body melting and distorting, stuff bubbling up under her skin so you'd think an alien might burst out at any moment. She starts slapping those eyelashes around — the ones you could rake your garden leaves with — says, "I'm laughing because my husband has also been called away on business."

Well, that was it. I had to do the doubled-over hobble to the bathroom. Remember that time I wet myself laughing in double chemistry at school and had to pretend the wet patch on the floor was my experiment boiling over?

I got back as quickly as I could but then the phone rang and it was Mac. He thought I was you. I was just about to explain when his phone cut out.

I went back to the window. Ed was looking at some photos and saying, "You know, you really don't need plastic surgery." Honestly, Ed is so pure — it just kills me. Then he goes, "But where's your husband?"

Cherelle goes, "Oh, I had him morphed out — you can do that now."

Well, I just had to get out there and have a look. So I burst out pretending I'd just woken up and had a look at the photos and there was Cherelle in her wedding bower — all alone. No Alex.

"You had Alex removed?" I said.

"Yeah," she said.

"Like an unsightly mole?" I said.

"Sure," she said.

"Because he went away on business?" said Ed.

I left Cherelle to answer that one herself. Next thing, there's a knock at the door to the hotel room. I ran over — Mac.

"Not funny," I said. "In my version of events, you are meant to be in L.A. with Honey. And, no, she's not here," I said. "That was me on the phone. And you can't come in." That was when I noticed that he looked different. Kind of sheepish.

"I need to talk," he said.

"To me?" I said.

"You'll do," he said.

Down in the lobby, we sat in armchairs the size of small ocean liners. Mac ordered coffee.

"I've never done this before," he said.

"What?" I said, struggling to get an eye line over the arm of my chair.

"This," he said, making back and forward gestures presumably to indicate communication. "You know — talking. I don't know how to start."

"At the beginning," I said. "It's quite easy — you just launch."

He couldn't. I had a horrible feeling he might be about to cry. I urged him to have a cigarette. He said he'd given up. I asked him if that was wise. Maybe it wasn't the best moment to give up smoking. Not my usual line on smoking, I know — but although I don't think he's capable of real crying, I was worried he might be about to ooze a couple of toady tears. A cigarette would have put an end to that.

"I must. I must," he said. Meaning give up smoking.

"You smoke for a reason," I said gently. "You smoke so you don't have to feel like this."

"It's about Della," he said.

Anyway, I'm afraid I can't go on because I regard the rest of what he said as having been spoken within the confidentiality contract that exists between therapist and client.

I'll write again soon.

Ven xxxxxxxxxx

PS Are you spitting mad because I left you hanging? I hope so. I've decided you'll never learn about running away unless you experience some negative consequences.

19

TALK about cliffhangers.

I was back in the Internet café. The smell of heat came in off the street. After I finished reading Ven's e-mail I got straight on the phone to her but she wasn't at Mac's and I didn't dare call the hotel in case I got Ed. I called Della instead.

"Hey," I said.

"Hey," she said.

"What's up with Mac?" I said.

"Why do you think something might be up with Mac?" she said.

"I checked my e-mail," I said, "like a good girl."

"Mac told Ven?" — amazement.

"He's changing," I said.

"Yeah," she said, gloomy. "For the worse."

"Tell me," I said.

"Okay," she said. "Long story short."

"No," I said. "Long story long. Start at the beginning."

"Okay," she said. "Well, the first sign of trouble was the night after the party. We got home about three a.m. — they're kind of part-timers in New York, whatever they might think. We had a good shag and all that, and Mac suddenly announced he was giving up smoking. I said, what would he want to do that for, and he said, well, because it was a dirty unpleasant habit. I said not to worry on my account — I kind of like that ashtray-mouth thing. And smoking can be quite manly in a man, if you know what I mean — I think it shows a healthy disregard for self and also it gives them something to do with their hands."

"Smoking for Procreation!" I said. It's a movement Della wants to start. Neither of us actually smokes but we always accept the offer of a cigarette when picking up men. Della claims the act of give and take with the long, slim, pointy thing is a primary courtship ritual. He offers you a cigarette. You put it in your mouth. He lights it. You're having sex.

Della believes the human race would die out without smoking.

"Anyway," continued Della, "I could see it wasn't really about the smoking — Mac's got this look in his eye, these days. Sheepish — it's the only word for it. Most unattractive. So I said, 'Look, Mac, don't get sex confused with love here. Yes, it feels good. Yes, it feels fucking amazing, frankly. But sex is sex is sex.'"

I could hear a clicking noise. "What are you doing?" I said.

"Plucking," she said. Della does that when she's tense. Plucks her eyebrows nearly out of existence.

I said, "It's rude to pluck on the phone." But she ignored me.

"So then," she said, outraged, "can you believe this? He starts interviewing me for motherhood."

"No way," I said.

"Yes way," she said. "The guy's approaching fifty, let's not forget. He asked me if I liked children!"

I said, "Well, maybe he's going to remake *Bugsy Malone* and he wants you to chaperone."

"I wish," she said. "It's his goddamn biological clock," then added, "He's broody," as if she were reporting some extremely unpleasant deficit in his personal hygiene standards.

"Outrageous," I said. And it was. Babies are about as mention-able in the lexicon of contemporary relationships as oral sex in polite Victorian society. "So you ran away," I said.

"No," she said, "I don't think that's it at all. I proceeded at a dig-nified pace to the airport — but that wasn't until I'd knocked the baby thing on the head by telling him there was no way on this earth I was ever having nipples the size of dinner plates. So then he goes off to work and I'm trying to get some sleep and he comes back! Lays this ring thing on me! I mean you should see this thing — it's the size of the fucking Taj Mahal."

"A diamond?" I said, breathless.

"Tiffany," she said.

"Shit," I said. I'm such a know-it-all, it's not often that I'm sur-prised. I enjoyed the rare sensation. "Then what?"

"Well, one thing led to another and at one point I kind of threw my arm out because you know we are very compatible on that level, Mac and I, and my hand hit the pipe and I heard this icy kind of cracking noise —"

"Hold up," I said. "Rewind. Pipe?"

"We were doing it in the shower," she said.

"You had the ring on?"

"Well, yes," she said, a tad defensive. "Just for fun."

"I see," I said.

"Anyway," she said, "Mac didn't notice a thing. But when I managed to get a look at it, the stone had sliced exactly in half. I didn't think you could break a diamond but apparently if it gets hit in exactly the right place you can." She sighed. "Broke right in two," she said. "I think it's a sign."

"What did Mac say?" I breathed.

"Oh, he said not to worry, it only cost five hundred thousand dollars." Sarcastic.

"You didn't tell him," I said.

Silence. Then — "I took a leaf out of your book. I got the next flight out."

"Where's the ring?" I said.

"Here with me," she said. "I've got to get it fixed."

"Well," I said. I couldn't think of anything else to say. I didn't think it was fixable.

"What do you think I should do?" Della said. Seven words that don't often come out of her mouth in that particular order.

"I don't know," I said. "We seem to have been transported to some kind of parallel universe, both of us, we don't know the customs, we don't speak the language. What to do . . ." I trailed off.

"What to wear . . ." Della echoed mournfully. "How's it with Alex?"

"New," I said.

"New?"

"I hardly know him."

"Does he go down on you?"

"Oh, stop," I said.

"Apparently that's the first question boys ask each other. 'Does she go down on you?'"

"You sound like someone from World War Two. Everyone goes down on everyone, these days," I said, wondering how we'd got on to this. I often wonder that when in conversation with Della.

"Oral sex is illegal in Utah," she said.

After we hung up I bought another Coke and sat there drinking it and wondering idly if Della's predicament was the end of my job with Mac — just as I had predicted. Then it occurred to me, with a jolt, that maybe I no longer had a use for my job anyway. Suddenly I saw myself living in L.A., turning my big American car out of the driveway into a broad, empty street lined with palm trees. I imagined Mac saying I could work for him in L.A. Then I changed my mind and had him getting me a fantastic job in the film business. Next it came to me, with a leap of the heart, that Ven would be there. Family togetherness on top of everything else! It must be meant to be!

I was just getting to the bit where I was giving birth to our first child in an American hospital — nicer décor, more effective pain relief, George Clooney in a green gown — when I started to feel dizzy. And then, all of a sudden — what goes up must come down — the euphoria flipped into something really quite unpleasant. The enormity of what I'd done came over me.

This had threatened to happen a couple of times before, but in the night — and I'd been able to stave off the feelings in Alex's arms.

Ed! What had happened to Ed? And what was I contemplating? Moving to L.A.? Me? Abandoning my life? For real?

Ohmygod.

I mean, what about my friends in London? Wouldn't I miss them? What about Theresa and the ponies? What about the rain and the BBC and the queue in the post office and black London taxis and Harrods and proper cups of tea and the unemployed? L.A. would have none of these things. What about my roots?

I was gasping for breath when Alex pulled up outside in a convertible Golf — top down.

"Where did you get it?" I said.

"I stole it," he said. "I wasn't in rehab for nothing."

"You rented it," I said.

"Get in," he said.

"Where are we going?" I said.

"Wait and see," he said. "Get in."

I did. He squealed the tyres away from the kerb. "Stop!" I yelled suddenly. He turned to me in alarm, still accelerating, his hair whipping across his eyes.

"Stop!" I yelled again.

He pulled over. "What's going on?" he said.

"I'm having feelings," I said.

"Feelings?" he said.

"Yeah," I said, "I do have feelings, you know."

He looked at me, worried. "Uh-oh," he said. "Is there a cure?"

"Alex," I said, "sometimes — sometimes I need to know where we're going."

There must have been an edge in my voice because he answered quickly, "La Posada," he said. "It's the best hotel in Mexico."

"I wish you'd told me," I said.

"I'm telling you now," he said.

"I'll miss Jesus," I said.

"He's gonna come visit," he said, and smiled.

"But . . ." I said, and hesitated.

And in that moment of hesitation I lost him. He swivelled the rays of his laser gaze away from me. A stack of colourful plastic baskets now revelled in its glory. I was jealous of the baskets.

"The thing is," I said, "I think I need to know where this relationship is going."

"Right now," Alex said, putting his foot on the accelerator, "it's going south."

There was the dusty empty road and the occasional glimpse of turquoise sea. There were white concrete hamlets with red tin Coca-Cola signs and Spanish-style churches.

And there was Alex.

How did I, I wondered, as I drove down the coast of Mexico with the wind in my hair and the man I didn't marry, how did I end up driving down the coast of Mexico with the wind in my hair and the man I didn't marry? How did that happen? Exactly? Remind me.

It wasn't that I thought I was with the wrong man. When I turned to look at Alex, his short fine hair whipping around his head, his tanned forearms holding the steering-wheel, his thick eyelashes, I just wanted to lose myself in him, to get inside his skin and disappear.

And, thinking that, I became a prisoner in my separateness. I was prey to all sorts of feelings — feelings, no doubt, engendered by my carnivorous thoughts, which were sucking my blood like the new improved extra strength mosquitoes they'd had specially waiting for me in the hotel room last night.

"Feelings aren't facts," Ven would say to me.

I'm not entirely sure what that means but I think it's something to do with mistaking a feeling as representing the outer world rather than the inner. The trouble with feelings is that they're so damn convincing. You can't rationalise your way out of them — a bit like when you go to a 3D movie and however much you tell yourself it's an illusion you still duck when the flying saucer comes flying at you.

When Alex pulled off the road and announced that we were going to visit a spectacular ruin called Tulum, I realised that the unpleasantly tense sensation lodged just behind my breastbone was actually fear. Good old-fashioned fear.

Okay, so now I had Alex.

Okay, so now I could lose Alex.

And we were on our way to do something as sensible and as ordinary as sightseeing together, with other couples, with other tourists. It seemed undoably sane.

Tulum turned out to be a Mayan temple, set against the Caribbean sea, rising up in delicate grey-white layers like ash when it is left to build on a cigarette. The warm thick walls of the Castillo bulge contentedly outwards, like they might be replete with the wisdom of the centuries. They seem full up, satisfied, at peace. After we'd done the tour I put my hands on the walls and let the distant presence of the people who had lived in that place nineteen centuries ago come close and touch me.

I remember once at school being shown a vertical line that represented the earth's history since time began. There was a little cartoon television on wheels that ran up and down the side of the line and plugged in here and there to show you what was going at any particular moment. The TV had to whiz nearly to the top of the line even to show you dinosaurs, and modern civilisation turned out to be a tiny speck right at the very very top. It made me feel like I was in one of those trick rooms where the perspective is all distorted.

Hanging on to those old warm walls, I had the same feeling. My insignificance is unimaginable to me. Unimaginable.

I knew Alex felt the same. So I didn't bother saying. Later, we sat side by side on the grass, our backs to the temple, and looked out to sea.

"Are you all right?" I said, after a while.

"Yes," he said.

"Are you sure?" I said.

"Yes," he said. "Are *you* all right?"

I hesitated.

"You know I wrote you e-mails when I was in L.A.," he said, "and just sent them out into the ether?"

"Really?" I said — astonished. "What did they say?"

"Oh, this and that," he said.

I often got the sense when he spoke that he was broadcasting from some far-off place, transmissions only being made after a crack team of editors and spin doctors had knocked them into shape and I got the impression I was only privy to a fraction of what he really thought. But, of course, that's what I found so attractive about him. There was nine-tenths mystery. Nine-tenths for me to colour in myself.

"Did you check your e-mails in that café back there?" he said.

"Yes," I said. "It's not what you think."

"What do I think?" he said. "I don't think anything."

Little silence.

"We're as old as the ruins," he said, with a smile. "You and I."

"What do you mean?" I said, catching a glimpse of the Enuff monster lurking behind a palm tree on the cliff edge.

"You know what I mean," he said.

"But it'd be nice," I said, "if you were specific."

It flashed through my mind that this wasn't really like me. I really wasn't used to this . . . this . . . The word "neediness" popped into my head. Oh, my Lord, I thought with horror, perhaps I'm becoming one of those Women Who Love Too Much.

"Remember when we first met," said Alex. He wasn't looking at me.

"In the restaurant," I said.

"We knew," he said.

"Did you know I'd get into the taxi?" I said.

"Yes," he said. "But if you hadn't I'd have come back in and got you."

"How?" I said — couldn't resist.

"I don't know," he said, disappointingly. "Some way."

"What was it about me?" I said. Oh, God, labouring the point.

"Are you fishing?" he said.

"It's just that I want to exactly understand," I mumbled.

"It's not to understand," he said. "It just is. Come on." He got up, took me by the hand and pulled me after him and away.

20

L A POSADA was the most lovely hotel. It was luxurious but also peeling and faded in the most comforting authentic way. It had cabins and jungly bits and a beautiful old mosaic-tiled swimming-pool with carved dolphins at each end and great big flat hammocks slung between trees in shady nooks.

It also had a half-moon white-sand beach with the obligatory lonely palm tree leaning into the sea.

In the daytimes I lay on the beach and thought about how I'd never really cracked this holiday thing. Holidays gave me too much room for existential *Angst*. Well, I think it was existential — the *Angst*.

I'm not too sure what existential means — something to do with the meaning of life. I do know it's very hard to fathom the meaning of life when lying on a sun-lounger with absolutely no discernible purpose.

My usual way of getting through the holidays is to read books voraciously until it's time to go home, lose myself in them. I'd found a little wooden bookshelf in the lobby, filled with dog-eared copies of doctor-and-nurse romances. I thought they might be a bit close to the bone so I searched until I unearthed a thriller and took it down to the beach.

There were several big white wooden sun-loungers and I pulled one up underneath some trees and settled down. If I lowered my book one centimetre my view was of a stunning expanse of blue sea. Half a mile out a curious hump-backed rock raised itself out of the water like a giant turtle about to lumber towards land.

I found I couldn't read — not one bloody word. Every time I started a sentence in the book my head finished it with something all its own. There was interference on the line. I tried to do deep breathing and let my thoughts pass like clouds. Some hope. My thoughts were like London clouds. Thick. Wall to wall. And totally intransigent.

I thought about how I should be happy. I thought I should be happy. I mean, I could make a good case for happiness but some-how the actual feeling seemed to elude me. I felt horny and excited and hopeful and womanly and powerful and scared and alive and more — but I didn't exactly feel happy.

Alex wasn't with me. Alex had found something wrong with the car. The problem didn't seem too terrible to me — something to do with the transmission. Transition? Whatever. I was all for calling the rental-car company but he insisted that would be nothing but hassle and seemed pleased with the idea of fixing it himself. Earlier I'd been out to see how he was doing and he was delightedly tinkering, wip-ing his fingers voluptuously on an oily rag. Like a boy with Lego. I could sense his satisfaction. It was quite sexy watching him but he had his head under the hood most of the time so I soon gave up.

We'd been at La Posada a few days now and — when I really thought about it — I realised that, in a funny sort of way, I hadn't seen much of Alex at all. He didn't like lying on the beach and he was always off investigating possible excursions or checking out the diving school or planning epic bicycle rides or something.

Just as I was thinking this, a man and a woman wind-surfed into my field of vision. She was tall, frighteningly firm, and had that kind of life-on-a-beach-gone-native look — Ursula Andress in a wet-suit. I recognised her as the girl who ran the beach activities — Marie Claire. She liked to be called MC for short. She would.

It took me a few more seconds to realise that the man she was with was Alex. She was teaching him to wind-surf and he clearly had a natural aptitude. He would.

I watched him proudly. Well, I tried to. Actually I got into wondering why on earth he would want to be with me when he could be with her.

Of course, I knew this wasn't a particularly rational thought. Maybe he didn't like her personality. Maybe she didn't like his. Maybe his feeling for me went much deeper than anything to do with inside leg measurements. But I didn't know for sure. And in the absence of not knowing there were a million painful possibilities to while away the hours with.

Which led me to wondering whether Alex would have run off with Marie Claire if she'd been on the neighbouring balcony on his wedding night. Whether my being with him was simply a matter of timing. Not that I was complaining or anything. Good timing is always a lot better than bad.

Not that I was running with any seriously sinister ideas about Alex's intentions re Marie Claire. The opposite, actually — I knew it was all in my head.

And then it occurred to me that I never did any of this crazy head stuff with Ed.

I should add at this point that I pride myself on not being the jealous type. There's a part of me, you see, that firmly believes I am the only woman in the world. And usually, because I don't fancy other women myself, I find it hard to imagine my boyfriend fancying other women. Like I find it hard to imagine being a man. But all the time I'm finding it hard to imagine my boyfriend fancying other women I'm simultaneously thinking all the women in the world are more attractive than me. And if that sounds like a contradiction in terms I can only say that my mind is a very sophisticated thing. My mind is capable of great feats of contortion — while riding a monocycle on a tightrope.

One favourite trick, for example, is to walk down the street and see a businesslike blonde passing on the other side of the road and to become convinced that my boyfriend, whoever it is at the time, would far prefer to be going out with her than to be going out with me. Almost to the point of pity — for my boyfriend that he doesn't get to go out with her.

Yet I'm never caught up in specific jealousies about old girlfriends or the like. Della's boyfriends usually foam rabidly at the mouth at the mere mention of a predecessor — she has to hide old photographs. I, on the other hand, always feel rather sorry for old girlfriends — they remind me of all those dog-eared scripts stacked on the shelves in Mac's office, all those films that never got made.

With Ed, though, like I said, jealousy was never much of an issue (lap-dancers called Cherry being the exception that proves the rule). Ed always had this sweetly crazy idea that he'd got lucky with me, like he couldn't do any better. He'd still get furious with me, obviously, but his fundamental position was one of . . . well, dare I say it? . . . gratitude.

So I never thought about Ed looking at anyone else. I felt totally secure.

Oh dear.

Big sigh.

No wonder it hadn't worked out.

We had grilled shrimps and ceviche for dinner at a table under the stars. There was a little plinking waterfall in the restaurant and a little plinking band in the corner. Guitars, though, which made a change from marimbas. When we sat down the *patron* came over and presented me with a beautiful tropical flower.

Alex talked about L.A., his life there and his plans. I found myself trying to second-guess whether I was included or not so eventually I took a deep breath and said, "And what about us?"

He said, "You're coming with me, of course."

It took my breath away. "Really?" I said. It was meant to come out kind of sarcastic, as in, "You think I'd just ditch my whole life for you?" but it ended up coming out pretty accommodating — probably because I was, of course, considering ditching my whole life for him.

"Sure," he said.

I just grinned like a fool. I couldn't help it.

"But I don't want to hang around here much longer. I need to get back," he said.

Took my breath away again.

"But," I said, foundering, "weren't you planning a two-week honeymoon with Cherelle?"

He leant across the table and took my hand. "We'll be together," he said. "That's the main thing."

Later in bed I made a hole for our heads in the zillions of pillows, wrapped my legs around his steely thigh and said, "I think we should talk about Ed and Cherelle."

"You do?" he said.

"Yeah," I said. "Clear the air."

"Does it need clearing?" he said.

"Maybe that's the wrong expression," I said. "Maybe I meant more like grab the bull by the horns or look the horse in the mouth — an expression like that."

"Is something wrong?" he said. I didn't answer so he added, "Apart from the obvious."

"What's the obvious?" I said.

"I'm not the person you married. And vice versa," he said. "That's the obvious."

"Nothing's wrong," I said. "Tell me about Cherelle."

"What do you want to know?"

"Why did you fall in love with her?"

"I dunno." He shrugged. "Ask Cherelle."

"She's not here," I said.

"I dunno," he said. "When I'm around Cherelle I think that maybe Santa Claus exists. I think that maybe that senior VP at the studio has a kind streak and my best interests at heart. I think that maybe I'm just a regular guy and not some kind of Stepford suit, as empty inside as a dried-out pumpkin."

"Wow," I said, "you must be missing her."

"Yeah," he said, "I thought she was my salvation. But it was an illusion. Santa doesn't exist. And the senior VP at the studio cares about the screen averages and nothing else."

"And are you a pumpkin?" I said.

"I don't know," he said.

"Were you in love with Cherelle?" I suddenly trusted him to be entirely honest.

He thought for ages as was his way and then said, "Not exactly."

"So what was it?" I said.

"I don't know," he said, after another while. "She kind of carried things along — it all got carried along."

"But what — you don't think you'd be happy with her?"

"On the contrary," he said. "I think I would be happy with her." Ouch.

"Put it this way," he added, "I don't think she would be happy with me." Little silence. "I don't want to make her unhappy. I don't want to live like that."

"Oh," I said. "I see." Then, after a while, "Won't you make me unhappy?" Like I didn't want to be left out of the unhappiness stakes.

"I might. But it'll be different."

"Why?"

"Because . . ." he said. "You know, the morning after our wedding I woke up with Cherelle in that hotel room and it came to me very clearly, this is not my dream. This is not my dream."

I wanted to ask him if *this* was his dream. But something stopped me. Anyway he changed the subject by leaning over and running kisses down my stomach.

After we'd made love, Alex turned his back to me to go to sleep. I wanted him to face my way. I wanted to go to sleep in his arms. I wanted to lie like spoons all night.

I didn't say anything. But he heard me anyway. "I always sleep on my left side," he said. Which wasn't really the point.

I closed my eyes. I couldn't help thinking that, when we let them, our bodies talked better than our minds ever could. Or ever would.

It wasn't until I was back on my lonely sun-lounger the next day, staring out at that funny turtle rock and not reading my book, that I realised we hadn't mentioned Ed at all. I guess Alex didn't want to know.

So I lay there and thought about Alex's idea of cutting short our stay at La Posada and going back to L.A. together to face reality. Every time I went there it hurt. It hurt that he wanted to cut short our honeymoon.

Honeymoon! The word gave me a jolt. I reminded myself we weren't on a honeymoon. But then I realised there was a part of me that felt we were . . . an unconventional honeymoon, but a honeymoon nevertheless. And then I felt that I couldn't tell Alex that his cutting-it-short idea had hurt because if he hadn't guessed that it would hurt he wouldn't understand why it hurt.

Then I got to remembering, I don't know why, the time when I was about nine and my dad took me out to buy me a coat. This was a rare and strange occasion and to this day I have no idea why it was him who took me out to buy the coat. We went to this trendy shop on the King's Road that had these amazing fake-fur coats for kids. I tried on two — one was a shaggy camel colour, the other a startling black and white ponyskin. I could tell my dad preferred the camel but I wanted the ponyskin. Wanted, wanted, wanted.

The more my dad explained to me why the camel was the sensible choice, the more I wanted the ponyskin. Then, out of the blue, he capitulated — I could have the ponyskin.

It was when he was paying for it that the first doubts set in. Now I'd got it, did I really want it? Would it be hard to wear? What would my friends say? It was like, now it was mine there was something wrong with it.

And I never did feel right about that ponyskin coat. Never. In the end I was relieved to grow out of it and see it carted off to Oxfam (I imagined some poor child in Africa starving and hot in my unfortunate ponyskin).

I don't know why this particular incident sticks in my mind. But it does. Sometimes I think I'd have been happier with the camel. Even though I'd have been yearning for the ponyskin every second. Or maybe because of it.

21

To: Honey@globalnet.co.uk
From: mmm@wigwam.com
Subject: ohmygod
Date: 5 May — 12.05 pm EST
Mime-Version: 1.0

Dear Honey,

I'm staying in Mac's guest room. He has taken to his bed with lovesickness. Or so he says. I think it might be severe nicotine withdrawal. He is going cold turkey. He says he has never spent a day in bed in his whole life.

His office is going crazy. Apparently they have it on good authority that the world will end if he doesn't attend his meetings scheduled for today. They tried to send (a) paramedics, (b) a psychiatric consultant. Baskets of fruit keep arriving. And someone sent a "new baby" basket by mistake — it's full of pastel-coloured rattles, talcum powder and stuffed bunnies.

I'm very tired too. We were out all night saving your marriage. Del, Paul and I, we think we're the Three Musketeers. Del's back — she's taken two weeks off work and come back to sort out the ring thing at Tiffany's. She's camping in Ed's hotel room. She says she can't rest easy in London.

Paul, to be honest, doesn't think you want your marriage saved but he came along anyway. I think he was scared he'd miss something if he didn't.

Della and I, however, are more and more convinced that you have fallen for the quick fix of instant gratification and will soon gorge your-self on the walnut whip that is Alex and want to come running back to the crunchy parboiled carrot stick that is Ed. If you see what I mean.

Although, frankly, that's more my take than Del's. Del was a bit dubi-ous about saddling up on your behalf. She thought that you'd cooked your goose and you'd better stew in the juice or some such Musketeer-ial sentiment. I argued that we'd only get grief if you came back from Mexico looking for Ed and he was gone. And told her to think of all the hours we'd have to spend on the phone listening to you and that a stitch in time could save nine. (The Musketeers speak a lot in proverbs.) It all started when I was finishing up my therapy session with Mac in the hotel bar. I noticed that Ed and Cherelle had come in together.

Don't panic. I think Ed was just being polite to Cherelle — like he is when he's not being rude — you know, humouring her. When I saw them I got on the phone, called for back-up — Del and Paul — and then went straight over and muscled in.

Cherelle was on her second margarita. I didn't like to say anything but I know she met Alex in a treatment centre for addiction and that means she's not supposed to drink. So I just raised an eyebrow.

Cherelle said, "I saw that eyebrow!"

"You did?" I said, trying to smooth it down again but it wouldn't really go. My eyebrow is truthful to the nth degree. If I ever had to do a lie-detector test they should hook the thing up to my eyebrow.

Cherelle looked at Ed. "I was never into alcohol," she said. "It was never my thing."

"Fine," I said.

"You know what?" she said, "I'm sick of self-improvement. I've had self-improvement up the ass. I've improved myself stupid. And what for?" I thought she was going to say, "To be jilted on my honeymoon, that's what for," but she remembered in time. "For nothing," she said.

My eyebrow must have still been up there because then she said, "Okay — I'm having a slip. So sue me." She drained her glass.

Ed said, "Steady."

By the time Paul had turned up with his smelly French cigarettes, Cherelle was taking up smoking too. Paul demonstrated his Simone Signoret technique for us — it involves picking teeny bits of tobacco off your tongue while angling the cigarette and doing little rabbit nibbles on your thumb and index finger.

"Yeah," said Del. "Otherwise known as foreplay."

Things moved along. I think Paul forgot we were meant to be the Musketeers — either that or he was operating subversively in the name of Young Love. He insisted we go to a nightclub where his friends were doing a tranny Three Degrees act.

I chatted to a Degree at the bar — he was quite beautiful in long black wig and pink rubber tube dress, with those incredible male bum bones thrusting against the rubber — and I said something about him being a tranny, which annoyed him because apparently he's a drag queen. I suppose the difference is that he's a gay man dressed as a woman not a straight man dressed as a woman. The whole thing's a PC minefield, I tell you.

Anyway, Cherelle was a few more margaritas down the road. She kept telling us not to let her eat the peanuts then eating peanuts and going, "Oops!" all guilty, as if the nuts had eaten her.

They sang "When Will I See You Again?" and Cherelle made Ed dance with her. It was kind of a slow dance and for a moment there I thought they were going to get smoochy. I mean, I didn't really think anything was going to happen — not really-really.

I just can't imagine Ed going for Cherelle. But, then, you never know with men. They have a horrible tendency to see the best in women and overlook the worst. Or, rather, their dicks do.

I told Del and Paul that I thought Cherelle was trying to seduce Ed while he was still an innocent and didn't know The Truth. Paul wasn't much help — he kept being sent champagne by some mystery admirer in the club. He said no one could be seduced by Cherelle since Cherelle's version of seduction was like a wall frieze in play school — all big colourful letters and exaggerated smiley faces.

Del took the view that Ed would never be seduced while there was still Hope with you.

As for me, I know Ed much better than either of them and he was definitely flattered by Cherelle's attentions. Definitely. Ed's problem, you see, is that he doesn't know how attractive he is. He's just flat-out amazed when anyone finds him sexy.

I made Paul get up and dance with me so we could overhear what they were talking about. The subject appeared to be room service. Cherelle was saying stuff like, "There is nothing worse in life than a hotel that has slow room service."

When the song ended we all went back to the bar and Cherelle got brought a glass of champagne by the bartender who said it was from a mystery admirer. We kind of hoped it wasn't the same mystery admirer who was sending Paul's champagne. But sending mystery stuff was obviously all the rage.

Cherelle had a look around and claimed she knew exactly who it was who'd bought her the champagne. Claimed a man on the other side of the room was sending sex vibes at her. We all looked over and there was a dark Latinate man over there with short legs and long arms.

Paul said, "What's your definition of 'sex vibes'?"

Cherelle said, "You know, when a guy holds your gaze too long — like for an inappropriate amount of time. It's creepy. I mean, he may as well be waving his dick at me. Look at him," she said, "he's more ape than man." And she started drinking the champagne.

I have to say I was kind of warming to Cherelle at this point but Ed, who'd been pretty quiet all evening, suddenly woke up and said, "You're going to drink that champagne?"

Cherelle said, "Yeah."

Ed said, "And you called him an ape?"

Cherelle said, "Yeah!" and glugged some more.

Ed just looked disgusted.

Cherelle did her eyelash thing at him but in slow motion, due to the amount of alcohol in her system, I guess. Then she said, "What are you thinking, Eddy?"

Ed went, "Nothing."

At this point a new glass of champagne arrived from the simian admirer across the way and Cherelle raised the glass at him across the room.

She caught Ed's expression and said, "Tell me what you're thinking. I know you're thinking something."

Ed said, "Okay. You're shallow. I think you're shallow."

"Oh, good, I'm not bored any more" — Della.

Then Ed to Cherelle: "Why are you flirting with me?"

My first thought was that Cherelle was going to faint. Some hope. She threw her drink in his face. "You don't know anything. I don't care if you are British!" she yelled.

We all looked at each other like — British? British? I didn't dwell on it. I had a horrible feeling about what was coming next. I grabbed Cherelle's arm but she flung me to the floor in one swift martial-arts move.

While I was down there, Cherelle said to Ed, "I am flirting with you because your wife — *wife*," the word seemingly having roughly the same cold and dousing effect on Ed as the glass of champagne a moment earlier, "is — what's the word you use? — shagging — *shagging* — my husband — *husband* — in Mexico."

"No, she's not," said Ed. His face was still dripping and it gave him a kind of tragic-heroic appearance.

Ed looked at me. I looked away as fast as I could.

Not fast enough. Or maybe it was my eyebrow giving me away again because Ed grabbed me and frogmarched me out the back. We went through a fire exit and came out in an alley behind the club.

"I think you need to take this really, really slow," I said, trying to talk him down. "I think you should take this like one minute — one second — at a time." I tried to sit him down. "Breathe," I said and patted his stomach. "Breathe into your belly like you're blowing a balloon."

"Fuck off," he said. "Have you been lying to me?"

I was the one who sat down. I'm not used to being in the wrong. It was a terrible shock. I sat on a stack of bread-delivery tray things.

Ed said, "I deserve to be treated better than this."

And he's so right. Ohmygod — he's so right.

So I ended up telling him the whole story about you and Alex, and I finished up by saying that the whole thing was probably just your way of avoiding intimacy because in a way Alex had operated as a strange sort of insurance policy against Ed really being The One, that the fantasy of Alex in the background kept you from seeing the reality of Ed and letting him into your life as the man you were going to love and who was going to be there for you. And that if Ed could see his way to understanding, then there was hope.

But he just said, "Fuck off." But not rudely. Then he said, "Ven, what are you doing all this for anyway?"

"What do you mean?" I said.

"Do you think I can't handle this myself?"

"No," I said, a little faintly.

"So what are you doing?"

He wasn't going to let it drop. I said, "I'm saving the world. Can't you tell?"

He said, "Making the bad things go away?"

"Yes," I said.

"Well, I'm an adult," he said.

"Then behave like one," I said.

"Okay," he said.

I felt like we'd made a pact or something.

Ed went. He didn't say goodbye. He just walked away. I didn't mind. I felt closer to him than I ever had before.

After I'd had a little cry, I went back into the club. The place was rammed all of a sudden. No sign of Cherelle.

When I eventually found Del and Paul they told me I'd missed the best bit. Cherelle had danced on a table and the long-armed man had stood below staring up at her adoringly.

"Where's she gone?" I said.

"Home," said Paul.

"With him," said Della.

I thought they were joking. They weren't. Then a tall, handsome Australian came over. He wanted to know where the girl with the big eyes was. The one he'd been sending champagne to.

So, anyway, this morning I went round to the hotel just to make sure Ed was okay. I mean, I hadn't forgotten about our pact but I thought he might want to talk — or maybe ask some questions about you and Alex. I mean, I thought at the very least he'd be in shock and I'd take him some Rescue Remedy.

I found Paul and Della in a little posse in the corridor.

"What's up?" I said.

"He's in there," they said, pointing at the door.

"Of course he's in there," I said.

"It's Cherelle's room," hissed Della.

"Ohmygod," I said, clocking the door number.

"Yeah, right — ohmygod," said Della.

"What's he doing in there?" I said.

"I think it's a kind of love-hate thing," said Paul, feeding Honoria some croissant from an abandoned breakfast tray. "You know, like Scarlett and Rhett — when she's refusing him sex and he 'takes her' and the next morning she's a new woman because all she needed was a good —"

"Paul," Della said, "what would you know about what a woman needs?"

"Darling," said Paul, and drew breath in preparation for launch.

"What's Ed doing in that room?" I yelled, before he could start.

"I came back here last night," Del said, "and Cherelle had apeman in some kind of strange arms-length defensive tackle. She was pushing his

Adam's apple into his throat with the index finger of her right hand. Ed was watching. And when she'd finished with apeman, Ed and she got talking. I went to bed."

"Guess," said Paul.

"Talking about what?" I said.

"I don't know," I said. I hate it when I don't know stuff.

"Honey and Alex, of course," said Della.

I looked at the breakfast tray.

Paul said, "He had croissants, she had granola. He had tea, she had coffee. He had melon, she had banana."

"I see," I said.

"Do you think they were up all night?" I said.

"Maybe," said Della.

"Do you think they — you know — did it?" I said.

"I would guess no," said Paul. "Judging by the banana."

"What?" I said, the world spinning.

"Joke," said Paul.

Della said, "How would we know if they 'did it' or not?"

Just as she said "did it" like that — quite loud — the door swung open and Cherelle stepped out. She just stared at us like we were paparazzi camped out on her doorstep, didn't say a word.

I thought Paul at least might have the nerve to say something but he was as speechless as the rest. After a moment, she turned and walked off down the corridor.

Paul said, "She's going to AA."

I said, "How do you know?"

Paul said, "I can tell."

Mac is groaning, which I think means he wants some attention. I have tried to get Della round but she won't come. She says she's going to get the ring made into two earrings and sell them and give Mac the money. I think she knows it's not about the money but she's in denial about the whole thing and that's one more nut I really haven't got time to crack.

Love you, Sis,

                                    Ven xxxxxxxxxxxxxx

22

ALEX found me on my sun-lounger. He was carrying two sets of snorkelling equipment. "Come on," he said, and held out his hand.

We swam out to the turtle rock in a party of snorkellers and Marie Claire — MC (she of the firm thighs) — followed us in the dinghy.

I had only ever snorkelled as a child on English beach holidays so when we got behind the rock and I put my mask on I thought — I don't know what I thought, actually, I didn't think anything much. I mean, fish are about as interesting to me as, well, fish.

I put my face in the water and a school of small electric blue fish swam right up and looked me curiously in the eye. Then they were gone again in the whisk of a tail. I took my face straight out of the water and yelped with laughter. It's not often you discover something new and delightful about life. I felt like you feel when you're a toddler and you discover about throwing your food on the floor.

I snorkelled for ages, couldn't get enough. I even saw a sulky octopus folding itself foetus-like into a hollow beneath some rocks.

I was so engrossed I didn't think about Alex, but just as I wondered where he was, I came across him. He was mask to mask with the long-legged MC. They were pointing out fish to each other and laughing.

I snorkelled on, staying very calm and adult. Alex and MFC (Marie Fucking Claire) snorkelled down deep together and at one point he pulled her by the hand to show her something.

When they came up for air I swam over to Alex and shouted into his ear, "You realise that's the equivalent of shagging the ski instructor?"

I don't know if MFC heard or not but she snorkelled off. Alex grabbed on to the boat and pulled his mask off.

"You're referring to what exactly?" he said.

"Alex," I said, "don't."

"What?" he said.

"Pretend you don't know what I'm talking about," I said.

"Okay," he said evenly.

"Listen," I hissed, pedalling madly with my flippers to keep myself up in the water, "if you don't want me that's fine — just say so. If you think us running off together is some great big mistake, well, fine — just *say so*" — that last bit a yell.

"Honey," Alex said, "MC and I were snorkelling." He said snorkelling as if it were something inherently innocent. He said it as if he could see no obvious link between snorkelling and catastrophe.

"Snorkelling!" I snorted, with all possible contempt.

"Yes," he said, "snorkelling." (The more we said the word, the more it sounded like some horrible yuppy euphemism for oral sex.)

"In fact," I said, "flirting. With Marie Fucking Claire."

"Flirting?" he said, with what looked like genuine surprise. Which doesn't mean to say he wasn't doing it — the flirting. But does possibly mean to say that he didn't know he was doing it.

Then he shrugged. "You're right," he said. "She's the equivalent of the ski instructor."

I think I was meant to gather from this that she was fair game for flirting and I shouldn't read anything into it.

I was getting sick of gathering things. I suddenly felt sorry for those Stone Age women who had to gather all the time. I'd prefer hunt any day of the week.

"You held her hand," I said.

"I — what?"

"Held her hand."

"This is absurd."

"I saw it," I said.

"Listen," he said, "don't you start with me." With definite emphasis on the "you."

"Oh, I see," I said. "This is what Cherelle put up with."

"Cherelle is none of your business," he said.

I flopped my head back into the water. When I came up I said, "Is flirting with MFC your way of pushing me away?"

"No," he said.

"Yes," I said.

The conversation wasn't really going anywhere so I swam off round to the other side of the rock. I wondered what it would be like to cry underwater but couldn't summon the energy. I wondered if the fish had feelings.

After a while a wild face swam across my vision. It was a familiar face, black hair straggling in upright tentacles clawing for the water's surface.

I came up with a shriek. So did the face — although it didn't shriek. I pulled off my mask.

"Hi," he said, like he'd just bumped into me at the supermarket, by the frozen-peas cabinet.

"Ed," I said.

He smiled. I like that smile.

"What?" he said.

"When you smile," I said, "it makes me think everything's all right."

"In that case," he said, "I take back the smile. Shall we go somewhere we can talk?"

When we got back to the beach Alex came out of the water looking like James Bond and I did the Alex — Ed — Ed — Alex thing and they did the "yeah, we've met" thing and nodded at each other in a gentlemanly manner and, my God, we were all so polite you'd think we were at the Queen's garden party.

Alex said to Ed, "Listen, don't get the wrong idea here." I kind of knew what he was trying to say, but in the heat of the moment it sounded wrong.

Ed said, "Oh, right. You mean you're not actually shagging my wife?"

This is the life, I thought. Standing on a Caribbean beach with two half-naked dripping-wet men fighting over me. I felt my Oscar-acceptance speech coming on — "And I would particularly like to thank all those people who slapped me down and told me I'd never amount to anything. All those boys at school who said, 'Nice legs, shame about the face.' All those disapproving aunts who thought I'd never make something of my life — I'd like to thank you all. Because, frankly, proving you wrong makes this moment even more satisfying."

"Guys — guys," I said, trying not to smile.

They both looked at me with contempt. They knew exactly what was going on in my head and they weren't having any of it. My smile drained. It's not fair — you don't even get to win when you're winning.

"I haven't come here to fight over you," Ed said scathingly.

"But how did you find us?" I said.

"Jesus showed me the way," he said.

Ohmygod. That bad. Turned to the Lord.

"He told me you'd switched hotels," Ed said.

"Oh, that Jesus," I said.

"I've come here because I think we should all face up to this situation like adults."

"That's fine by me," Alex said.

"I think we should have everything out in the cold light of day," Ed continued.

"This is the Caribbean," I said. "I think you'll find there's very little cold light of day."

Ed said, "Oh, I think you'll find we can rustle some up."

"Thank you, Ed," I said. "Thank you very much." I felt livid. I felt like killing him. Ed's the only person in the world I've ever really felt like killing. I pulled a towel around me and ran back to my room.

When I got there, I got in the shower and screamed. I couldn't help it — I just screamed one big huge horror-movie type scream.

23

CALLED Ven at Mac's.

"Have you read *The Road Less Travelled*?" she said.

"No!" I said, feeling another scream coming on.

"I'll have it Fed-Exed down to you," she said.

"Don't," I said.

"Well, if you take that attitude I won't. But actually you only have to know what the first sentence says. 'Life is difficult.' There — don't you feel better already?"

I said, "Do you think you might actually be mad? You know, clinically. Mum used to say that Great Aunt Nora was mad — she was in an asylum and everything. I think maybe you got the gene."

"You see," said Ven, "if you start from the position that life is or should be easy, then you are constantly disappointed — and constantly in the victim position. If you start from the position that life is hard, then you are pleasantly surprised when there's enough hot water for a bath. I was wondering where Ed had got to."

"My life," I said, "is in ruins."

"When you're playing victim," Ven went on, "everyone else becomes either persecutors or rescuers since —"

"I am not," I interrupted, "a victim. Thank you very much."

Silence.

"Sis," I said, "I need help."

More silence.

"Imagine that you are in exactly the right situation at exactly the right time in your life," she said.

"Ha!" I said.

"Imagine it," she said.

I shut my eyes. "Okay," I said.

"Imagine that you are there to learn something that will take you forward in life."

"That would be nice," I said.

"It's important to make mistakes," she said. "We all make them. It's true, some mistakes are bigger than others. Some mistakes are huge enormous whoppers —" She brought herself up short. "Sorry — forget I said that. Mistakes are fine. Really. They're signposts."

"D'you think?" I said, a warm glow starting.

"I know," she said suddenly, spoiling it, "think of the whole thing as a very elaborate episode of *Blind Date*."

"Ven!" I said.

"Honey," she said, "I can't sort this out for you."

"Whaaaat?" I said. "Since when have you not been able to sort something out?"

"Since — since . . . Do you want to talk to Della?"

"Della's there?" I said.

Della came on. "You fucking wuss," she said.

"Hi. Hello. Love you too."

"Mac's not here," she said. "We're trying to find the receipt for the ring so that I can return it."

"For God's sake, just give him back the ring and tell him you're not going to marry him."

"I can't."

"Yes, you can. He can't exactly make you marry him."

"You don't know Mac," she said.

"I do," I said.

"Well then," she said. She had a point. "I hear Ed has turned up."

"Yes," I said.

I heard whispers and scuffling.

"There's someone at the door," Della said. "Ven's getting it. It won't be Mac — he wouldn't buzz. So — who's your man, Alex or Ed?" imitating the *Blind Date* voice, "'The decision is yours.'" Then I heard her say, "Come again?" but not to me.

There was a bang. The phone obviously got dropped. I said, "Hello," a few times and eventually Ven came on and said in a whisper, "This woman's just arrived. Oh! My! God!"

"Who is she?" I said.

"Mac's wife," Ven said.

"She can't be," I said, but even as I said it I knew she could. "What's Della doing?" I said.

"Hugging her."

The call ended pretty abruptly at that point. But I did feel a bit better, knowing that I wasn't alone in my fucked-upness, knowing people all over the world were fucking up right along with me . . . I was grateful for that. In fact, I felt a little rush of love towards Ven and Della and suddenly imagined buying them both Prada bags as a gesture of my undying affection. But even as I thought about it I knew I'd never actually do it.

There was no sign of Alex. I threw on my sarong — now looking quite authentically weathered — and went over to Reception to find out where Ed's room was. I didn't know what I was going to say but I definitely wanted to seize the moment while I still had a bit of heart left over from my talk with Ven and Della.

I was directed to Ed's room. All was quiet — and dark. He appeared to be napping. I wasn't exactly surprised. Ed always seems to be asleep at the opportune moment. He's like Winnie-the-Pooh or something. Ed could sleep in the eye of a hurricane.

I went in and sat on the bed. The person in the bed sat up with a yell. I yelled too. It was Cherelle.

We stared at each other. "It's so nice to see you," I said eventually. That was the kind of mood I was in.

"You, too," she said. I don't think she meant it.

"Why are you here?" I said.

She said that she had come to burst me from her energy field.

"Okay," I said, and took to pacing the room Sherlock Holmes style. "We can do that. Are you and Ed . . . ?"

"Oh, no," she said. "Ed and I don't like each other. Do they have worthwhile room service here?"

"I don't think they have room service at all," I said, and took a swig of water from her Evian bottle. "Why don't you like Ed?" I said.

"Well, what I figure is that in a pure essence kind of way I do like Ed. But my ego doesn't like Ed because Ed doesn't like me."

"I see," I said. "So, have you come here to fuck us up? I mean — I'm not saying we don't deserve to be fucked up."

"That's a very negative attitude."

"You have a positive attitude?"

"I figured," she said, "I could spend the rest of my life wondering what I did wrong. Or I could come down here and find out." And with that she burst into tears. Abandoned sobbing, actually. I didn't know where to look. I thought maybe I should go over and put my arm round her but then I thought that would be a bit inappropriate.

In the end I said, "You didn't do anything wrong."

And I meant it, actually. I wondered how to get this through to her. "Alex and I," I said, "we're —" I couldn't think of the words. "We're screwed-up people," I said. "It's got nothing to do with you." Then I said, "Alex loves you. He's told me." But that made her wail even more.

"Are you two happy together?" she choked out, between sobs.

I found myself making a face like you do in school when you hear you've been called to the headmistress's study. Luckily, Cherelle wasn't looking at me. I put my hand up and smoothed my facial muscles back into shape.

I said, "I can't answer that question," but she just lay there and waited for an answer. So eventually I said, "That's like asking Einstein if two times two equals four."

"Excuse me?" she said.

"It's too simple."

There was a little silence. Then I said, "That's what it's meant to be about, isn't it? Making each other happy."

"Well, it's not supposed to be about making each other unhappy," she said, cheering up a bit at this evidence of my stupidity.

I swigged some more Evian.

"So," I said, "what now?"

"We all talk," she said. "We have, like, group sharing."

"Are you serious?" I said.

"Serious as a heart-attack," she said.

"They are outside," I said to Alex, "knocking on the door."

"Both of them?" he said.

"Yes," I said.

"Tell them to go away."

I opened our shutters and stuck my head out. Cherelle and Ed were standing there framed in bright pink bougainvillaea like they were in a wedding bower. I remember thinking they made a good team.

"He won't play ball," I said.

"Tell him we have to talk," said Cherelle.

"They want to share," I said to Alex.

"Ask Cherelle which bit of 'no' she doesn't understand — the N or the O," said Alex, practically climbing into the wardrobe in his eagerness to escape.

I asked Cherelle.

Cherelle made a face. "I used to say that to him," she said. "Listen, I'm way too hot out here. I have to get back to my air-conditioner." She went off looking downcast.

Ed came over to me at the shutters. "Hi, baby," he said.

I went out on to the verandah. "Ed," I said, "this is terrible. Don't do this."

I couldn't continue because a waiter arrived at that moment with a tray of tea and set it down on the verandah table. Alex must have ordered it.

The waiter left. "Have some tea," I said.

"I miss you," Ed said.

Arrrrrrrgh! I screamed, but not out loud. Inside. Pain. Ohmygod — it hurt so much.

Is this guilt? I wondered. I'm not sure I ever had much cause to feel guilty before. No wonder there was so much talk about it in the Bible though. I'd had no idea. But then again maybe it wasn't guilt I was feeling. Maybe it was loss. Whatever it was, I wanted it to go away. I wanted Ed to go away. But I poured him a cup of tea and picked it up to hand it to him. "Ed," I said, "please give up."

"Oh, don't worry," he said. "I'm giving up. Thank God. I should have given up years ago. I should have given up when I first realised the extent of your self-obsession. When I first realised that you weren't ever going to grow up. You're like a pre-pubescent teenager who thinks you're the first person in the world who ever felt any pain. Well, you know what? You're not special and different. You make everything about you. Everything! Everything's about you trying to prove to yourself that you're all right. Well, you know what? You are all right. No big deal. Now maybe you can grow the fuck up."

I said, "Was that one sugar or two?" My hand must have been shaking. The tea-cup was clattering in its saucer.

Ed turned on his heel and left.

"Please go home," I said, to his departing back.

"Try stopping me!" came the reply.

*   *   *

Back in our hotel room, Alex was reading unconcerned on the bed.

"Did you hear any of that?" I said, giving him the cup of tea.

"What?" he said.

"Nothing," I said.

I sat down on the bed. "Wow," I said. "Do you think childbirth is this painful?"

"It's a different kind of pain," he said.

You see, he knows what I'm talking about. One might think that emotional pain wasn't physical pain, but in that moment it *was,* and the epicentre was slightly to the right of my heart.

"We'll go on an outing tomorrow," Alex said, "and when we come back they'll be gone."

I joined him on the bed. "You don't think it's even remotely a good idea that we should talk? The four of us?" I said.

"There's nothing to say," he said. "We all know what went on."

He went back to his book. He'd found an old copy of the very erudite *Blue Guide to Mexico,* and he was reading it from cover to cover — the small print takes you through the museums pot by pot. He was already nearly half-way through.

"Cherelle thinks she did something wrong," I said.

"I'm going to write her a letter," he said.

"She wants to know if we're happy," I said.

"It says here that Coba is the least-visited sight in Mexico," he said. "With any luck we'll be the only people there."

"Listen," I said, after a moment, "I've been meaning to say. If you ever regret being with me — even for one second — I want you to tell me."

"Okay," he said, "and vice versa."

"Okay," I said. "I mean, if you ever find me selfish . . ."

"Selfish?" he said. He shut his guidebook, perplexed.

"What is it you want from me?" he said.

"I don't know," I said. "Something."

He looked at me for quite a while. "You know what," he said gently, "we need to take things slowly."

"Don't be daft," I said. "You're talking about two people who eloped in a helicopter on the strength of a kiss."

He said, "I mean between you and me. You know what I mean."

"Is this because of the Marie Claire incident?" I said. "Because I probably got that a bit out of perspective."

He smiled. He put out a hand and stroked my hair. "It's going to be okay," he said.

"I know what you're going to say," I groaned, "you're going to say you need some space!"

He didn't deny it. He rolled me into his arms.

"You've had all the space in the world," I said, thinking of how it had been the last couple of days. "You've had football bloody stadiums."

"Some people, you know," he said, "need space."

"I know," I said, with a phoney bright-idea inflection, "why don't I go and live in London and you can live in L.A. and then you'll have some space!" — triumphant.

There was a little silence. He still held on to me. Like he wasn't going to let go whatever I said. After a while he said, "You know I'll always love you whatever happens."

I just lay there letting the words run through my mind. I don't know why they felt like a death sentence.

24

A S IT turned out we weren't the only tourists at Coba but it didn't really matter. The ruins of the ancient town were spread wide in the form of little humps of stones, run-down and defeated in their fight to escape the suffocating net of dense jungle.

Jungle has always made me nervous. Not that I've been to the jungle much. I should say, the idea of jungle makes me nervous. All those unseen creepy-crawly things. It was muggy and buggy and the birds — I usually like birds — the birds were what can only be described as deafening.

But then we suddenly came across a lake.

"Coba means Town of Wind-ruffled Water," Alex said.

"That's beautiful," I said. More beautiful than the thing itself, which had a milky grey puddle-like quality. And no wind.

We climbed an immense, flaky stone staircase to a crumbly Mayan temple at the top. I felt hot and cross, and overcome suddenly with sightseeing ennui. I've suffered from this since I was a child — I blame my father making enthusiasm compulsory. The symptoms are boredom, heaviness, lethargy and an overwhelming desire to go home and watch *The Simpsons.*

"The Toppled God," said Alex, pointing out a sculpture at the temple's entrance.

"The Toppled God?" I said, waking up a little.

"Yeah," said Alex. "He's big in this area. He's highly esteemed. And," he went on, leading me inside the temple, head buried in his guidebook, "of the numerous *stelai* found here, grave column twenty is described as being 'splendidly equipped.'"

"Awesome!" I heard a familiar Californian voice say. "God answered my mail."

"Certainly well hung," said an English voice, even more familiar.

Alex grabbed me and pulled me behind one of the tombs. We crouched there like idiots while Cherelle and Ed perused the various graves.

"I feel like I'm in *The Sound of Music,*" I whispered to Alex.

Actually, it's been my lifetime's dream to be in *The Sound of Music* because, although Theresa had been a good proxy mother, she had never sung to us about brown-paper packages tied up with strings.

"Shush," said Alex crossly.

"Schnitzel with noodles," I said.

"What?" he said again, irritated, not listening.

"Schnitzel," I said again, louder. It sounded like a sneeze.

"Here," he hissed, handing me a tissue, "please be quiet."

I don't know if it was the sightseeing *ennui* or the desire to annoy Alex but something made me go on. "Bright copper kettles," I whispered.

"Warm woolen mittens," came from the other side of the grave column.

So — a bit like Liesl — I gave a little gasp. And there was Ed smiling at me and the game was up. Alex and I had to come out and it was all very embarrassing, to say nothing of hot and sweaty. The place was like an oven. Cherelle looked like a melted candle — she's not very good in the heat.

"It was my idea," Ed said.

"I thought you were going home," I said to him.

"I'm not going to give you up," he said.

"Sounds like another song?" I said.

"No," he said. "Just a bad line."

"It's okay," I said. "You're allowed to say bad lines in real life. Just not in the movies."

"Excuse me," said Alex. And walked out.

We followed him.

It turned out that Ed and Cherelle had come in a taxi but when we got to the car park their taxi had gone.

"I must have manifested for it to go," Cherelle said. "It was the taxi from hell. No air-conditioning. Air-conditioning is a basic human right in a country like this. And the guy was playing music at full volume and then — get this — smoking! Can you believe? I nearly died. It's barbaric. You know what? In a hundred years' time we won't be able to believe that people really put those cancer sticks in their mouths."

"Didn't stop you doing it in New York," said Ed, causing Alex to look at Cherelle sharply. I had a feeling this was the first time they'd really met eyes.

"Oh, that," she said. "That was a parallel universe. You guys will have to give us a ride back to the hotel. Does your vehicle have air-conditioning?"

"Of a sort," said Alex, letting the Golf's roof down.

"Alex," said Cherelle, "I cannot ride in this thing with the top down. I will die of heat."

Alex looked at her. Here we go, I thought. A domestic. But to my amazement he just put the top up again.

We all got into the car together.

"Cosy," Alex said.

Cosiness — as it turned out — was the least of our problems. The car wouldn't start. We had to try to get someone to give us a lift but there weren't many cars there and the few there were couldn't fit us in. Apparently buses only run to Coba on days of the week with the letter T in them and no one knew if this was the days in Spanish or English.

Eventually Alex cadged a lift on the back of a moped to go and call the car-rental people. But none of us could stand the thought of being left behind in that heat. Cherelle went to "the bathroom" (behind a bush) and practically sat on a snake. She was seriously a woman on the edge.

Long story short, we all got lifts on the back of mopeds with some Canadian students. That bit was fun, actually. They dropped us at a little village on the road where there was a phone.

As it turned out there was no chance of rescue by the car-rental company until the next day so we checked into a run-down guesthouse on the beach.

I say "checked in" — Cherelle got the last room, which had only one single bed, and absolutely wouldn't hear of anyone else coming in there with her. She was very indignant — said we obviously had no idea how much heat is generated by the human body. A lot, apparently. She got the manager to give her his electric fan and went into her room to worship it. Alex and I were given a mattress out on the deck to sleep on and Ed was allocated the hammock.

Alex and I ate refried beans for supper in the village — he'd insisted we sneak off. He was terrified of the idea of all four of us having dinner together. When we got back I rigged up a mosquito net over our outdoor mattress.

Cherelle was still in her room so I went to look for Ed. I found him sitting on the beach in the low evening sun throwing shells mournfully into the surf.

We sat for a while side by side.

"Do you think you can ever forgive me?" I said eventually.

Ed said, "I don't think forgiving is something you can just decide to do."

"I should stop trying to make this better, shouldn't I?" I said.

"Yes," he said.

There was a little silence. Then he said, "I'm not saying forgiving doesn't happen. It happens. Just suddenly one day — it happens."

Sometimes I think Ed must be the nicest man on the planet. I said, "You mean if you ended up meeting Milla Jovovich on your way back through Mexico City airport and you never would have met if you'd never been dragged down here by me and you ended up spending the rest of your life living with her in conjugal bliss, then you might be able to forgive me?"

"Exactly," he said. And he smiled. I was glad he smiled. "I'll survive," he said. "You know that. I will survive."

"It's funny you should say that," I said.

"I just want to go home now," he said. "I want to go and stand in one of my gardens and see how the camellias are doing and get drizzled on."

"You're homesick," I said.

"Yeah," he said.

For some reason this made me want to cry. I tried not to but my mouth went into a stiff line and my eyes went bleary and Ed knows me so well. "Hey," he said, and went to put his arm round me, then remembered and didn't. "You got what you wanted. You got your dream come true." He said it like he was genuinely trying to cheer me up.

"Yeah," I said, "it was my dream."

Ed said, "Did you think about Alex all the time you were with me?"

"Of course not!" I said. "He was in the back of my mind. Way in the back. He was like — I don't know — a distant mountain in the landscape. I never thought I'd meet him again. And, anyway, I thought I'd imagined it with him — I mean, I never thought —"

"You thought you couldn't have him so you settled for me."

"It wasn't like that," I said. Except it was, sort of. But saying it like that made it sound so awful. And it hadn't been awful. "It didn't feel like 'settling' for you," I said. "It felt so nice."

"Not nice enough," he said.

"It was totally nice enough," I said. "It just wasn't —" I wished I hadn't started the sentence. I couldn't finish it.

"Say it," Ed said.

"Well, you know," I said, "that thing — whatever that thing is."

"It," he said.

"Yes," I said. "It."

We threw a load more stones into the sea.

"If," he said, after a while, "if you hadn't had him in the back of your mind, this 'mountain,' how do you think it would have been between us then?"

I rolled on to my side and looked at him. "What are you getting at?" I said.

"Do you think maybe you would have fallen in love with me?"

"I did," I said.

"I mean properly," he said. "It."

"You're amazing," I said.

"What?" he said.

"You amaze me," I said.

"Why?" he said.

"You just do," I said.

I stood up and stripped down to my bikini, which had been doubling as underwear, and went and got into the sea, even though it was nearly dark. I felt like getting underwater. I wanted that kind of aloneness. I wanted to feel my body just being my body. Surviving. I was tired of thinking. Too much thinking.

When I came up for air the stars were out. The stars always help me get perspective. Maybe that's what they're there for. Maybe that's why people get so crazy living in cities — because they can't see the stars.

I floated in the water and I looked up at the stars and I let my life flash before my eyes, my life back in London. But I kind of cut it together and edited it fast and sexy like it was a trailer for a movie and by doing that I made it what I wanted it to be or what I thought it should be. But trailers don't do it for me any more, that coffee-commercial kind of stuff.

So I let myself see my life how it really was and I let myself imagine that it would only ever be how it really was. Messy and inconsistent and — well — sometimes it was awful but sometimes my friends made me laugh and sometimes I got high just being alive and driving my car in a rainstorm. And then I thought that maybe that was good enough.

I thought about not letting myself have what I've got. I thought about being caught up in all this stuff about what should be and not noticing what is. It's a bit like when you get old and you wish you'd known how lucky you were to be young. When I was twenty I thought I was hideous — a freak. Now I look back at photos of myself at twenty and I can't believe how pretty I was. Now I think thirty is the end of the world. Although when I'm fifty I'll look back and —

I think I've always lived life as if the path were about to run over the edge of a cliff. The fact that the cliff never actually comes doesn't change the logic. It's always just those few paces ahead.

When I finally came out of the water a breeze had got up and my fingers were wrinkled like shelled walnuts. I think that last happened when I was about eight years old and my mother wouldn't let me out of the bath unless I'd washed my neck. I had a thing about not washing my neck.

When I got back to our mattress under the verandah I looked up to the sky one last time but the stars had gone. Completely gone. Like a door being shut. It took me a few moments to work out that a breeze had sprung up and the sky had abruptly clouded over.

Alex was lying in bed under the mosquito net reading the goddamn guidebook.

"Does that guidebook really, really interest you?" I said.

"I wouldn't read it otherwise," he said.

"I don't understand," I said.

"You don't have to."

"Did you speak to Cherelle?" I said. "Or are you really going to write a letter?"

"I spoke to her," he said. "We had a talk."

"And?" I said.

"She's going to be fine," he said.

"But tell me what you said," I said, taking off my wet swimsuit and getting under the mosquito net and between the sheets naked. I wished I didn't have to sleep naked out in the open, but I didn't have much choice.

Alex hadn't answered my question. "What did you talk about?" I said.

"There are some things," Alex said lightly, "that are private between a husband and a wife."

There was a long silence. I felt the cliff edge looming.

"I can't believe you just said that," I said.

"I didn't mean anything by it," he said. "It was a joke."

"Freud said there's no such thing as a joke," I said.

"Hey," he said, "I'm not asking you what you and Ed discussed."

"I kind of wish you would," I said. "Don't you want to know?"

"Not really," he said. He leant over and kissed me gently on the forehead. "I trust you," he said.

And then he turned away so that he could catch the light better on his book. "Did you know," he said, "that the revolutionary hero Pancho Villa sold the movie rights to his battles to Hollywood? Real battles. He'd wait to start the battle till the light was good enough for the cameras to roll."

"Humph," I said.

"That was in 1914," he said. "Sleep well."

I woke up to the drumming of rain. The noise was different from the noise of rain in London. Each drop sounded enormous. It was pitch dark. Then I realised that Alex was talking to someone — and I thought maybe the voices had woken me up, not the rain.

"Don't worry about it," said Alex. "She's asleep."

I kept my eyes firmly closed — some reflex action from childhood: when in doubt, pretend to be asleep.

I heard Ed's voice say, "I'm really sorry about this but it's really, really wet out there."

Alex said, "It's okay," again sleepily. Next thing, I felt Ed arriving in the bed on the other side of me. He was careful not to touch me. Alex settled down with his back to me.

To say I stiffened would be an understatement. I lay there between them as frozen as a fish-finger. I held my breath. I opened my eyes — darkness. I didn't dare move my head. I didn't think sleep was a possibility. I pretended to breathe. I was forced to. I wondered if I was actually getting any air. I wondered how I was going to get through.

I decided to entertain myself by imagining recounting the story to Ven, Della and Paul. I beefed it up a bit — gave the whole thing a bit of a rewrite. I imagined Ven's OH! MY! GOD! I imagined it so well that I nearly laughed and I gave a little stifled snort. Alarmed, I choked it back. Alex's breathing was even, he appeared to be asleep. Ed — I couldn't tell.

A couple of minutes passed and then this foot arrived underneath my foot. Ed's foot, to be exact. It was warm and it was smooth and it fitted perfectly underneath my foot and sort of held it, if you know what I mean. I stopped breathing again. But then, I thought, I know that not-breathing thing goes nowhere, so I started again.

And with each breath I could feel myself drifting further into a world where it was okay to touch feet with your ex-lover, now your husband, while in bed with the Love of Your Life. The cells in my foot started to take in the oxygen and to expand and relax and as this happened Ed moved his shin so that it lay against the back of my calf, and the warmth and the relaxation moved all the way up to my knee and I drifted into a world where it was okay to touch lower legs with your ex-lover, now your husband, while in bed with the Love of Your Life.

And as that happened Ed moved his firm thigh against my soft one and now I was waiting for more and it seemed to take too long until he moved so that his chest lay against my back and his arm came quietly around me and gently held my waist and every cell in my body breathed again and I melted against him as we lay there, his cheek resting tender and vulnerable against the back of my neck.

Blissed out, my thoughts finally faded as I'd so wanted them to earlier and I just drifted in being human again and when I woke the next morning I couldn't remember having gone to sleep. Ed had gone but I was aware of a fuzziness around me, an aura — a kind of afterglow.

Alex arrived, all booted and businesslike. "Been up since six," he said. "Do you know what time it is?"

"No," I said.

It turned out it was half past eleven. I do that sometimes when I need to. I just sleep and sleep. Regeneration.

"You could have brought me a cup of tea," I said.

"I didn't think of it. The car guy has been. We're free."

"Free?" I echoed, thinking it was a strange choice of word.

"They've gone," he said.

"What?" I said. But I knew.

"The car guy was going back to Cancún. They decided to get a ride with him. Ed said he'd originally planned a trip with you — to drive across to Merida and see Chichen Itza on the way. Well, they're gonna do it. Then catch a flight out of Merida."

"Together?" I said.

Alex said, "Chichen Itza is amazing. We should try and get over there. But maybe not today." He smiled.

I tried to digest the news. I knew why Ed had been so keen on that particular trip.

"You know Ed was in this bed last night?" Alex said, interrupting my thoughts.

"It was raining," I said.

"Even so," said Alex, with a grin.

I felt like slapping the grin right off his face. I wanted to say, "You let Ed sleep in the bed! You let him! You set us up! You bastard!"

But of course I didn't because I didn't really think it was true. It was just a good line. Anyway, I never do dramatic stuff like that. It gives too much away. Anger is vulnerability, Mac used to say.

Alex was looking at me, quizzical. Oh God, he could read me like an open book.

Get out from inside me, I wanted to say.

"Weird guy, Ed," Alex said, shaking his head, and started to walk away. Like he knew I was coming for him.

I said, "Wait. Where are you going?"

"To get you a cup of tea," he said.

"Too late," I yelled after him, and thrashed about uselessly, caught like a mosquito in my own net, blindingly white and bridal in the brilliant sunlight.

25

WHEN we got back to La Posada that afternoon I went and stood in the shower. I thought it might help. When I came out Alex was on the phone booking flights to L.A.

"Hey," I said, when he'd finished.

"I need to get out of here," he said.

"What about me?" I said.

"You're coming too," he said.

"What makes you so sure?" I said, which startled us both equally.

He said, "We need to get out into the world — see if we can make a life together."

"See if we can?" I said. "What about London?"

But I knew as I said it that it wasn't going to work in London. I wasn't willing to be responsible for making him live under the clouds. I wasn't willing to test his love that much. "Forget I said that," I said.

"I'd like to leave tomorrow," he said.

"You'd 'like to'?" I said. "You just booked flights — without asking me!"

"Well, I'm going," he said — recalcitrant little boy.

"You're going," I said.

"Are you coming with me?" he said. "Yes or no?"

I called Ven at Mac's and got Della. "I'm going to live in L.A.," I said. "I'm calling to say goodbye," I said.

"Goodbye," Della said.

"Don't you care?" I said.

"Why does that feel like a trick question?" she said.

"Alex and I have talked and I've agreed to try and make a go of it in L.A. We've got nowhere to live. I haven't got a job. But, you know what they say, all you need is love."

"All you need is a green card, a shit load of money, a Mercedes, a security fence, a pool, friends in high places and reliable staff."

"Thanks for that vote of support," I said. "Couldn't you just be nice for once, like other people's girlfriends? Couldn't you be sort of warm and cuddly and 'I'm sure it'll work out'-ish?"

"I could," she said, "but I've got my period."

"Oh, right," I said, as if that explained anything. It was startling somehow to think of Della bleeding.

"You sound weird," she said. "What's going on?"

"No. It's okay," I said. "Ed finally went this morning."

"Oh," she said.

"It's going to be okay," I said. "It's just — you know — a wobbly bit. Not surprising, really, considering everything."

"That sounds like the comforting stuff I'm meant to say."

"Yes," I said. "Listen and learn."

"Your voice is weird," she said.

"Will you stop saying that?"

"Okay."

"And listen, don't tell Mac yet."

"Okay," she said. "I've got to go."

"What's going on?" I said.

"I'll tell you later — I've got to go."

"Where's Ven?" I said, but Della had already hung up.

"Tell her I miss her so much," I said to the dial tone.

When I got off the phone to Della I felt worse than when I'd started. There was nothing for it but to phone Theresa. I'd been putting this off since the Great Escape — but I couldn't feel this bad and not phone Theresa.

"Listen," I said, when I got her, "don't worry but I didn't go on honeymoon with Ed — I ran off with someone else instead."

"Don't worry?" she said.

"I know it sounds bad," I said, "but it's not as bad as it sounds."

"How is that?" she said.

"You see," I said, "he's not just anyone, he's the Love of My Life," I said.

"Not the American guy with the blue eyes who picked you up in a restaurant, made you drive him to the airport and never called you again?"

"Must you put it like that?" I said.

"Honey — sweetheart — take it slowly," she said. "Don't make any life-changing decisions. In fact, come home and think about it. Come and stay with me for a bit."

"I can't," I said, "we're going to live in L.A."

"Are you in a fit state to make a decision like that?" she said.

"Oh, please, don't be the voice of reason," I said.

"Come home and think this over. And if he's the love of your life he'll wait a couple of weeks for you. Come home to Trees."

"But it's everything I've ever wanted," I said.

"But, Honey," she said, "you've never known what you ever wanted."

Silence.

"Come home," she said.

"Okay," I said. I couldn't think of another way of getting her off the line before I started to sob.

"I'll be waiting for you," she said.

"'Bye," I said — quivering.

"Honey," she said, "if you go to L.A., I love you anyway."

I sat on the edge of the bed and cried like a baby. Just hearing Theresa's voice had caused my whole elaborate fantasy to flop down with a wet splat like an overblown soufflé. Sometimes I think reality is the most painful thing in life. And that's a terrible thing because reality is the only thing in life. When you come to think of it.

You know those books you read when you're a kid where they find a magic door or something that leads to another country, an enchanted place where none of the normal rules apply? Well, when I was a kid I found that place in my head. I found that I could fantasise myself into a whole other family and a whole other life. And although what I imagined wasn't technically real, the imagining created real sensations in my body and real feelings in my heart and those became a very convincing framework through which I perceived — or misperceived — the day to day reality of my life.

I mean, I knew what it felt like to be a prima ballerina taking her curtsies on the world's stage. I knew what it was like to sing to the camera on *Top of the Pops.* I knew what it was like to win the Derby on my faithful pony. I knew what it was like to be kissed by James Dean.

I wanted to lead all those lives. And I thought life owed me all those things. And that only those things would make it okay.

And then when my parents died I didn't know how to deal with their loss without being overwhelmed by it. But I didn't want to die with them. I wanted my chance at curtsies and prizes and kisses. So I fantasised even more. Their death became like this big no-go area. And the easiest way of not going there was to go into fantasy.

I had been constantly aware, these past few days with Alex, of the pain of reality. There was nothing wrong with him except all the things that are wrong with everybody. But just being with him was painful because he kept doing and saying things that proved to me that he was him — that he existed separately from me, that he had his own life and that I couldn't do with him as I pleased like I could if he'd existed only in my head.

After I'd dried my eyes, I went and joined Alex in the restaurant. We didn't talk. We were like a couple who've been together so long they've run out of things to say. I couldn't eat either. I was in shock, I think. My senses were heightened like I'd been up all night taking drugs.

When I sat down he leant over and took my hand. I tried to kiss him so I wouldn't have to look him in the eye. He stopped me. He wouldn't let me get away with a stunt like that.

There was an elderly American couple at the next table. The two of them kept smiling at us indulgently and eventually the woman leant over and said, "Just married?"

I smiled and said we weren't actually married.

They tut-tutted genially and the man hollered, "You'd better marry her!" jovially to Alex.

Alex said, "As a matter of fact I'm married to someone else."

That shut them up.

Alex said he was going for a walk so I went back to our room and tried to read my thriller. I was wired though. Itching for something. Every minute seemed like an hour. Eventually I went out to look for Alex.

I found him sitting side by side with Marie Claire outside the beach hut. They were just sitting there on this bench swinging their legs in the moonlight. When Alex saw me standing on the edge of the surf he said goodbye to Marie Claire and came over. He didn't say anything. He wouldn't.

I said, "You know something?" I said, "You never ask me any questions. Have you noticed that?" I hadn't quite formulated this complaint before but now that it had leapt out of my mouth it seemed profound.

"Questions?" he said, genuinely perplexed. "We did questions."

"Questions about me," I said. "You never ask me anything about me. How can I go and live in a strange city with someone who doesn't know me?"

"I do," he said.

"I don't think so," I said, "not really.

"There's something between us," I said.

"Sure is," he said.

"I mean," I said, "something not right. Something . . ." I didn't know how to describe an atmosphere I experienced as a kind of anxious tension in my gut. "It's not comfortable," I ended up saying. "I mean, I've had more relaxed times with the tax-assessment officer."

"Now that's not kind," he said.

"But you know what I'm talking about," I said. "Don't you? You can feel it too. Can't you?" He looked away, he couldn't meet my eye. "It feels —" I couldn't go on.

"It feels?" he said.

"Empty," I said.

The truth gave me a jolt like an electric shock. Him too, I think. I decided to throw down the gauntlet. "Would you change your plan to go back to L.A?" I said. "Would you stay here so that we can get to know each other?"

He didn't say anything. He didn't need to. I could see the negative in his eyes. I could feel it all around us in the air.

"I don't want it to be like this," I said. "But I don't think you're really there for me."

"I'm here," he said,

"But not *there*," I said. "Not really," my voice rising. And suddenly I found all the longing and wanting and fear and pressure of the last week expending itself like a blast from a steam train. I let it go with relief.

"Let's cut to the chase here," I said. "This is about the fact that you can't face up to commitment. Sorry to be so mundane. But it is mundane. It's so incredibly mundane. You've been leaving me since you got me and we've both known it. You're just plain old running away. This whole thing has just been one big running away."

And with that I ran away. Down the beach. He caught up with me and yanked me round to face him. "You know what?" he said. "You just described yourself."

Back in our hotel room we made love like we were the last man and woman alive. Our sex was like that. It was always *Gone With the Wind* and never *When Harry Met Sally*.

After a decent interval he rolled over with his back to me. That was how he went to sleep.

"You know I used to call you the Love of My Life," I said, "that's how I used to refer to you. It was kind of a joke. Not."

"I've always believed in that soul-mate thing," he said.

"And am I it?" I said.

"Yes," he said, without turning over. "Am I it?" he said.

"You're it," I said. And then, after a moment, "I want you to remember that."

He murmured imperceptibly and I waited as he went to sleep, as he drifted away from me into that place where he was complete and whole just as he was, without me.

You should never go to sleep after someone has said, "I want you to remember that." In fact if someone says, "I want you to remember that," you should demand an immediate explanation, confiscate their passport, and not let them out of your sight for several days.

When he'd been asleep for a good twenty minutes I got out of bed and gathered my things. It didn't take long. I didn't exactly have a whole load of stuff. I took the car keys and wrote Alex a note. It said, "I've borrowed the car. I just had to do this. I hope you understand." As far as notes went it was useless but I just wasn't able to explain further and I reasoned that it was better than nothing.

Out in the car I had an irrational fear that Alex would hear the engine starting and come rushing out. Of course he didn't. Maybe

I was disappointed. A tiny bit. I consulted the map. There was a big main road to Merida but taking it meant driving up to Cancún and going round two sides of a triangle rather than going much more directly on the smaller roads. I set off on the small roads. It all looked quite simple on the map.

I'd been going only about half an hour when I saw the fireworks way off in the distance. It gave me heart to think there were people out there. People celebrating.

I was driving through all these deserted little villages, each one heralded by the car hitting a speed bump and me flying up in my seat and whacking my head on the roof of the car. Mexican speed bumps. Imagine if they took the kerb of the pavement and laid it across the road. Well, that's what they were like.

Apart from once, when I went the wrong way at a T-junction and ended up driving down a dust track through a plantation, the route seemed quite straightforward. My car was the only vehicle on the road. I didn't see another.

I passed through a small town where the church was an extraordinary burnt yellow colour against the midnight sky and the bells were ringing. There were signs of life here — donkeys and old men standing on the side of the road. For no particular reason it seemed. They stared at me as I drove by.

I was beginning to get a little snow blind with all the driving, seeing only the few yards of road ahead, when suddenly the fireworks were right above me. Out of nowhere there was colour and music and fire and people, people everywhere. I stopped. Children in bright feathers with painted faces were running towards the car and then were right there knocking on my windows.

I seemed to have driven straight into the middle of some sort of festival. There were flaming torches and a milling crowd and scary painted masks leering at me.

It was too bizarre to be really frightening. And, anyway, I felt strangely detached. The little bubble of my car separated me from

the world. Everything outside might have been an illusion pro-
jected there for my amusement.

I left the village and drove on. And on. I was worried that I was
lost. I was scouring the roadside anxiously for signs to Chichen Itza
when I saw the sign to Tixcacalcupul. Something jolted in my
brain. A little flash of electricity that ran from one synapse to
another and made the hairs on my arms stand on end.

This unpronounceable place, believe it or not, was somewhere I
had to go. I don't remember making a decision, I just felt my hands
turning the wheel. I drove in the direction the sign indicated. It was
that simple. When I got to the village itself another fiesta was in full
swing.

This time I was careful not to drive into the middle of it. I left
my car at the edge and walked down the side of the church to
avoid the revellers. At the back of the church there was a little
cemetery within four white walls, like a little enclosed house. The
gates were open and I wondered briefly if maybe it was the day of
the dead and all the ghosts would come dancing out. If I'd stayed at
home and thought about doing what I was doing I wouldn't have
done it, if you see what I mean. It would have scared me witless.
But right there in the moment I felt no fear whatsoever. I went into
the little cemetery.

Inside, the layout reminded me a bit of pigeon-holes: everyone
had lots of mail. Some of the little drawers had plastic flowers sticking out, some had candles burning and others had little laminated
photographs stuck up like postcards.

The plaque was on the wall at the far end. It was a little com-
memoration plaque for a small air crash. It was brass and it had a
date on it, then something in Spanish — or was it Latin? — and
then nine names. My mother's name. And my father's. On separate
lines.

I stood there looking at them. Feeling my eyes in their sockets
and my body in its skin. That's what I felt. I think I expected to feel

something really huge. But it wasn't like that. I just stood there. I went on standing there. And then, very slowly and gently, like the way evening comes or something, the understanding came to me that this was my mother's name and this was my father's name and that they were dead. I mean, obviously I'd known they were dead, but it hadn't been this kind of knowing. The knowledge resonated through me with that painful firm ground feeling that truth brings.

They were never coming back. They really were never coming back. Not ever. I didn't realise until that moment that I had actually been expecting them to come back. But I had been. So in the exact moment that I found them, I lost them again.

I was glad when I started to cry. I was so frightened I wouldn't. I had the mad thought of taking one of the red plastic candle-holders and collecting my tears in it. For some reason I wanted to have those tears for ever. But in the end, of course, I just used an old tissue I found in my pocket.

A while later it came to me, as I sat crying and cross-legged on the little patch of grass in that funny little cemetery with my back to the marble with laminated pictures of the dead to keep me company, that I liked it there. And that I felt at home.

A great rose blossom of a firework showered through the sky above me and I sat with my head back and watched it rain down. I was so glad to be alive and so glad to feel love and to know there was love that I'd lost and love that I hadn't lost.

I've never been big on the love thing, you see. I was always a bit like Prince Charles who famously said of love, "whatever that is." And I was irritated by all that all-you-need-is-love stuff. I'd kind of agreed with Della: all you need is love and a Mercedes and friends in high places.

But, sitting in that place, I felt myself reluctantly beginning to see what all the fuss was about. There was no denying that I had a very specific feeling in my chest and the only word that I could think of to describe it was — love. When I thought of Ven, for example, the feeling swelled and I cried more.

And then, finally, I thought about Ed and how I'd find him some-how. How I couldn't let him go without telling him properly that I loved him. So as he'd know I meant it. With this real kind of love. And tell him that Alex might be my other half but that I couldn't live with Alex. I didn't want to. It was too painful, being so alike.

And then, I thought, when I'd sorted the whole stupid mess out and made Ed understand, well, then, maybe I'd get me to a nun-nery. The pure and simple life. It kind of appealed.

The tears kept coming but just gently and wetly. I'd given up wiping them. I felt like I was drifting. I didn't want to leave. I looked up at the dark sky and it was like I could see the earth turn-ing and feel it holding me. I put my arms around myself and I thought, I'm okay. It's okay. I'm here and I'm okay.

I must have fallen asleep. When I came to consciousness again the air was warm. The marble beneath my head reflected the palest of pale, pink and fragile morning light. I didn't move. I was curled on my side, comfortable beyond belief.

I felt there was someone there. The someone squatted down. I sat up, eyes still closed. The someone put his arms around me and I said, "Oh, good — you're here."

We stayed like that for ages. Ages and ages, and then I took his hand and opened it and placed my screwed-up snotty tissue on his palm. "That's for you," I said. "A present."

Ed said, "What is it?"

I told him it was my tears.

When we walked out to the car it was all very dawny and dusty and morning-after-the-storm-ish. Epic, actually. I felt like I was in the closing moments of a spaghetti western and was hobbling home in tattered skirts, having learnt the hard way that a woman's a woman, a man's a man and, anyway, you can't keep a Charles Bronson type down.

There was a little bar on the road just opening up. "Let's have *huevos*," I said, "and refried beans." I was suddenly starving.

We sat waiting for our eggs at a rickety lino-covered table and drank coffee — so thick and dark it was hard not to drink the grounds. Ed said that Alex had found me gone and called him at the hotel in Chichen Itza, guessing that I'd probably headed that way. When I hadn't turned up Ed had made an informed guess at my route and what might have happened when I'd got to Tixcacal-cupul. So he drove out.

"You were going to bring me here," I said, "weren't you? When you planned the honeymoon."

Ed smiled.

"I didn't mean to come here," I said. "I was looking for you. I was coming to find you."

Ed kept smiling. Like it was Christmas.

"Where's Cherelle?" I said.

"She stayed in Cancún," he said. "Waiting for a flight home."

"Is there any chance," I said, "that you could understand? About all of this?"

He just looked at me.

"It's like I'm driving along," I said, tracing it out with my finger on the table-top, "and I have to make a detour — but the road still brings me back to you."

"What was the detour?" he said. "Tixcacalcupul?"

"The detour was Alex," I said.

He thought about it for a while. "Is this the bit," he said eventually, "where I get my revenge?"

26

WHEN I arrived at Mac's, fresh from JFK, a small welcome-back party was in full swing. Mac, Della, Ven, Paul — they were all there.

"Sorry the cold fish turned out to be a red herring," Paul muttered into my ear, as he gave me a hug.

"What?" I said.

"Young love," he said.

"Oh, I see," I said, "yes."

Della came over with champagne. Shook the bottle and sprayed it over everyone shouting, "She's back!"

"Steady," I said.

Ven sat beside me, put her arm around me. "We must talk," she said, in her most salacious voice. Eyebrows working overtime.

"We must," I agreed.

Mac waved hello at me with his cigarette then produced a tall peroxide blonde. "This is Chiquita," he said, "my current wife."

I looked at Della. She gave me a wink. Which was new, actually.

She'd never done winking before. Maybe it was a New York thing. Maybe she was changing. Maybe we all were.

"Hey, pretty girl," said Chiquita, "I heard about you."

"Wife?" I said to Mac. "Wife?"

Mac said, "It's a long story."

Della said, "It involves Bertolucci, L.A., an Italian film retrospective, and a mad group outing to Tijuana. Oh, and too much mescal and drunken wagers and impromptu weddings in Vegas come into it somewhere."

"And the blow-job of the century," put in Mac.

"Which didn't save the marriage," put in Della pointedly. "When I introduced Mac to his wife, he had trouble placing her. He thought the whole thing could be ironed out with a little legal sleight-of-hand and some paperwork."

"But now I'm suing," said Chiquita.

"She's going to really drag it out," said Della eagerly, and put her arm through Mac's.

"Are you two back together?" I said.

"But of course," said Della. I looked at Mac. He was busy smoking. He seemed happy enough. When there was a moment, I took Della to one side. We went into the bathroom. "What about the ring?" I said.

"Oh, I gave it to Chiquita," she said.

"What did Mac say about that?" I said.

"What can he say?" she shot back. "He can't go round asking half the world to marry him."

"You're the only person he's ever wanted to marry," I said.

Della evaded my eye and Ven put her head round the door. "Do you like the colour?" she said. The room had been recently mosaic-tiled, floor to ceiling, a loud lemon yellow.

"Yellow," I said.

"Well, actually, it's kind of a lime green too. For harmony," said Ven.

"It reminds me of the colour of urine," Paul said, appearing suddenly, "after taking vitamins. Ven's a big *feng shui* hit," he went on. "All Mac's starlets are lining up to be told they must put the bed in the kitchen and generally have their apartments ruined."

At which point the doorbell rang. Everyone looked up in alarm.

"That'll be the Love of My Life," I said. I went out and pressed the buzzer for the downstairs door.

Everyone gathered round. "Who?" they all said.

"The Love of My Life," I said.

"Ohmygod," said Ven. "Oh! My! God!"

"He's been at the hotel," I said, "collecting our bags." And then I opened the door to Ed.

On the way to the airport I told Ven and Della a bit about what had happened in Mexico, and Ven said she'd go and visit Tixcacal-cupul — if she ever learnt how to pronounce it.

When we got to the airport she gave us a little talk concerning the unlikely event of a sudden drop in cabin pressure and that we should fit our own oxygen masks first before attempting to help others. I thought she was concerned for our in-flight safety but the whole thing turned out to be a metaphor for maintaining a healthy marriage.

"I'm glad you guys are back in love," she said.

When we got to Departures, Della said, "So it's goodbye. I wish I could cry but I can't. Too much of a bitch."

"Aren't you coming back to London?" Ed said.

"Maybe," she said, "but I expect I'll become a lady who lunches." She looked resigned.

Ven made Ed and me pose for a photo.

"Oh, no," said Della. "There it is again."

"What?" Ven said.

"That real love thing. I can feel it coming off them." And she shivered like someone had walked over her grave.

*　　*　　*

When we got home Ed and I went down to stay with Theresa for a few days. She'd said she'd be waiting and she was.

It was a balmy summer evening with the cows lowing in the fields and all that sort of thing. After we'd had tea with Theresa, I took Ed up to the attic where I unearthed my cigar box and showed Ed the never-getting-married vows, and the four-leaf clover. They'd been on my mind, those vows. Mainly because of all the times I'd fervently wished I'd kept them.

It was almost dark up there so Ed had to open the little dormer window to read the sacred document by the last of the sun. No sooner had he finished laughing at my idiocy than he threatened to tear the thing up.

"No!" I said, and grabbed the yellowing piece of paper. He gave me a look. He had a point. As usual. So I held my vows up by the window and just let them go, let the paper blow away in the breeze. We both watched it scuttling down the roof and out across the garden. It was kind of whimsical. But effective. (I hope.) Then I gave Ed the four-leaf clover. I decided it was for him.

When I woke up the next morning I felt like I'd come a long way. A long, long way. For one thing I didn't know where I was for a moment, what country I was in, who I was with. I opened my eyes and the first thing I saw was a pair of Ed's boots by the bed, his comfy crumpled Timberlands leaning slightly to the left and as familiar to me as my own thumbs. They looked so contented and snug, like they'd found their purpose in life. Looking at them, I knew that I was where I was meant to be and that everything was going to be okay.

And then it came to me — empty shoes! I hate empty shoes. I searched myself for signs of revulsion. None. I thought maybe I'd been cured, maybe the adventures of the last few weeks had operated as some kind of aversion therapy, like when people come face to face with a tarantula and are thereby cured of lifelong arachnophobia. But then I thought of Mac's loafers in the wardrobe in Chelsea and thought I probably hadn't been cured at all.

"You're The One," I said.

Ed stirred, mumbled something half awake, then rolled over and got close. He liked that.

I gave a big sigh. I do that sometimes. I don't know why. "You're definitely The One," I said.

"Oh, yeah?" said Ed, waking up a bit. "I thought *he* was The One."

"The thing is," I said, "what I never told you is that there's The One — okay — but then there's The Other One. He seemed like he was The One but actually you're The One and he was The Other One."

"You're making this up," he said. "I could just as easily be The Other One."

"No, no," I said, "you're The One."

"If there's The One, why isn't there The Two? What if The Two comes along?"

"Don't be silly," I said.

"Silly?" he said. "I think if anyone's going to accuse anyone of being silly —"

"Don't you want to be The One?" I said.

"Well, frankly," he said, "it's been nothing but trouble. How about we abandon the whole theory?"

"Revolutionary," I said.

To: Honey@globalnet.co.uk
From: alexlyell@hotmail.com
Subject: hi
Date: 21 August — 9.42 p.m. PST
 Mime-Version: 1.0

Dear Honey,
Just one last thing. We spend all this time and effort wondering who to love and if we love them enough. But the hardest thing is being loved. That's the hardest thing of all.

Guess who was in the seat beside me on the plane home?
See you in our next life,

Take care,

Alex

With many thanks for encouragement, inspiration and support, to:
Jenne Casarotto, Alison Dominitz, Su Fletcher, David Heyman,
Tracey Hyde, Sarah Lutyens, Maria Matthisen, Sam Miller,
James Purefoy and Carolyn Tristram. And with love to
Polly, Milly, Flora and Nat.

Honeymoon

by Amy Jenkins

A READING GROUP GUIDE

Amy Jenkins on the TSSW

Aren't you sick of the thirtysomething single woman? Don't you wish she'd get run over by a bus after one of her Chardonnay-swilling girls' nights out, never to return to her aromatherapy en suite bubble bath, all that's left of her and M&S ready-meal for one crushed to a red and sticky pulp in the gutter? Or perhaps in a more generous mood, you'd have her turning forty and sinking grace-fully into the silent oblivion of confirmed spinsterhood. (Forty being officially The End of Hope.)

Where did she come from, this siren of self-sufficient yet unsat-isfied womanhood? Ten years ago, we hadn't even heard of her. Now she is ubiquitous.

A marketing, consumer, zeitgeist phenomenon fueling books, TV shows, advertising campaigns, and zillions of column inches. She has the job, the flat, the car, the Manolos — she is the girl who has everything except a date. And, the question on everybody's lips, why, oh why, can't she get one? Well, if she did find a man she'd no longer be a Phenomenon, with a capital P; she'd lose her edge. For another, she doesn't really want one. Not really.

You only have to watch one episode of *Sex and the City* to dis-cover this simple truth. Thirtysomething single woman (TSSW) thinks she wants a man but she doesn't really. Not right here, not right now. TSSW doesn't want the man she can have. He's either a compromise — she was seduced at first by how good he was at putting up shelves but now she sees his ordinariness. Either that, or maybe he's suffocation — all over her like a rash. But it's all just excuses. It's the old knight-in-shining-armor syndrome dressed up as something new. Men aren't seen as men — they're not seen as equal and vulnerable fellows. Men are treated as commodities. They are the stuffing for the girlish dreams that have to be made to come true.

So TSSW only wants the men she can't have and that's exactly why she likes them. She can smell them out at a hundred paces — even if they appear initially to be bearing roses and professing undying love. It's easy to love someone who isn't going to be there for you. It's easy to blame him when he goes. But who picked who? There's a wise saying: Getting what you want can be the hardest thing of all.

This is the real problem, but TSSW doesn't want anyone looking too closely at her dirty lingerie, so she says: "There are no men." Or "All the men are gay." Or "Men are inadequate human beings with no communication skills" (formerly "All men are bastards"). Or "All the nice men are taken." Or "Men can't commit." This is the oldest trick in the book. When you don't want to look at yourself, deflect the blame outwards. It works like a dream. It's TSSW who can't commit. She just thinks she can. She's actually the female version of the "male bastard" commitophobe bachelor type who women have been hurling themselves against for centuries. But at least Mr. Commitophobe is usually unapologetically honest about his nature. TSSW is not. She is anathema to herself. She doesn't know her own soul.

As women, they are so deeply imbued with the idea that they are the ones who want commitment and men don't that they can't make head or tail of this new version of themselves. The received wisdom being that men are congenitally promiscuous, compelled to scatter their sperm far and wide to increase their chances of procreation. Personally, I like the new anthropological theories that say that the opposite is true. Women didn't see much use for men other than to provide children and the odd bit of hunting, and so it was men who were forced to invent marriage as a way to keep some power over their offspring — who were, after all, the only guarantee of something to eat in old age.

Times changed, men ran the show, and women were generally obliged for social and financial reasons to seek the safe haven of marriage. The unlucky were obliged to be realistic, obliged to compromise. Now the trouble for TSSW is that times are changing again. Those old social and financial imperatives are fading fast. I'm not saying compromise was ever easy. You only have to read Jane Austen to know that it's always been hard to compromise. Bad news is — it just got harder.

At this precise moment in history, TSSW is imbibing a particularly heady cocktail of cultural juices old and new. On the one hand she has grown into a force that fulfills her like she never dreamed possible. On the other, she was born into dreams that aren't possible to fulfill.

TSSW is not well enough prepared for relationships to be hard work. Which they are. As a culture, we still operate on the romantic love model, brought up to think that love between a man and a woman should bring us a happy-ever-after kind of bliss. If you think about it, there are a million movies about the struggle to find Mr. or Mrs. Right — the thrill of the chase — and virtually no movies about the struggle of relationship itself.

Happy ever after. Are you happy? TSSW is asked. Am I happy? She asks herself. Sure, relationships can be joyful, warm, companionable, and fun. They also tend to be the place where we most comprehensibly meet ourselves, where we become aware of our hang-ups, our fears, our desires, our pain. You can see how TSSW might easily decide she was "happier" with her Chardonnay, her aromatherapy bubble bath, and her ready-meal for one.

And what gives me the right to lecture poor old TSSW like this, you might well ask. Well, for one thing, I am one. And is there hope for the future? Er, therapy, or maybe sprawling singleton communities like Sun City old people's home in Arizona, outside the city walls. Er . . . maybe not.

Personally, I'm banking on the Internet. Soon I hope to be able to order up a man to my exact specifications and have him arrive, guaranteed next-day delivery, on my doorstep. Second thoughts, that might be too intimate. Why don't I just relate to him online? Virtually. Wearing gloves.

Reading Group Guide Questions and
Topics for Discussion

1. Do you believe that there will only ever be one love of your life?

2. Did you think the various settings of the book — London, New York, the Caribbean islands — contributed to Honey's final decision about the outcome of her love life?

3. Can old-fashioned romance still exist now that people such as Honey and her friends rely so much on e-mail and cell phones instead of waiting for love letters to arrive in the mail? Do you think Honey would have had the same ending to her story without these things?

4. Would Honey have made the same choices without the aid of her sister? How has your family gotten in the way of one of your romances or, alternatively, moved one right along?

5. Do you think it's possible to be in love with two people at the very same time?

6. Did Honey make the right choice? Do you think she will have regrets? What would you have done if you were Honey?

7. Is there a point in your life when it's time to discard fantasy romances? How much of Honey's ultimate choice was about a fantasy? How much of it was about a particular time in her life when she felt the need to make a major decision?

8. Was Honey's final decision a compromise? Can you influence your own destiny when it comes to love?

The Boys of My Youth
by Jo Ann Beard

"Utterly compelling . . . uncommonly beautiful. . . . Life in these pages is an astonishment. . . . *The Boys of My Youth* speaks volumes about growing up female and struggling to remain true to yourself."

— Dan Cryer, *Newsday*

This Body
by Laurel Doud

"A frisky, riveting debut. . . . With Doud's brightly visceral prose and deft sense of trigicomedy, *This Body* proves equally engrossing for the senses, soul, and mind."

— Megan Harlan, *Entertainment Weekly*

White Oleander
by Janet Fitch

"Quite simply, *White Oleander* is amazing. It's the kind of book you don't want to put down. It's full-bloodied, alive, breathtaking, frightening. . . . This incredible novel is the story of what it is to be extraordinary women."

— Rohana Chomick, *Tampa Tribune-Times*

Available wherever books are sold

Hangover Soup
by Louise Redd

"A funny, sassy, sexy, moving book about love, sex, friendship, sports, education, alcoholism, marriage, and commitment; in short, something for everyone."
— Theodora Schmid, *Tampa Tribune-Times*

The Pilot's Wife
by Anita Shreve

"From cover to rapidly reached cover, *The Pilot's Wife* is beautifully plotted, tensely paced, and thoroughly absorbing."
— Heller McAlpin, *New York Newsday*

Talking to the Dead
by Helen Dunmore

"Brilliant and terrifying, an unbeatable combination. . . . We aren't released from the author's spell until the very last line."
— Carolyn Banks, *Washington Post*